Stolen Vows

TWISTED ARRANGEMENTS
BOOK ONE

CASSIA QUINN

Wednesday Ink

Stolen Vows

*To all the girls searching for their White Knight,
in hopes he'll carry you off to his dark castle.*

Content Information

Dear reader, before you turn the page, please know that this is a romance with dark themes and potentially difficult situations.

Please read the entire content list here: http://cassi aquinn.com/twisted-arrangements/

XX
Cassia

Stolen Vows Playlist

Bad Guy - Billie Eilish
Natural - Imagine Dragons
I Like Me Better - Lauv
Greedy - Tate McRae
Hot N Cold - Katy Perry
Slow Hands - Niall Horan
Never Be The Same - Camila Cabello
Shivers - Ed Sheeran
Those Eyes - New West
Don't Blame Me - Taylor Swift
I hate u, I love u - gnash, Olivia O'Brien
Would've, Could've, Should've - Taylor Swift
Like I'm Gonna Lose You - Meghan Trainor
Thinking Out Loud - Ed Sheeran
Listen on Spotify

Contents

Sophia

Tonight my family's announcing my engagement to Nikolai Kozlov, second in line to rule the Kozlov Bratva in New York City. In three short months I'll be his wife. An arrangement agreed upon by my father and Nik's uncle to form a stronger alliance.

With clammy palms, I smooth down the front of my dress for what must be the hundredth time as I stare into the full-length mirror. I shouldn't be nervous, but I am. I've been fortunate enough to date my fiancé for the past nine months, if you can call going on all of four dates in that timeframe *dating*.

Honestly, he hasn't shown much interest in me at all. But at least I was allowed to meet him before our wedding day, some girls are not so lucky. I should be grateful. And yet... Tonight's engagement party has brought the reality of my situation crashing in, breaking against me like a wave on jagged rocks.

All of this is happening too quickly. I'm not ready.

"You look beautiful, Sophia."

My gaze flicks over my shoulder in the mirror and lands on my sister's sweet face. "Thanks. Though, how I look is the least of my concerns tonight."

Her brow pinches as she walks fully into my bedroom. "What do you mean? Tonight is extremely important to all of us." Arianna perches on the edge of my bed, her back ramrod straight, and her hands folded. She's stunning in a satin dress that brings out the green in her hazel eyes. I'm the oldest, but Arianna is the epitome of the perfect mafia princess.

She continues, "Your marriage to Nikolai Kozlov will set Ginevra and I up for good matches of our own. We're relying on you to pave the way for us. The connections our family will make through your marriage will further cement our authority in this city. No one will dare cross us or the Kozlovs again."

"You sound like Papa." I roll my eyes. Arianna has always fallen in line with whatever our father says. Whereas I doubt Ginevra, our youngest sister, is excited about the prospect of a *good match*. In fact, she's probably downstairs already causing trouble right now.

Though everything else Arianna says is true. I am paving the way for them, and in the process helping to strengthen my family. I'm the eldest daughter and this is my duty. My own dreams are irrelevant.

Dreams of college, of a normal life, of having any real say in the direction of my life... Those are not possible for me.

Arianna crosses her arms and levels that authoritative look on me that so closely resembles Mama's. She's a year younger than me, but most people mistake us for twins. We have the same deep brunette hair with a hint of auburn and are of a similar stature. Though my eyes are dark brown, lacking the myriad colors in her hazel irises.

I turn away from the mirror to study her more closely. Something about the intensity in which she delivered her little pep talk is nagging at the corners of my mind.

"Are you listening to me? We *need* this union, Soph."

"You know something," I practically accuse. "Look at you, you're all tense—well, more tense than usual."

She tosses me an exasperated glare.

I ignore it. "What's going on? Why is my engagement party tonight so important to you?" I lift a brow, both questioning and inflicting my older sister authority on her.

She glances away, and I know my assumption is correct.

"The aunties were talking yesterday, and they let it slip that Papa's been hinting around at betrothing me to someone very soon."

Not the aunties again.

"Those old bats just like stirring up trouble. You're only twenty, and I'm not even married off yet. Surely Papa will wait until my wedding is over before he starts scheming for his next son-in-law." I *tsk*. "Besides, you know gossip is a sin, right?"

"*Idle* gossip is a sin. In our world it's the only way to get information, skewed as it may be at times." Arianna leans forward. "But I refuse to sit by and have absolutely no clue about what's being decided for my future."

She has a point. *Our world.* I sometimes forget how we don't live life like normal people. At least, not since we were young children. Being pulled from private school and having tutors come to the house since the age of thirteen, so we're not influenced by the outside world, is *not* normal. Spending the past three years studying to be the perfect wife and preparing for our engagements is *not* normal. Most people are in college during this time of their lives.

Above all else, arranged marriages are *not normal.*

Yet here we are. I am fifteen minutes away from taking the first step toward my arranged marriage to a man I've been out with a total of four times—four times in nine months--but know him well enough to know that I won't be happy as his wife.

But I have no choice.

I've never had a choice in anything. I was born into this family and this is my role to play. Mama hopes I'll come to love him, like she did with Papa. I don't have much hope for that.

At least Nik isn't as bad as other men. He's young, only five years older than me, and handsome. If he never opened his mouth, I might actually enjoy his company. Unfortunately, Nik is full of opinions. Ones I have to live with.

Arianna doesn't seem to notice my inner musings

—or my dread. She says, "The worst part is, they told me his name. Papa wants me to marry Liam Baron." Her pink cheeks are visibly pale. "He's the Black Baron's younger brother. I hope it's false gossip and nothing more."

Those words pull me out of my own self-pity, redirecting my concern to her. "Liam Baron? *Blake* Baron's brother?" His name alone makes me shudder. She nods. "I don't believe that for a second. You know the aunties aren't always right, they're probably trying to scare you for a laugh."

She doesn't look convinced, and neither am I.

To have Papa create ties with the Russians through marriage is one thing, but Blake Baron, known as the "Black Baron", is a man no one with any sense would want in their sphere—not to mention their *family*.

While the different families, whether Italian, Russian, or Irish, rule over their own domains, Blake Baron is both outside and above their influence. He deals in secrets. Sometimes those secrets turn into blackmail and ruin. He's worse than any mafioso.

We used to be close friends with the Marino family until the Black Baron ruined them so thoroughly that they disappeared. More like they were wiped from the face of the earth, never to be heard from or seen again. That was five years ago and to this day no one knows if they're in prison, witness protection, or simply dead.

The cold fingers of horror crawl up my spine. Papa couldn't possibly pair Arianna with a member of the Baron family. Though as I have that thought, one of my father's phrases echoes through my head: *"Keep your enemies closer than your allies."*

He would do it. He'd marry one of his daughters into that family just to be closer to Blake Baron. With the illusion of asserting some kind of control over Baron's power.

"Anyway, it doesn't matter." Arianna stands, smoothing the back of her dress to get the wrinkles out. "Tonight is your night. We should go down, everyone should have arrived by now."

A sudden, hot fury replaces the cold dread.

"*It doesn't matter?*" I repeat her words. "We're talking about your life, your future. Of course it matters. You can't just let Papa do anything he wants with you. You're a person, a human, you deserve to be treated like one."

"You're letting him do what he wants with your life and your future," she snaps. Her heated gaze pins mine. "You don't even like your fiancé, but you haven't told Papa."

"I can handle Nik. You don't have to worry about that." I'll never be happy with him, but he's predictable, so I know what I'm getting myself into. Honestly, my fiancé could be a lot worse, he could be a Baron.

She scoffs. "We all know exactly what kind of man Nik Kozlov is. He won't let you go to college, like you want. He'll keep you pregnant, locked up in his house, his own personal broodmare."

"What other choice do I have?"

"None!" She lowers her voice so we're not accidentally overheard. "That's my point. You have no choice, and neither do I. So, stop telling me to stand up for myself, when you're not even willing to voice your own concerns to Papa."

"Fair point." I sigh. "I'm sorry. I always figured as the eldest daughter, I'd be the one to make the sacrifice for us. That you and Ginevra would get it easier, maybe even be able to marry for love, or do something else with your lives. It seems I was wrong."

"Oh, Sophia, I'm sorry." She steps close and flings her arms around me. I hug her back. "I know this is hard for you, I shouldn't rub your face in it."

"It is what it is. This is our life and all we can do is make the best of what we're given." I inhale her rose water perfume. "We should go downstairs."

Nodding, she releases me and moves toward the door. "I'll see you down there."

When she's gone, I push away my negative thoughts and straighten my spine. This is the life I was born into. I'm a mafia princess. In so many ways I'm privileged, with wealth, manners, and a predictable future set out in front of me. I never have to worry about the necessities of life. My family has taken good care of me, and soon that responsibility will fall to my husband. One day, when I'm old, my own children will make sure my remaining years are comfortable.

That's how it goes, generation after generation. Even if, God forbid, I become a young widow, my family ties are strong. There will always be someone there to take me in.

My gaze wanders around my spacious bedroom

taking in the walk-in closet full of designer clothes and shoes, the silk bed sheets, and the towering bookshelf full of hardbacks. In less than three months this won't be my bedroom anymore. I'll be married and living with *him*.

Shaking away that unsavory vision, I make my way downstairs to what's supposed to be an intimate engagement party with close family and friends, only to find that my father invited all of his business associates. It seems the Kozlovs did too.

The mansion is bursting with people, music, and conversation. As I walk through the crowd, countless people offer their congratulations. I smile and nod as if I want to be here. In my head, I'm willing my legs to stride toward the engaged couple's designated table instead of running for the door and out into the frigid late February night.

As I approach, my gaze lands on my fiancé. Nikolai Kozlov is a six and half foot tall, blond haired, blue eyed Russian immigrant with a jawline that could cut glass. At least he's easy on the eyes. And at twenty-six, he's not too much older than me, at least we're in the same decade.

I've heard plenty of horror stories of young women being forced to marry *very* old men, all for the sake of an alliance. I count myself lucky for not being one of them.

Nik stands as I reach our table. His gaze flickers down my body, lingering at my breasts before rising to meet my eyes. I register a flash of lust followed by thinly veiled annoyance. Something about my appearance doesn't meet with my fiancé's approval. Instead of fear or anger, I'm filled with a sudden irritability.

Clamping down on that emotion before it can run away with me, I sit in the chair Nik pulls out. Such a gentleman. Too bad his good looks and basic manners don't reach far beneath his exterior.

"Good evening, *moy angel.*" His voice is laced with the faintest hint of a Russian accent.

I force a smile at him as he takes the seat beside mine. "Good evening." My gaze darts to the two massive guards standing a couple of feet behind us. Did he really think it necessary to bring his security detail to our engagement party? I guess so. After all, we're not married. The deal between my father and the Russians is not yet sealed.

Apparently, a polite greeting is all we have to say to each other. Nik's attention focuses on the men who come up to talk with him. Mine drifts around the elegantly decorated room overflowing with flowers, champagne, and over-the-top expensive decorations.

The entire scene screams of extensive wealth and questionable taste. It tells everyone here tonight that the Pontrelli family, my family, is one of new money, influence, and power.

I catch sight of Arianna with our younger sister, and cousin Ravenna, across the room. As I watch them, Ginevra swipes a Prada clutch from one of the tables and wraps it in her shawl. Her movements are so smooth and quick that if I'd blinked, I would have missed it.

Inwardly, I sigh.

My lips press into a thin line and I subtly shake my head. One of these days, she's going to get caught and there will be hell to pay. I'm not sure what's wrong with Gin, or why she steals. When I've confronted her about it before, she said she does it for the thrill, the rush of the danger of potentially getting caught. Honestly, I think she's simply seeking attention.

A set of broad shoulders in a black suit catches my attention, dragging my gaze away from my sisters and cousin. At first, I'm not sure what drew me to this particular man, he's one of many in a sea of men dressed in dark formal wear. Then he turns and I immediately recognize him.

Roman De Luca. His perfectly styled dark hair is trimmed shorter on the sides than the top. The shadow of stubble shades the lower half of his face which boasts a straight nose, strong jaw, and lush lips. He's gorgeous in an aristocratically roguish kind of way.

All I really know about him is that he's an extremely wealthy business associate of my father, everyone finds him mysterious, and despite his good looks he's an absolute monster.

I've heard he owns a major shipping company, but I doubt that's the extent of dealings. He's probably deeply involved with smuggling illegal goods into the country, although I don't know for sure. Because of his business, and ruthless tactics, he's earned a few whispered nicknames: Poseidon and King of the Sea among them. People say that if you cross him, your shipment will end up at the bottom of the ocean. Some even think he controls the tides and the storms.

I think they're crazy. He's a man, not a God.

Though when his stony gaze collides with mine, the rest of the room seems to fall away. The conversations all around hush, growing faint, and my pounding heartbeat fills my ears. The hairs on the back of my neck prickle. My breath is caught in my throat as his eyes bore so deeply into mine that I swear he's looking straight into my soul.

I can't breathe. I can't look away. And I don't dare blink.

He holds me captive, mesmerized like a snake charmer. Or perhaps like a lion staring back at his petrified prey.

My lips part, and his gaze falls to my mouth, breaking the spell between us. I close my eyes and suck in a much-needed breath of air, trying to regain my composure. When I open them, he's gone, leaving me wondering if I imagined the entire experience.

"Sophia."

I startle, glancing up at my fiancé. "Sorry. What?"

Nik shakes his head and sighs. "I was saying that we should dance. Come." He reaches out and I take his hand. Standing, I glance around the room one more time for Roman but he's nowhere in sight.

On the dance floor, Nik takes my hand and places the other on my waist. We move in time to a slow song.

"You look very nice tonight," he says, holding me closer. His huge palm envelopes a good portion of my ribcage.

"So do you. Very handsome." I smile politely up at him.

"I do wish you'd worn a different color dress though, maybe something blue or green. It would look better with your dark hair than this red color. Plus, red makes you look cheap. Like a whore."

My cheeks heat, but my steps never falter. "I'll keep that in mind for the future."

The four dates I've had with Nik in the past nine months have taught me that he always speaks his mind. Which I appreciate. Honesty is a good, rare trait in a man, from what I've heard. Sometimes, I just wish he wasn't quite so blunt with his hurtful opinions.

"Wear blue next time. It won't make your hair look so red under the lights." His hand skims lower, to the curve of my ass, as if testing my boundaries. "This red dress makes men think impure thoughts... You're still a virgin for me, aren't you, *moy angel?*"

I swallow hard as his fingers dig into my butt cheek. "Of course." It is one of the terms in our betrothal contract. I am to remain a virgin until my wedding night with Nik. If I'm not, then our engagement is called off—along with whatever deal he's brokered with my father.

The song comes to an end, and Nik releases me. He leads us back to the table, his expression neutral, like he didn't just grab my ass in front of everyone.

I take my seat and pick up a piece of warm bread from the basket. I open my mouth to take a bite, when Nik snatches it away.

"Excuse me?" I say in protest, drawing attention from the nearby tables. I plaster a smile on my face to mask my outrage.

"You don't need that, my darling." He dumps the breadbasket on a passing waiter's tray. "You don't want to get fat. Honestly, your mother's ass is big enough for the both of you. I don't want my wife to turn into that."

I bristle further, glancing across the room to Mama. Gorgeous, vivacious, and...

"She's a size six, Nik."

He shrugs. "I like my women—" he cuts himself off. "My *wife* will be slender. Not a cow like the Pontrelli matron."

He just called my *mother* a cow. Thankfully we're alone at this table for two, so no one overheard him—this time. I cringe.

"If my father ever heard you say that—" I start.

"He didn't. And you won't tell him." Nik leans in. "You're to be *my* wife, Sophia. *Mine.* Your loyalty is to me first and your family second. Do not forget that." Someone catches his attention over my shoulder, and he calls out something in Russian.

As Nik stands up and walks away from our table, my skin prickles with the sensation of being watched. I turn around, but can't pinpoint the source. A hundred people are in this room and yet I know that *he* is looking at me again. So he hasn't left after all.

My stomach does a strange kind of flip-flop that leaves me feeling nauseated. I swallow hard and twist around in my chair. My skin morphs from chilled goosebumps to blushing heat. One more glance around and my heartbeat stutters.

There, from the shadows of a corner, I swear I see

the outline of none other than Roman De Luca, staring right at me, his gaze all consuming.

I quickly look away.

Why is Roman watching me? We've never spoken so much as a single word to one another.

Just like the Black Baron, Roman De Luca is not a man I want attention from. I may find him mysterious and intriguing—in the same way a person is drawn to a caged tiger at the zoo. Something pretty and dangerous to look at, but no one wants to be trapped in the cage *with* the predator.

Make no mistake, Roman De Luca is the deadliest of predators in my world.

The smooth amber liquid barely burns as it glides down my throat. I eye Davide Pontrelli, head of the Pontrelli family and a long-time business associate of mine, over the rim of my scotch glass. The din of the party is muted by the thick walls of Pontrelli's office.

He sits across from me, behind his executive desk, his face impassive enough to hide his thoughts. Except I can tell by the tick of his left eye that he's about to pull a gun on me.

Pontrelli's hand disappears beneath his desk as he says, "You know full well I can't give you what you ask. Breaking off the engagement with Nikolai Kozlov would devastate my family's standing. Our word would be worth nothing. No one would trust us ever again."

"I see." I ease back into the soft leather chair, cradling the glass between my palms. "If you don't willingly give me your daughter Sophia, I will have no choice but to seduce her and ruin her virtue before her wedding. I believe that would break the contract you have with Kozlov." I sneer at having to say his name aloud.

Pontrelli's face darkens. "You wouldn't dare defile my daughter."

I don't bother to suppress the vicious grin that tugs at my lips. For a chance at revenge, I'd defile every precious virgin daughter in all of New York City. But I don't have to because there's only one girl that leads to Nikolai Kozlov's ruin, and her name is Sophia Pontrelli.

When Pontrelli told me about his daughter's upcoming nuptials I paid little attention, until I realized her fiancé is none other than Kozlov, the one man I'd sell my soul to the Devil for, if it guaranteed Kozlov's ultimate suffering. Luckily, I don't have to go that far. It seems my chance for revenge has fallen right into my lap.

Pontrelli studies me, his right hand remains out of sight. "I know this isn't about Sophia, you've never spoken to her, much less looked her way. So, I'm assuming this has something to do with Nikolai Kozlov. Is there bad blood between you two?"

Bad blood doesn't begin to cover it. It barely scratches the surface. For what Kozlov did to me, I will see him suffer for years, destroy everything, every hope and dream he's ever had, then watch as he dies a broken, bitter man.

I want everyone he trusts to turn against him. For

everything he holds dear to shatter and be swept away. For his own family to shun his very name.

"Something like that," I admit to the man in front of me. "My business with Kozlov is of no concern to you."

Pontrelli purses his lips, obviously disagreeing with me. "No, but this does concern my daughter. My daughter is my business."

"Fine." I drain my glass and set it on the side table. "You can have her back once I'm done with her. If I'm gentle, she might be in good enough shape to sell to someone else."

"How dare you?" Pontrelli abruptly stands, the revolver in his hand pointed at my chest. "You will not so blatantly disrespect my family. I said *no*. This conversation is over. Get out. Now." He cocks the gun.

I wave him off. "Don't be a fool. Believe me, you don't want to face the consequences of killing me."

Pontrelli's hand is steady, his finger resting on the trigger. "All I see are the benefits to having you out of the way. I get to keep my arrangement with Kozlov, someone more agreeable will rise up to take over your company, and my daughter will be safe."

The chuckle that rises from my chest is dark and devoid of humor. "You're only overlooking one thing. I have a life insurance policy with Blake Baron."

Dropping the Black Baron's name alone is enough to make Pontrelli pale. A visible tremor overtakes his hand.

"You're lying."

Slowly, I shake my head. "I'm not. Baron and I go

way back. We're good friends. Whoever puts a bullet in me will face the wrath of Baron, and we all know he can topple empires—even one as thriving as yours. Look what he did to the Marino family. And they were even more powerful than you are today." I cock my head to one side. "So, think hard. Do you really want to kill me?"

Pontrelli thinks about it for all of two seconds before he lowers the gun. The defeat written across his face warms my cold heart.

"Good decision. Now, shall we talk terms?"

He lowers himself into his chair, looking much older than his fifty odd years. Truth be told, I didn't expect he'd be this reluctant to give up his daughter. Unless of course it's breaking the agreement with Kozlov that he's so upset about. That makes more sense.

"What do you want?" he asks, pouring himself another scotch. When he offers me the bottle, I wave it away.

"It's simple. You'll tell your daughter that she has a new fiancé. The wedding plans can remain the same, she'll simply be walking down the aisle toward me instead of him." If we even make it to the altar. Ideally, I'd like to have this mess over and done with before enduring that insufferable public display of lifelong commitment that's ultimately meaningless.

"This will hurt my family's reputation. We may not recover from it. The Kozlovs will see it as an insult, and they could go so far as to start a war over this. We just came to an agreement with the Irish, we can't anger the Russians now."

"Leave the Kozlovs to me." Soon enough every one of them will be turning their backs on Nikolai, then he'll be alone, and right where I want him. With absolutely *nothing*. "As for your reputation, once we show the world how unworthy Nikolai Kozlov is for your family, once his own turn their back on him, no one will question your decision to break off the engagement."

"How are you going to do all of that?" He clearly underestimates me. What a fool.

"Why, with the help of Blake Baron, of course. Who else has the power to tear apart the Kozlov Bratva?"

He visibly swallows. "I see. In that case, I will inform my daughter of this change in plans."

"Good." I stand up and adjust my cufflinks. "Do it tonight. I don't want Kozlov around her for a second longer than necessary."

With that in mind, I go in search of my fake fiancée. She's a temporary means to an end, nothing more. I can't wait to see the look on Kozlov's face when I tell him that she's now *mine*. That I've stolen her away from him and there's nothing he can do about it. Little does he know, this is only the beginning of his end.

I'm practically giddy as I rejoin the party. Step one of my master plan is almost complete. I can practically taste the sweetness of victory. The next few months are going to be wonderful. I've waited *six years* for this moment, and I'm going to savor every moment of what's to come.

Starting now.

I search the main room, but neither the girl nor Kozlov seem to be in here anymore. Where could they have gone? It's too cold to be outside, so they must be somewhere else in the house.

Moving from room to room, I scan the crowds. Though I see many familiar faces, none are the ones I'm looking for right now. A couple of acquaintances try to stop me for conversation, but I side-step them and mutter incoherently about urgent business.

I enter the last public space on the ground level, my search fruitless. Where the fuck did they go? Somewhere private? Are they lovers?

I wouldn't be surprised. They've been dating for the better part of a year.

That very thought has me grinding my teeth. Though if they actually have feelings for each other, then my plan will be doubly hurtful. As it stands, I doubt Kozlov cares for the girl at all. Me stealing her away from him is nothing more than a slap in the face. The first of many things in his life he won't be able to control any longer.

However, if they are lovers, if he does care for her, then I'll further enjoy watching them both suffer the loss of the other. They can spend the last of Kozlov's days pining for each other. Or perhaps I can think of something worse.

By association with that wretch, the girl is my enemy as well. If she's fallen for Kozlov I will happily ruin her and send her back to him, broken beyond repair.

Yes, that's perfect. Now all I need to do is find her so that I can figure out if she's in love with her ex-fiancé.

I'm about to double back, when I spot Kozlov's goons hanging around the perimeter of the smaller room. Another sweep of the space shows Kozlov's not here, but he must be nearby. That's when I notice the short hallway.

A commotion caused by some drunk partygoer catches the goons' attention long enough for me to slip past them and into the darkened corridor. It's quieter here. There are two doors on either side and one at the end of the hall.

Quickly, I make my way to the far end and press my ear to the solid wooden door. Sure enough, from inside I hear a deep baritone followed by a higher pitched wail.

That cry momentarily short circuits my brain. Before I can formulate a plan, my hand is on the knob and I'm barging through the doorway.

I stop short as I enter a library. Near one section of the bookcase, Kozlov grips the girl by her upper arms, shaking her like a doll.

"You're drunk. Let me go!" She struggles against him, terror distorting her pretty face.

Kozlov backhands her, sending her sprawling to the floor.

"This is what happens to sluts who wear red," he says to her right before he notices my presence.

His eyes flick up to my face. But my attention is on the girl. Seeing her cowering on the floor like that, terrified and vulnerable, makes my blood run ice-cold. A crimson haze halos my vision. He doesn't know it yet, but he's touching what's mine. I don't like other people touching my things.

I lunge at him, tearing him away from her, a snarl erupting from my throat. We're both over six feet and muscular, but I seem to have superior strength tonight as I shove his entire body into a built-in bookcase with enough force that several tomes topple to the floor. My fist smashes into his nose with a satisfying crunch. Blood splatters across my white shirt.

I don't care. I don't want to stop until his face is unrecognizable.

The Devil has given me this moment. The chances of catching Kozlov in an intoxicated state, and without his goons nearby, are slim to none. Yet here he is, too inebriated to properly fight back.

My knuckles split as I hit him again and again. Somewhere in the room a woman's voice is shouting, but I pay her no mind. That is until she wedges herself between us, her face swimming into view, and my next swing freezes midair.

"Stop! You're going to kill him." At first her words don't make sense. Kill who?

I blink, refocusing on the brutalized face in front of me. Kozlov. I don't want him dead—not yet. Being beaten to death is too quick, too merciful of a punishment for him.

Fuck. I rarely lose control like this.

Stepping back, I take in a deep breath and count to three, as I watch Kozlov's body slide to the floor. His chest rises and falls, indicating he remains alive, simply unconscious.

"Thank you for...for stopping him," the girl says, claiming my attention. Her round, red-rimmed eyes look up at me with so much gratitude that my heart gallops. She's so naive that I can practically smell it in the air around her. It's the stench of innocence, of optimism and unshattered dreams.

I straighten to my full height and tug down on my tuxedo jacket to smooth it. If I'm going to see my plans through, there are some things she needs to know about me. The first being that I'm no savior.

"I didn't do it for you." My tone is edged with shards of ice.

She blinks a couple of times as her empty head tries to make sense of my meaning. I see the moment she understands. Her bright, open brown eyes dim, their inner light closed off to me.

The second that light is gone, I want it back.

Inwardly I shake myself out of that thought. What the fuck is wrong with me? I don't give a shit about her, her eyes, or hurting her feelings.

She makes a move toward Kozlov, like she's about to check on him, and I snap. "Don't touch him."

Her gaze darts to mine. "He needs a doctor."

"Are you an idiot? Why do you care what he needs? He hit you." I practically snarl at her, growing tired of her stupidity. How much of an airhead is she, caring about the man who physically assaulted her mere minutes ago?

Her eyes narrow on me, and her lips thin. I'm sure she's holding back what she really wants to say to me. I can only imagine how banal her cutting remark would be.

"He's drunk, he didn't know what he was doing. Besides, he's still my fiancé," she mutters, glancing away.

I ignore how her words make my stomach twist into knots. *No, I want to tell her, you don't belong to him any longer.*

There will be plenty of time to explain later. For now, I need to get her out of here. "Your father wants to see you in his office. Now. Go."

She levels those angry chocolate brown eyes on me. "Nik's bodyguards will kill you for what you've done to him, you know that right?" She moves toward the door, her fingers resting on the handle. So obedient.

"Don't be ridiculous."

She turns to face me. "I'm not being ridiculous. It's a fact. Especially when I tell them what happened." Her eyes flash with menace, right before she slips from the room, presumably to alert Kozlov's goons. Though I doubt she'll do it. She's too sweet to throw a man like me to the wolves.

Or is she? Is she going to hold a grudge because I hurt her precious feelings?

When two pairs of heavy boot steps sound from the hallway, I have my answer. What a vengeful little creature. She has more of a spine than I give her credit for.

Their footsteps draw closer.

Shit. I've made a mess for myself. While his goons might think twice about harming me, I'm not willing to risk it. Those thick-necked types aren't exactly known for their reasoning abilities.

So, I draw the Ruger I always keep on me, lean casually against the sofa, and wait for them to enter.

One after the other, they step into the room and assess the situation. Slowly, by my standards. When the beefier of the two goes for his gun, I shake my head, giving him pause. Maybe he's smarter than he looks.

"Your boss is drunk. He brought this on himself. Now get him the fuck out of my sight before I decide to finish the job."

The goons scowl at me before doing as they're told. I wait while they lift a moaning, semi-conscious Kozlov between them and carry him through the French doors that lead into the garden. No doubt they want to avoid being seen practically carrying Kozlov's intoxicated, battered body away from his own engagement party.

Will there be hell to pay for this later? I sure hope so. I want Kozlov to come at me with everything he's got. Even though it won't be enough to stop me, it will make getting my revenge even more satisfying.

Now all I have to do is find my way back to Pontrelli's office and claim my prize—and the first domino to fall—*Sophia*.

Silently fuming, and more than a little shook up, I walk through the crowd of guests toward my father's office. Roman's voice haunts me with each step. '*I didn't do it for you. Are you an idiot?*'

Why I thought, for even the briefest of moments, that Roman De Luca was my white knight, I haven't a clue. This first encounter with him has told me everything I need to know. He's rude, arrogant, and ruthless. I honestly believed he was going to kill Nik. But he wasn't doing it for me, which begs the question: Then why? What does he have against my fiancé?

Nik. A shiver runs down my spine and my gut twists in a way that makes me regret the couple glasses of champagne I've had this evening. I've never seen Nik act like that before. He was extremely intoxicated, but that doesn't excuse his behavior, no matter what I said to Roman.

My arms hurt where he dug in his fingers and

shook me. Does Nik often get wasted? Will he come at me like that once we're married?

I fix a polite smile on my face for those who pass by, but inside my heartbeat pounds against my ribcage as I consider the horrors married life with Nik will bring. He was rough, hurting me and seeming to enjoy it. That's what scares me the most—his enjoyment. If Roman hadn't come in when he did....

Taking in a steadying breath, I rap on Papa's office door and enter when he calls out.

"You wanted to see me?" I ask, curious, quietly latching the door behind me before striding toward his desk. I'm curious why he'd send Roman to come get me, as well as why he wants to see me in the middle of this party. Any business seems like it should be able to wait until morning.

"I did." Papa gestures for me to sit.

I move toward one of the leather armchairs, then halt when the door opens and in strolls none other than Roman De Luca. My breath catches in my throat, pulse whooshing in my ears, as I stare at his blood splattered shirt.

What is he doing here?

My eyes widen as he stalks towards me, and I have to tilt my head back in order to hold eye contact. Which I boldly do. All the while the rest of my body is frozen in place, except for my glare. He isn't worth the effort of my good manners.

He stops in front of me. His stony hazel yellow eyes scrutinize my features as I unwittingly inhale his scent. My nose drinks it in spicy bergamot, sweet tobacco, and something more subtle, like vanilla. The mixture goes straight to my brain, momentarily addling my mind. If I didn't despise this man so much, I might find him intoxicating. Addicting.

Then cold, harsh reality sets in. He's here for a reason. I fear it has something to do with me.

Finally, I find my voice. "Papa, what's going on?"

He rises from his smooth leather chair, glancing at me then Roman in turn. "Sophia, this is Roman De Luca, a colleague of mine."

"We've met," I say dryly.

Papa shoots me a warning glance for my tone, then clears his throat. "Sit down. Please."

We sit, and I awkwardly perch at the edge of my seat. Whatever this is about, it can't be good. The tension in the room is palpable, and my brain is contorting itself with the numerous scenarios of why I'm here with Papa and Roman. Not a single one of the reasons I come up with makes any sense.

Papa pins me with his stern gaze. "There's been a change in plans. While your wedding will continue as planned, your engagement to Nikolai Kozlov has been called off."

My brow creases in confusion. How can I get married without a groom?

"In his place," Papa continues, "you're now engaged to Mr. De Luca. You will immediately—"

I shoot out of my seat. "*What?* No, Papa, you can't give me to this...this monster!" Horror grips my chest and gives it a harsh twist.

Roman quirks a brow, the curve of his lips show his amusement at my distress. What an asshole.

Papa glares at me. "Sophia, sit down. You will do as you're told. This is important and you will not mess it up." His tone is firm, and I do as I'm ordered. But I'm not going down without a fight. This simply cannot be happening.

"He did this, didn't he?" I point an accusing finger at Roman's smug face. "Why? Why are you doing this to me?"

His only answer is to give me a bored stare, as if this entire situation, and me, are beneath him.

Fine. I turn my attention to my father and fold my arms. "I won't do it. I won't go with him." For the first time in my life, I stand my ground. I'm disobeying Papa. I've always done as I'm told, but this time... There's a line, a boundary, I never knew I had, and this has pushed me over the edge.

I'd rather burn in Hell for all eternity than marry Roman De Luca.

In response to my father's silence, I restate my position, "You can't make me do this."

Papa glances away, at the same time as Roman snorts a laugh. In his deep rumble, he says, "This is a business deal between your father and I. Be a good girl and do as you're told—or I'll make you."

Dread wraps its claws around my lungs and squeezes. It clenches so tightly that for several seconds I can't breathe. Roman holds my gaze and I feel like a mouse in the presence of a giant cat, out in the open with nowhere to hide. Even seated he manages to be intimidating. Behind that cool exterior is a monster ready to snap. I know it. I just witnessed it when he beat Nik bloody.

This evening is turning into a nightmare.

I'm not sure what comes over me, but when I open my mouth, my voice is steady as I say, "You can't make me."

My tone is hushed, but the words are defiant.

Roman immediately picks up on the challenge. Twisted satisfaction flashes in his eyes as his cruel lips turn up at the corners, and I know I'm doomed. He is not the type of man to back down. I should have known better.

"Papa, please." I beg, not taking my gaze off of the predator before me. "I won't do this. I can't. You don't understand—"

"This is not up for argument or debate, Sophia! It's been decided. It's necessary. Now go say your farewells to your mom and sisters. You're leaving at once."

I shake my head, standing and slowly backing away from them toward the exit. I need to get out of here, away from both of them.

Being engaged to Nik I could handle. I knew what to expect from him, especially after tonight, and in a strange way that made him safe—predictable. But this man... How can Papa toss my life, my future, into a business deal with a man like Roman De Luca?

There's only one explanation: Roman coerced my father. Is it blackmail?

Roman uncurls from his chair, standing to his full,

impressive height. "You'll either walk out of this house with me, or I will carry you out. The choice is yours."

My jaw pops open at his blatant threat.

"You wouldn't dare." I swallow hard, preparing to make a run for it.

"Oh, I would." He takes one step forward.

I bolt for the door, but Roman moves quicker than I expect. Large, rough hands tear my grasp from the knob, and he unceremoniously tosses me over his shoulder. I thrash, rumpling his bloody tux.

"Put me down! You monster!"

He rumbles a laugh, swats my ass, then carries me in his iron grip through the main hallway and out the front door. No doubt drawing attention from our guests as I continue to shriek, my cheeks aflame with humiliation. Though from my upside-down position, I cannot see their stricken expressions as we pass by.

In the circular driveway a limo waits for us. Roman shoves me into the back seat with him and closes the door. The locks immediately click into place. Even so, I fumble with the locking mechanism, and repeatedly yank on the door handle. I try the window control. Nothing will budge. I'm trapped. Kidnapped from my own home.

Slamming my fists against the glass, I scream, "Help!"

All the while Roman watches me with amused interest. That asshole is enjoying this, he's entertained by watching my terror or suffering. I was right about him. He is wicked.

The car begins to roll forward and we pull away

from my home. Only then do I realize that I never had the chance to say goodbye to my mama, sisters, and cousin. Am I ever going to see them again? Yes—at my wedding.

There's no point in screaming any more. No one's around to hear, and even if they were, not a single soul is coming to my rescue. In the span of half an hour my life has veered so far off course that I barely recognize it as my own. I'd recently gotten my head wrapped around the idea of being Nik's wife, only to have that future torn away and replaced with one much worse.

To add insult to injury, Roman doesn't seem affected in the least. He sits across from me, legs spread wide, thumbing through his phone as if he didn't just act the part of a tornado and upend my entire world.

I don't even think he likes me. So why is he doing this? What benefit is it to him to steal me from not only Nik but my entire family?

Did Papa cross this man in some way?

Is Nik his enemy?

Am I being used to get back at either or both of them?

I don't have any answers, and until this man starts talking I'm not likely to get any. So, clenching my teeth, I try my best to ignore the big brute by staring out the window.

The trip takes about an hour before we turn onto a long, winding driveway that climbs into forested hills. Roman De Luca's private estate, lit with numerous lamps, is even more impressive than my father's place.

We are truly out in the country now. Private, remote, isolated. Dread settles in my gut, knowing there's no easy escape from here.

I suddenly have the feeling of being completely, devastatingly, alone.

As if to compound my fears, snow begins to fall in huge puffy flakes and sticks to the frozen ground. Normally I love the snow. The way it blankets the world, hushing all other sound, transforming a familiar landscape into an enchanted wonderland.

But right now, the sight of snowflakes makes me feel trapped. At the rate it's falling, we'll have a couple of feet before morning. I glance across at Roman. Maybe what they say about him holds some truth, and he can control the weather—especially storms both out at sea and inland.

It's a ridiculous thought, I know.

But if ever there was a Greek God in a man's body, he'd look and act like Roman De Luca. Gorgeous, yet heartless. I guarantee it.

The limo pulls up in front of a brown stone mansion and the car doors unlock. The sharp click eases some of the pressure in my chest. There's nowhere to run now, but I let myself out, every inch of me aware of Roman climbing out after me, his heat pressing into my back.

I shiver in the sudden cold. My satin dress offers little protection against the freezing temperature and icy flakes that melt on my skin. The white flurry is so thick I can barely see the front of the house.

"Come." Roman places a light touch on my lower back and guides me through the front door.

Inside, the foyer is warm and smells of wood oil. Like the exterior, the interior is formidable and masculine. Rich, dark wooden and leather furniture occupies the space. The floors are black and white marble, the walls have paneling all the way up to the soaring ceiling. Lamp light casts an amber glow over the scene. The space is grand yet soulless, just like my giant captor who inhabits this place.

The driver deposits several suitcases by the door—my suitcases. It seems Papa had instructed someone to pack my belongings. He was determined to send me away. That knowledge is like a sucker punch to the stomach. The back of my eyes sting, but I refuse to let a single tear fall in front of Roman. He doesn't deserve to see the pain he's inflicted on me.

This is my new life, whether I like it or not.

Roman moves further into the house. With nothing better to do, I decide to follow him. I need answers.

"Why are you doing this to me?" I ask as we enter the kitchen. It's also all dark wood and gleaming marble. Impressively appointed with a commercial sized refrigerator and a twelve-burner stove that would make a chef weep with joy.

Roman glances over his shoulder and lifts a dark brow. "Doing what to you?"

"I'm not in the mood to play games. You know perfectly well what I'm talking about. Why did you take me from my home? Why do you want to marry me? You don't even know me."

Roman scowls as he pours bourbon into two glasses, then slides one to me across the enormous, glossy black and white marble island. I pick it up, grateful to have something to occupy my fidgety hands. I'm not used to confronting the men in my life, but this must be done.

"My reasons are none of your concern." His answer infuriates me.

"None of my concern? *None* of my—" I cut myself off with a huff, then decide to let out my frustration. "This is my life! I'd say everything going on right now is my concern. Now answer the goddamn question."

Curiously eyeing me, he drains his drink in one swallow, then refills his glass. "What happened to the sweet, quiet, obedient girl who defends drunken abusers and sics goons on the man who saved her?"

My cheeks flare at his description of me, but it's not enough to deter me for long. "She's checked out. You don't get sweet and quiet from me. And you certainly won't get obedient. Ever."

His features darken. "We'll see about that."

"Yes, we will." I match his glare with one of my own. Where is all this strength coming from? I'm normally not this combative.

"The sooner you stop fighting me and accept your new reality, the easier this will be for both of us. We're engaged. Your place is here with me. And you'll do as you're told, like a good girl."

I set the glass down with an audible clink. Fury

makes my hands shake. This man is completely insufferable. I hate him with every fiber of my being.

"Like hell I will. I wasn't asked about any of this, and I'm not going to just roll over and submit to you. You'll have to find a different woman if that's what you want."

"I don't think so." His lips curve up in a feral grin. "Be a good girl or I'll have to punish you."

My pulse skitters. He sounds like he would enjoy punishing me. I'm in way over my head here, but I can't bring myself to back down. I've been an obedient daughter all my life and this is where I end up? Engaged to a man at least ten years older than I am, all because of a business deal? Hell no. I never agreed to this, and I never will.

"You are not going to lay a single finger on me." I pick up my glass and swallow the contents, seeking some liquid courage to see this through. I never set boundaries, and see where I ended up because of that oversight? I've had enough.

Enough is enough.

"Is that what you told Kozlov before he had you backed up against a wall?" Roman drains yet another glass of scotch.

"You really like rubbing what happened in my face, don't you? Then here, you'll probably enjoy seeing these too." I thrust my arms toward him so he can clearly see the darkening bruises from where Nik had hold of me.

I still can't believe he became so physically violent.

The whole memory feels more like a dream than reality. That wasn't the Nik I've come to know.

Glancing up at Roman, I try to read his expression. He's staring at the marks on my upper arms, and something dark and dangerous lurks in his eyes. A muscle in his jaw pulses.

Then he's stalking around the island, coming closer, until he has me pinned between his massive form and the marble countertop. Every cell in my body is aware of him, his heat, his scent, the danger that oozes from him like a wave crashing against me. A tingle of electricity shoots over my skin, and I shudder. Once again, I'm frozen in place. Trapped.

His palms settle on my arms, his thumbs slowly circling the bruises. I gasp when the contact sends a prickling sensation up my spine. It's unlike any fear I've experienced before. My nipples pebble and heat pools between my legs. Surely that's an odd fear reaction?

I try to shake off the strange feeling. I can't let his overwhelming presence take me off course. I clench my jaw and try to break contact, but his hold tightens.

"Tell me, did you agree to marry Kozlov? Or were you obeying your father's orders?"

"I... I agreed to the match." Reluctantly.

Hostility flashes through his gaze. "Do you love him?"

"No. I don't know him well. Obviously." My answer is honest. I couldn't come up with a lie right now if my life depended on it because Roman's soft caresses are all I can focus on. His gentle touch is at odds with the pure loathing I see in his eyes.

"Do you want to go back to him?" he asks, his tone giving away none of the roiling emotions he can't hide from me while our gazes are locked.

I swallow hard. Would I return to Nik, if not for Roman?

"If I have to marry someone, I prefer the devil I know than the monster I don't."

"You think I'm a monster?"

I nod.

"Yet, I'd never do this to you." He releases my arms. Raising one hand, he skims his knuckles across my cheek, touching a sore spot. I sharply inhale at the unexpected pain. "He hit you."

Yes, Roman witnessed Nik backhanding me right before he stepped in. I hadn't realized it left a visible mark until now.

Roman brushes my hair away from my cheek, his fingers a gentle caress. My skin heats and my lips part at the affectionate gesture. Any moment now, my heart is going to burst from my chest, it's pounding so hard and fast.

How can this man's words be so harsh, yet his touch so caring? His presence both intimidating and protective? He makes me want to smack him for his cruel mouth, and lean into his heady scent.

He promises punishment, yet he'd never hit me.

I'm so confused. No man has ever made me feel like this before.

"You can think whatever you want about me, I

don't care." He leans down, his breath warm against my ear. "But very soon, you're going to get to know me much better than you ever knew Kozlov. Then you can decide which one of us is the real monster."

I shiver from the intensity of his words.

"And you most certainly won't be needing this." He takes my hands in his. Slipping Nik's engagement ring from my finger, he pockets it.

Abruptly, he takes a step back, breaking the spell he'd cast over us—or was it just me? Surely he felt it too. The crackling energy between us, the way all the oxygen vanished from the room, he must have felt it.

Before I'm able to clear my head enough to realize that he still hasn't answered my questions, he leaves the kitchen. All I can do is watch his broad back disappear into the darkened hallway.

Never have I felt so alone, or confused, as I do right now.

CHAPTER 4

My palms tingle from where I touched the girl's smooth skin. What possessed me to rub my hands up and down her bruised arms, I'm not sure. All I know is she felt good. Too good.

Too tempting.

Once again, I had to remind myself that she's a pawn in my elaborate game with Kozlov. She's nothing more than a means to an end. One piece of Kozlov's life that is now mine, that he's not getting back. She deserves to be punished for agreeing to be his wife.

Then why do I have the urge to wrap her protectively in my embrace and never let her go?

She's mine temporarily, not mine *permanently*. Some deep primal part of myself is not fully understanding the situation. Once this is over, I'm letting her go. She can go back to her uninteresting life. Her father can find a new match for her. She's none of my concern at that point.

I heave a sigh as I drop into the leather chair behind my desk. It's late, but I won't sleep soundly until I can get the girl's warm honey scent out of my nose, and the next part of my plan is in motion. So I fish out my cell phone and call Baron. He never sleeps.

"De Luca," he answers in greeting.

"Baron. Have you received the information I had Niall send your way?"

"Yes. I have it right here."

I lean forward, resting both elbows on my desk. "And is it what you need to start bringing Kozlov down?"

"More than enough. I'll start by crashing his investments, then move closer and closer until every single one of his personal and professional relationships are destroyed. This evidence will get the FBI's attention. Give me a couple of months and no one will dare touch him out of fear of being tainted by association. But it will cost you, De Luca."

"Yeah, I know. How much?" I'm willing to pay any price he comes back with to see Kozlov completely destroyed. It's a shame I can't do the devastation myself, but at least I will witness it in a front row seat.

"I consider this type of job priceless."

"I don't have patience for your games right now, Baron. Name your damn price," I growl into the phone.

"My price is a favor. One that I can call in at a later date."

I sigh. "What's the favor?"

"It's yet to be determined."

I scowl. I hate owing undefined favors to be fulfilled at some later time. If this were anyone other than Blake Baron, I'd decline. However, I know that whatever he may request later will be worth it for what I want done now.

"Fine," I agree. "As long as it doesn't put me and everything that's mine at risk."

"It will be within your skillset. I don't ask favors of people who I think will fail in delivering upon them."

"Then we have a deal." I can no longer hold back the wicked smile that forms on my lips. This is it. Everything is falling into place. "Keep me up to date. I want to know what to expect, and when, so I can fully enjoy the show."

Baron grunts in response. "You're fucked up. It's one of your better qualities. Will do."

He ends the call.

I lean back in my chair, letting the reality of what I've put in motion fully sink in. The clock is ticking, a countdown to Kozlov's ruin, and music to my ears. I've waited six long years for this day. All I have to do now is keep up this charade with my temporary fiancée and watch Kozlov fall. Then, in less than three months, my life will be mine again.

I'm looking forward to peace. A time in the future when I will no longer be consumed by this need for revenge. My days will be quiet, my sole focus on my company, and a different woman in my bed every week if I want. I've been too focused on my plans and my company to give much thought to women until now.

But that's the perfect life.

No wife, no children, and above all else, no one to betray me.

Waking my computer, I initiate the bank transfer to Niall Bane in payment for the information he provided to Baron. Niall owns a security company with an army of private investigators on his payroll. If you want information on anyone, Niall is the man for the job.

But digging up dirt is as close to the criminal underground as he's willing to get. If you want something done with that information... that's where Baron comes in. He's not afraid to get his hands dirty for the right price.

As soon as Niall is paid, I pop up his contact via text.

ROMAN DE LUCA:

Baron confirmed receipt of information. I've paid your fee.

NIALL BANE:

Received. If you need anything else, you know where to find me.

I close the app and set my phone on the desk.

Done, and done.

"You must be Miss Pontrelli," says a middle-aged woman, dressed in a simple black uniform, as she steps into the kitchen. "I'm the housekeeper, Diana."

Her friendly smile immediately puts me at ease. Since Roman disappeared earlier, I've helped myself to another pour of bourbon and been lost in terrible, spiraling thoughts.

"It's nice to meet you, Diana. Please, you can call me Sophia."

"Very well, Sophia." She gives me an assessing once over. "You must be freezing in nothing but that delicate dress. Come, I'll show you to your room."

"Thank you." There's no reason to be rude to the staff. They probably secretly hate Roman as much as I do.

She leads me back through the foyer to the curving double staircase, then along a wide hallway to the last door on the right. The room itself can only be described as grand. A king bed sits among robust furniture. One door leads to a walk-in closet, the other to an enormous ensuite. The double French doors open onto a private balcony overlooking a terraced backyard that fades into dense forest.

Diana motions toward my suitcases. "I had your luggage brought up. If there's anything else you need, either come downstairs or press the call button on your nightstand. Can I get you anything else right now, Miss Sophia?"

I've probably had a little too much booze but I'm not hungry. If anything, I just need a good night's sleep. So I tell her, "I'm fine for now, thank you."

She nods. "Very well. The cook's name is Luis. At some point, you might see Rafael, the groundskeeper, though he is quite reclusive. In fact, I'm not sure if I've laid eyes on him yet this year and it's almost March. Anyway, we occupy the East wing of the house, so we're never far if you need anything."

"What about Roman? Where does he spend time at home?"

"His office is on the main floor, and his bedroom is right across the hall from yours."

The thought of him sleeping so close makes my skin prickle with the awareness of his proximity.

"Thank you," I say again.

"You're very welcome. Goodnight, Miss Sophia." She retreats from the room, leaving me to my own devices.

I immediately go for my suitcases. In the side

pocket, I find my phone and turn it on. It chimes as text after text, and a slew of missed calls appear on the screen. Most are from my sister Arianna, a few are from Ginevra and my cousin Ravenna.

I quickly scan the texts before swiping over to press the call button. Arianna answers on the first ring.

"Sophia, are you okay? Papa told us what happened. I can't believe he just let that man carry you off like that! Mama is giving him hell."

"I'm fine. He took me to his home in the country." At least, I think I'm okay, all things considered. "I don't think it's Papa's fault. I'm pretty sure Roman's blackmailing him or something."

"Of course. That makes more sense." Arianna *tsks*. "He should never have started doing business with a man like Roman De Luca."

That piques my interest. "What do you know about him? What do the aunties say about him?"

She hesitates, and the moment of silence sends a chill down my spine. Usually Arianna is forthcoming about the gossip she hears. If she's hesitating to share what she's heard, then it must be horrible. This is bad. Really bad.

"Arianna?" I prompt. I don't really want to hear what she has to say, but I have to. I need information, even if it's gossip.

She sighs. "You have a right to know, especially since you're in his house. I'm sorry I'm the one to have to tell you this, but... Roman De Luca is a very mysterious man. He comes from old money. That shipping business he owns, he inherited from his father. He's an only child. His father is dead, but his mother is still alive. That's all I really know about him, that's fact." She pauses. "Then there are the rumors."

I mentally brace myself. "Go on. Tell me."

"Okay. Take what I have to say with a grain of salt. I'm not sure how much of it is true. But, you know, there's usually a kernel of truth in these types of rumors."

"Arianna," I bite out. "You're stalling. Tell me what you've heard."

Another sigh.

"Okay, okay. Years ago, Roman was married."

Oh. I blink, taken by surprise. He seems like the perpetual bachelor type. Brooding and moody, a loner who generally hates people and hides away in this secluded estate. I never would have guessed he once had a wife. Who would marry a man like him?

Arianna continues in a low voice, "Supposedly it was a love match." *That's doubly shocking.* "But it didn't last for very long until things went horribly wrong. He became possessive and jealous, and when she tried to run, he hunted her down. He killed his own wife. Worse, her body was never found. It's probably buried in the woods at his country estate."

Oh my God. His country estate is exactly where he's taken me. Is his late wife buried in the gardens out back, or deep in the woods that surround this place?

I glance over my shoulder and peer into the shadowy corners, half expecting a vengeful spirit to come flying out of the wall. Does she haunt this place? My arm hairs stand on end, an otherworldly chill seeping deep beneath my skin.

Did Papa know who he was giving me to?

"Sophia, are you there?"

I startle. "Yes, I'm here. I'm just...processing."

"He's a wife-killer. He committed *uxoricide* and got away with it."

"Yes, I understand, thank you." I begin pacing at the foot of the bed. "What am I going to do?"

Roman wouldn't answer my questions earlier. I don't know why he wants to marry me, but what if he wants to make me his wife in order to murder me and bury *my* body in the woods? Is he a serial killer? How many other women has he married and offed?

Arianna speaks in a hushed voice, "If I were you, I'd run."

"Run where? Papa won't take me back while Roman's alive. No one will help me."

"We will."

I frown at my phone in confusion. "What do you mean, Arianna? Who's *we*? You're always on Papa's side, he won't let you come to my rescue."

"I'm not on his side when it comes to this. What he did was wrong, even if he didn't have a choice. Either way, I'm not going to sit back and do nothing when your life could be in danger. Ravenna is here. She and I will come for you. The consequences be damned."

Once again, I stare at my phone in shock. Arianna never cusses. She must be really worked up about this, which makes me feel less alone. I have my sister and my cousin on my side.

"Hold on. Let's back up for a minute. What if the rumors aren't true and he didn't kill his wife? Are you sure he was ever married?" My head is spinning as I try to sort through all the information, implications, and possibilities.

"I've heard about his wife from several different people, not just the aunties, so I'm pretty sure he was married. I'm sorry, but given his reputation—which everyone knows about—do you really think he didn't do it? He's ruthless and unforgiving. The facts are he was married, and his wife disappeared. *Poof*, gone."

"You're freaking me out, Arianna."

"Good, because you need to get out of there before it's too late. I don't want to lose you. He already murdered one wife—who he was supposed to be *in love* with. What do you think he'll do to you if you displease him? He's a tyrant, Sophia."

I've seen first-hand how brutal Roman can be, and I don't doubt he killed his wife in a fit of rage. He's a cruel man. I'm sure his own mother regrets bringing him into this world.

"What's the plan?" I cast my gaze upward, praying that Arianna does have an actual plan to get me out of this mess.

"Okay, so you need to share your location with me, then we're going to take Ravenna's car and pick you up. Just get to the main road and we'll find you. Keep your phone with you so we can text."

I nod even though she can't see me. "What about after that? I can't go home."

"No, you can't. Ravenna says she'll take you in."

"Is Cian okay with that?"

A pause. "She says he'll have to be. You'll have to hide at her place for a while and no one can know you're there. I know it's not ideal, but as long as Roman is searching for you, you can't come home without putting all of us in danger."

"I know. But what if Roman figures out I'm at Ravenna's house?"

Ravenna's voice comes on the line. "Don't worry about it. Cian is the head of the Irish mafia and richer than God. If we have to, we'll hide you away in Ireland. I just hope it doesn't come to that."

Inhaling a shaky breath, I steel my nerves. "Okay. I'll head out tonight. It took us about an hour to get here, so you should leave soon."

"I will. Share your location with Arianna's phone, we're leaving now."

"See you soon." I hang up and text her my location. She should be here in less than sixty minutes, unless—

Shit, I forgot about the snowstorm.

Sprinting to the window, I peer through the glass. The grounds are blanketed in white, but the wind has calmed down and the falling snow drifts lazily from the black sky.

I can do this. I will make it across the estate and out to the main road.

With my mind made up, a ray of hope on the horizon, I dress in a pair of wool slacks and a cashmere sweater. Going through the contents of my luggage, I find that all I have are high heels and slippers. Neither are a good option for this weather, not to mention the terrain. I'm going to have to find, and steal, someone else's shoes.

The back door is off the kitchen, and I swear I saw a mudroom. Someone has to stash their boots in there. I cross my fingers and pray to God that my assumption is accurate.

Fortunately, my father's staff packed my long fur coat. I drape it around myself and cinch the waist closed. Wearing two pairs of socks, and a scarf wrapped around my head, I'm ready to make my escape.

I crack open the door, and peek out. The hallway is quiet and empty, so I slip from the room and tiptoe along the corridor to the stairs, with my heart in my throat. Surely Roman's security is top-notch. It's only a matter of time before he gets wind of what I'm up to and sounds the alarm.

As I creep down the stairs, a distant voice tells me Roman is somewhere deeper in the mansion, probably on a business call, as I can't hear the other side of the conversation. The steps are well built, barely creaking as I make my way stealthily to the ground floor.

I stride toward my destination, my palms grow clammy and my pulse whooshes in my ears. It's past midnight. The rest of the household staff must be in their wing of the house by now, settled in for the night.

Not so much as a mouse moving in this tomb of a house.

I squeeze my phone in the pocket of my fur coat to reassure myself it's still there. I'm so close to getting out of here that I can practically taste my freedom.

Except this freedom is tainted by knowing I'm putting others in danger. What I should do is go on the run, far away from here, where not even my family can find me. I'd be on my own for the first time ever. But that's better than staying here to suffer who knows what fate Roman has in store for me. Or letting him tear through my relatives, punishing them, until he flushes me out of hiding.

It's too much to think about right now. My first objective is to get out of this house. Then I can worry about my next move.

I make it to the back door, holding in a whoop of triumph when I spot a pair of rain boots nestled in a tidy niche. I slip my feet into them. They're a full size too large, which tells me they probably belong to Diana instead of one of the men. At least I'll be able to walk in them. Even run if I must.

My hand grips the doorknob, ready to turn it, when Roman steps out of the shadows of the adjoining pantry. A startled cry escapes my mouth. Though it's dark, I swear Roman's yellow-hazel eyes burn with fury.

"Going somewhere?" he drawls, his tone soft and deadly.

Instead of answering him, I twist the handle and

bolt through the doorway. He spews a series of curses as he lunges after me.

He's hot on my heels. His menacing presence presses against my back. I half sprint, half fall down the stairs to escape him.

My feet land in deep, untouched snow, but I don't let it slow me down. I turn left and sprint across the manicured garden to the obscured tree line with everything I've got. I refuse to be caught. My boots pound the uneven earth. I pump my arms and focus on the dense woods ahead.

Roman shouts at me, but I pay no attention to him. Wind whips my hair into my face, stinging my eyes. My nose and lips are already growing numb from the cold.

Still, I don't let up. My life literally depends on making my escape.

I crash into the forest, blindly running through the quickly accumulating snow. My only thought is to get away from Roman. To escape my ugly fate. To run toward my sister and freedom. To live another day.

Low hanging branches smack me in the face and shoulders. As I run farther away from the estate's lamplight, the darkness seems to swallow me whole.

Is it my imagination, or is the snow falling more heavily now?

Breathless, I come to a stop behind a huge tree trunk. Not only is the snow denser, it's swirling around in all directions in the biting wind. If I stay out here too long, I'll likely die from exposure.

Maybe this was a mistake. What was I thinking coming out here at night in the middle of a snowstorm?

Only one word explains my reasoning: Desperation.

That is my only excuse for acting like a complete idiot and putting my life in danger.

Staying inside with that monster is more dangerous, a voice whispers in the back of my mind. Yes, it is. I'll gladly risk the weather. It can't be too far to the road.

I take off running again, and as the elements continue to beat down on me, I grow panicky. In no more than a couple of minutes, I've lost all sense of direction. Hell, I can barely see where I'm going. In the morning, someone is going to find my frozen body in these woods.

You're smarter than this, Sophia. Think.

Taking a huge risk, I use the flashlight function on my phone. Hopefully, I am far enough away from the house that no one will spot the illumination. The light doesn't go far, but at least I can see my surroundings a little more clearly.

I emerge from the dense forest and breathe a sigh of relief. Up ahead is an open field, and beyond it are moving spots of golden light. Headlights. That's the main road!

I quickly make a beeline for it. My boots pound the white powder... leaving easy to follow footprints? Nope. They are concealed in a matter of seconds by the snowfall. At least that's another blessing to count. Roman won't be able to track where I went, or how I escaped. He can never know that Arianna and

Ravenna helped me. Though he's guaranteed to suspect as much.

As I run, I notice that the ground now feels different beneath my feet. I can't quite explain how it's altered. I'm not getting the same traction—

A series of ominous cracks split the air.

And the earth shifts beneath me, opening up.

Then I'm plunged into water so cold it instantly freezes the blood in my veins. The world around me grows darker, the weight of my fur coat pulls me down to the murky bottom and the promise of death.

CHAPTER 6

Roman

"Sophia! Stop!" I call after her, but she keeps running. "Goddamn it!" The stupid girl is heading straight for the lake, which this time of year should be frozen, but there are no guarantees.

With another curse, I take off after her. Between the dense forest, the snow, and the darkness, I momentarily lose track of her, until she broadcasts her location with a small beacon of light. I tear through the trees, but I'm too late. She's already running full speed across the lake.

My palms itch in anticipation of what I'm going to do to her once I catch her and bring her home. Her ass is going to be so raw that she won't be able to sit properly for a week.

I'm beyond angry with her for not only trying to escape, but for putting her life in danger. She's a damn fool. When this is over, I'll teach her a lesson she'll never forget.

Then I hear it. Like the roll of thunder clashing with the snap of a whip. One moment the girl's there, and the next she disappears, swallowed by the lake.

My heart stops.

The world around me seems to slow.

Everything pauses, as if holding its breath, before sharply inhaling. One moment I'm on the shore and the next I'm diving into the frigid water.

The shock to my body causes momentary paralysis, before instinct takes over and I swim for the sake of survival. Except I'm not headed up for air, I'm moving deeper, desperately seeking the mindless creature who sank like a fucking stone.

My lungs begin to burn. My muscles are so cold they start to cramp.

Where the fuck is she? I refuse to surface without her. This stupid girl is going to kill us both.

Finally, my fingertips brush against cold, wet fur, and I know I've found her. Gripping her arm, I tug her upward until I can grab her around the waist. Then I kick off from the lake's floor and break through the water's icy surface. More frigid air assaults my lungs.

Sophia coughs and sputters as I drag her from the water. She's breathing, which means that my search for her must have not taken that long. Though it felt like I was underwater for ages. Since drowning didn't kill either of us, my guess is that the cold will, soon enough.

We have to get back to the house.

I lift her into my arms. She weighs a ton in that drenched fur coat, so I tear it from her back and haul her against my chest. Carrying her bridal style, her small body shaking uncontrollably against mine, I make it back to the mansion in mere minutes.

At least she's continuing to shiver, that's a good sign.

I climb the stairs two steps at a time, ignoring the wet, muddy footprints I'm leaving in my wake, and the water droplets dripping from both of us. Once I reach my bedroom, I nudge the door closed with my boot.

The girl is shaking so hard she can barely stand. So I hold her upright while stripping the sodden clothes from her quaking body. Her teeth clatter so loudly they drown out all other sound in the room. Her skin is cool to the touch.

Her eyes are closed, but she's conscious, barely. Not lucid enough to resist me as I manipulate her body. I'm sure if she was fully herself, she'd be fighting me right now, even though it would do her more harm than good.

This is *not* how I envisioned the first time I undressed my fiancée.

Scooping her up, I lay her in my bed, beneath the thick comforter. Then I make quick work of discarding my own clothing and slide under the covers with her. I haul her body against mine. My arms and legs wrap around her petite frame.

While I'm not that much warmer than her, I *am* warmer. The exertion of jogging home, carrying her in my arms, has managed to stave off the worst of the cold. Plus, I'm naturally hot-blooded.

My natural internal inferno soon heats our little

cocoon. The girl's shivers and chattering teeth begin to subside, her body relaxing into mine, and I inhale her pleasant honey scent.

At any moment, I expect her to pull away. To regain her senses and try to escape my hold. Instead, she snuggles into my chest as her breathing grows steady, indicating she's asleep. I quickly check her pulse. It's strong and steady. She'll be fine in the morning.

Not an inch of space separates our flesh from one another. Her skin is warm and smooth against mine. I sweep damp hair away from her face while I hold her. She feels amazing in my arms, so much so that I don't even mind the way her hair has drenched my pillow. Careful not to wake her, I swap it for a dry one.

Now that we're both out of immediate danger, questions plague me. Why did she run? Besides the obvious answer: She doesn't want to be here. But is that reason enough to risk her life in the woods, in the snow?

I don't think so.

Perhaps she's more impractical and dim-witted than I originally thought. Which is a pity. She's gorgeous, but obviously not very bright.

Though the way she spoke to me in the kitchen, and the defiance she showed at her father's house, suggests she does in fact have a sense of self-preservation. I see intelligence in her eyes—especially when she's glaring daggers at me. So why would she do something this stupid?

I bury my nose in her hair, drinking in that

summer honey scent, and my eyelids fall closed. Since she's asleep it's easy to pretend she wants to be in my arms, that she's enjoying the closeness as much as I am drinking in the sensation of making contact with another human. I don't remember the last time I held someone like this.

Actually, that's not true, I do remember. It's been six years—maybe longer.

At the realization that I haven't been naked with a woman in over half a decade, blood rushes to my cock and I'm instantly, achingly hard. I groan as it presses into the space between my abdomen and her soft stomach. My eyes roll back in my head. I bite down on my bottom lip, resisting the urge to rock my hips and spurt cum all over us. At this point, it wouldn't take much to set me off.

I should get up. She's safe. She doesn't need my body heat anymore.

I should *really* leave her be.

But I don't.

Ignoring my throbbing cock, I immerse myself in her scent, the sensation of her skin against mine, the firmness of her body in my arms. Fuck, am I really this starved of human touch that I'll torture myself, with a woman I don't particularly like, just to feel her body close to mine?

I shy away from the obvious answer to that question.

Instead, I let myself relax into her soft curves. It's late, and since I never sleep more than a few hours, I'll be up by six, and gone before she so much as stirs. She'll never know I was here.

Because that would end in a catastrophe.

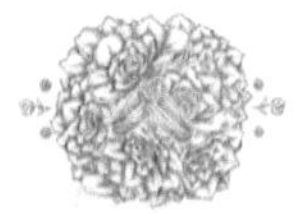

"**G**et off of me!" A shrill, feminine voice screams into my ear a second before I'm shoved off the bed and land on the floor. The impact jolts me fully awake. Though my mental faculties are not yet operating at one hundred percent, because I immediately leap up, presenting her with a full-frontal view of my raging morning wood.

This elicits another shriek from the girl. Her wide, innocent eyes glued to my cock. Unfortunately, *that* look on her face initiates a series of dirty thoughts so vivid that my dick twitches like it has a mind of its own.

I turn away, giving her an unhindered view of my backside instead. Is that really any better? No.

With a curse, I find a pair of boxers and slip them on. They do little to conceal my hard-on.

Turning back to face the girl in my bed, my gaze slides past her horrified expression to the light streaming through the gap in the curtain, then to the bedside clock. It's almost ten in the morning.

I overslept. That's an understatement.

I have never slept past six in the morning, not since

I was a teenager, no matter how late I'm up the night before. And I was still deeply asleep when she so rudely woke me up.

Vaguely, I recall dreams involving the girl's sweet mouth wrapped around my cock. Apparently, I was unwilling to wake from that delight.

Fuck. I drag my fingers through my hair. What is happening to me? I try to shrug it off as a peculiar set of circumstances that have thrown me off course—momentarily. I need to pull myself together.

"What are you doing in my room? In my *bed*?" she demands, drawing the covers up to her chin to cover her nakedness.

A smirk touches my lips. "This is *my* room and *my* bed, principessa."

It takes her all of three seconds to glance around the space before her jaw drops open in horror. I have the sudden urge to shove my cock between those parted lips.

"Why..." She clears her throat. "Why am I in your room?"

"You don't remember what happened last night?"

Her forehead bunches in thought. It's fucking adorable.

Shit, I'm losing my goddamn mind. Nothing about this woman is adorable. She's the bane of my existence at this point.

Hastily, I grab fresh clothes from my closet and dress. I'd normally shower first, but today there's no time. I need to get myself under control, and that little vixen out of my bed before I do something we'll both regret.

"I remember," she says as I emerge from my closet. "You rescued me?" That sounds more like an accusation than a thank you.

"Yes, I did. You're welcome."

She shoots me a withering glance. "I'm sure you didn't do it for me. So why should I thank you? We both know you're not the knight in shining armor type."

That gives me pause. Yes, I've made certain to give her that impression. Now that she has it, I want to rip it away from her so she'll look at me with that same adoration I saw in her eyes in the library.

Why? I have no fucking clue.

So, I double-down on her original impression. "You're right, I didn't do it for you." I grab a pair of cufflinks off the nightstand, and continue, "I need you alive for a little while longer."

The blood visibly drains from her face, even her pink lips pale.

I eye her. "Why did you run last night? Do you really think I'm so much of a monster that you'd rather brave the wilderness than stay a single night under my roof?"

"I don't *think* you're a monster. I *know* you are." Her gaze spews a mix of fear and hatred.

Oh, this is going to be good.

"Is that so? Why don't you tell me what you think you know about me?" I level my stare on her.

She licks her lips. The sight of her pink tongue

sends another jolt of arousal to my neglected cock. It's not helped by the fact that her hair is *come-fuck-me* disheveled, and she's naked in my bed. If she hadn't shoved me out of it, this morning had the potential to go in an entirely different direction. One I need to stop thinking about.

She mumbles something incoherent.

"What did you say? Speak up." I step closer to the bed.

"You murdered your wife."

I recoil as if her words are a physical blow. A lot of people believe that rumor, but no one has dared to say it to my face.

Until now. Until her.

"Is it true?" she asks, leaning forward. Strangely, there's a glint of hope in her chocolate brown eyes.

Oh, is she giving me the benefit of the doubt? I don't need her fucking charity. Or anyone else's for that matter.

"It may as well be true," I snarl. "Don't ever bring up my wife again. Are we clear?"

"Or what?" Her chin tilts at a stubborn angle.

My glare deepens. "Or I'll bury *your* body in the woods."

She gapes at me as I storm from the room, done with this conversation. Fucking gossips. I loathe them. They think they know everything about me, when they don't know the half of it. If the girl wants to believe every word they utter, that's on her. I'm not going to defend myself against their half-truths. I don't need to justify my actions.

I already know there's a special place in Hell waiting for me.

By the time I've seen my plans through, I may even qualify for an upgrade. Or would it be considered a downgrade? Hm, I wonder. Either way, I'm sure it'll be the best VIP service the Devil has to offer.

CHAPTER 7

Sophia

The moment Roman leaves, I wrap a blanket around myself and sprint across the hall to my own room. Turning the deadbolt, I heave a relieved sigh, then head for the shower because I smell like the bottom of a murky lake.

Arianna and Ravenna are probably out of their minds with worry. They had my location on the cell, but when I went under water it probably blipped out.

Crap, how am I going to get in contact with them? I doubt Roman will let me use a phone since I tried to escape. He won't trust me at all now.

As I wash, my brain cycles through images and snippets of our conversation. He rescued me—for his own benefit. But the fact remains that he dove into a frozen lake in the middle of the night to pull me out. He risked his life. That sounds suspiciously heroic to me.

He's defensive about his late wife and the circumstances surrounding her death. Though he neither admitted nor denied his role in her demise. So that's still something to ponder.

I turn around to wash the shampoo from my hair and close my eyes. The image of Roman's long, thick, throbbing dick instantly invades my mind. I swallow hard. I've never seen anything quite like it.

Did I do that to him? Make him hard? Or do all men wake up aroused?

I really shouldn't be thinking about my captor's cock. What is wrong with me? Seriously.

Quickly, I finish showering, and dress in a comfortable pair of designer jeans and a cashmere sweater.

A commotion in the hallway draws my attention. I press my ear to the door. It sounds like several people are arguing, and I think I recognize...

I pull open my door, then practically launch myself at Arianna, unable to believe my eyes. She's here, with Ravenna, they came for me. Instantly, I realize they shouldn't have done that. They're putting themselves in great danger by being here.

"Are you insane?" I whisper into Arianna's ear.

She pulls back. "This was Ravenna's idea not mine."

I glance over at my cousin. Her arms are crossed and she's giving Roman the death glare, while he manages to look both irritated and bored. Diana hovers nearby. From her unsettled countenance, I'm guessing my sister and cousin pushed their way into the house.

Arianna draws my attention back to her. "We waited for you last night, and when you didn't show up, we came to the gate. Where we were rudely turned away by security. What happened?"

"I fell through the lake."

Her brows shoot up her forehead. "Are you okay?"

"I'm fine." I glance at my captor. "Roman rescued me."

Arianna's jaw drops. "What—"

"I'm very busy," Roman barks. "Conclude your business and get out."

"Give me my cousin and we will happily leave you alone." Ravenna stands tall and faces Roman.

"I can't do that."

"Can't or won't?" My cousin questions, pure challenge in her tone.

Roman sneers down at her. "Both. You wanted to see that she is alive, and there she is. Now get out."

"Fine. I'll pay you for her. How much do you want?"

Roman's chuckle is low and edged with danger. I'm afraid that Ravenna has pushed him too far.

He gets in her face, though she remains rooted to her spot. "I don't want money. I don't want anything you could possibly have to offer me. And if either of you interfere again, your family will never find your bodies. I have no issues making enemies with the Italians or the Irish, or anyone else for that matter. So leave. And never come back here again."

I take Arianna's shaking hand in mine. "You're such a tyrant," I tell Roman. "These are my best friends, you can't throw them out of the house. Not while I'm supposed to live here too."

He considers me for a few seconds with that intense stare. If I didn't know any better, I'd think I took him by surprise. Though I'm sure nothing ever takes Roman De Luca by surprise.

"You think I'm being unreasonable?" he asks, frowning.

"Did my use of the word *tyrant* tip you off? Or are you simply that intuitive?"

The momentary flash of amusement in Roman's eyes gives me pause. It's gone so quickly that I'm already beginning to doubt what I saw. Does he think I'm funny? Impossible.

"Very well," he says. "Your family may visit you here. But if you try to escape again, Sophia, know that I will hunt you to the ends of the earth. I will leave no rock unturned, no family, friend, or acquaintance alive in my search for you. Do you understand?"

I nod. Once.

His meaning is crystal clear. I'm not going anywhere. I can't without putting everyone I know and love at risk. Roman wants me, and that's exactly what he'll get.

I draw Arianna by her hand into my room. Ravenna follows us in. As I close the door my gaze clashes with Roman's, the message in his eyes is as clear as his words, a warning. I nod again.

"What a horrible man!" Arianna sits primly at the edge of my bed. "I'm so sorry, Soph. This is terrible."

"I think I'll live."

"You'd better. Because if you don't, I swear I'll wring his neck."

"We'll both wring his neck," Ravenna adds. "I know these things can be difficult, but try to make the best of it. Cian was...challenging in the beginning, but then we fell in love."

I scrunch up my nose. "I'd rather drink molten lava than think about falling in love with Roman De Luca. He's the absolute worst. Except..."

They gaze curiously back at me.

"Never mind."

"I don't think so," Arianna says. "You can't leave us hanging like that. Except, what?"

I sigh. "This stays between the three of us. Okay?"

They nod.

"Nik hit me, at our engagement party, and Roman nearly beat him to death." I pace the room, ignoring their shocked expressions. "I've known Roman for less than twenty-four hours and he's saved me twice. I'm sure he has nefarious intentions, but...I'm conflicted. He's an overbearing, rude brute. I'm not denying that at all. There's just something *else* about him too. I can't explain it."

"Sophia, he murdered his own wife!"

I shake my head. "I don't think he did it."

"And how did you come to that conclusion?" Arianna folds her arms.

"I asked him about it this morning."

"Oh my God, are you crazy? Roman has *killed* people for less than that."

"Well, I'm still alive."

Arianna gasps. "I know what's going on. You have

Stockholm Syndrome. I can't believe it. This is terrible."

Ravenna's husky laughter fills my bedroom. "Arianna, you're such a sweet innocent thing at times."

My sister's gaze narrows on our cousin.

Undeterred, Ravenna continues, "Sophia has clearly met a man who intrigues her. There's no shame in that." Her expression sobers. "Be careful. A man like him can bring you the highest highs and the lowest lows. Their gravitational pull is so strong that you can lose yourself as you orbit around him. Remember to protect your heart while you experience the amazing things he will do to your body."

My cheeks heat. A vivid picture of Roman's cock appears in my mind's eye.

"Ravenna!" Arianna is thoroughly appalled.

Our cousin smirks. "Don't worry, Arianna, I'm sure you'll marry a good boy who won't do any of those naughty things to you."

"I sure hope so."

Ravenna and I giggle.

Quickly, easily, we fall into our usual norm. We spend the rest of the morning chatting about everything under the sun. Diana brings us lunch. Then we say our goodbyes.

As soon as they leave, I feel disconnected again. Lost. Lonely.

I'm about to go mope back to my room, when Diana approaches me in the foyer. She holds out a brand-new cell phone. I glance questioningly at it, because Roman wouldn't allow this, would he?

She presses it into my hand. "All of your information has been restored from the backup."

"But..." I'm so confused right now. Is this a trick? Some kind of mind game?

Diana must read my distress clearly on my face. "It's fine, Miss. Roman's orders."

"Thank you." I take the phone, it's my only lifeline to the outside world.

She smiles, then goes about her business.

Roman's orders? Wouldn't it be easier for him if I had no means of communication? Or is he so sure that his earlier threat latched itself deep in my bones, that I wouldn't dream of running away again?

This gesture is either arrogant or thoughtful. Unfortunately, I'm not sure which.

Sophia

I didn't see Roman again until that night at dinner. I spent the rest of the day recovering in my own bedroom. I tried to read, but my mind was a jumble of thoughts and memories.

Memories of how I'd fallen through the ice, believing I was going to die. Then the complete trust I had in Roman when he pulled me from the lake. The feeling was so powerful, so all-consuming, that in the moment I'd forgotten why I'd run away. I felt protected in his arms. I just knew that everything, that *I*, was going to be okay.

Of course, I couldn't tell my sister and cousin that this morning. The small parts that I did disclose to them already felt like too much. Is Ravenna right? Am I intrigued by this mysterious man who always leaves me feeling some intense emotion whether it's hatred or gratitude? I'm certainly not indifferent around him.

I glance across the table at Roman. Dark head

bowed over his plate of grilled chicken salad, scrolling through his phone. I swear he never stops working. At least, I assume he's working. He could simply be using the device as a means to ignore me.

"What do you do for work? You own a shipping company, don't you?" I ask him, wondering what can possibly take up so much of his time.

His head jerks up, almost like he forgot I was here. I suppress an eye roll.

"I run De Luca Global Trades." He clears his throat, setting his phone on the table beside his plate. "It's an import export company that's been run by my family for several generations."

"And...what does that have to do with my father? You two work together, don't you?"

"I work with a lot of people." He leans back in his chair. "I assist with importing goods into this country and have ins with the port authorities. To the mafia, the various bratvas, and everyone else I work for, I'm indispensable to their business."

Arrogant much?

"So, you're a smuggler?"

He scowls. "I suppose you could put it that way."

Roman reaches for his phone, bows his head over it, and resumes ignoring me while we eat. I guess that conversation is over.

In the full twenty-four hours that I've known him, he has alternated between hot and cold so many times that I'm beginning to get whiplash.

He's rescued— I mean, *not* rescued—me twice. His touch does funny things to my body and brain, making me crave more. Then he ruins it all with his threats.

'I'll bury your body in the woods'

Or worse, kill my entire family.

I cock my head, studying him. Except, before all of that he'd stated that, *'it may as well be true'*, to the question of murdering his late wife. Which is not the same as an admission of guilt. No, this complicated man is hiding something. He has secrets. The mystery of those secrets lure me in, begging me to unearth them.

Why? I'm not entirely sure.

I'm not the best judge of character perhaps, but I think I'm okay at it. Now that I'm sober, calm, and have had the entire day to think about recent events, I don't peg Roman as a wife killer. This morning I said as much, and my intuition around it has only gotten stronger throughout the day.

I also have a sneaking suspicion that he is, in fact, a white knight, cleverly disguised as this arrogant, surly, reclusive man. But why? Why does he hide his true nature beneath this prickly exterior?

Since I'm not going anywhere anytime soon, I aim to find out which version of him is the real Roman De Luca. Is he a hero or a villain?

I can't think of a better pastime. The puzzle will certainly keep me from getting bored.

So far in the hero category, I have: two rescues, caressing my bruises, telling me he'd never hit me, giving me a new phone, and... that's about it.

In the villain category: Assaulting my ex-fiancé—

though this could be seen as heroic, kidnapping, smuggling, verbal threats, snide comments, calling me an idiot, rude behavior all around, and holding me captive in his house.

He needs to make quite the effort to tip the balance into the hero category. At this point, it's not looking so good. But I'm not willing to give up just yet. For the sake of my own sanity, I can't give up. Perhaps he needs a push, or a reason, to do good rather than evil.

"Why are you trying to flay me open with your stare?" he grumbles, finally glancing up from his phone.

"I don't think you killed your wife," I blurt. One of us has to be open and honest or we'll never have a conversation that lasts more than a millisecond.

He frowns. "Good for you." His attention returns to his phone's screen.

I lean forward. "I think you arranged our betrothal to get back at my father, or maybe Nik, but deep down you really did it because you're lonely."

His gaze flicks up to meet mine. The expression on his face is unreadable, carefully guarded by that neutral mask. His eyes search mine, but I can't tell what he finds there. Honesty, perhaps?

"I liked you better when you were running scared." Ah, now we're back to villainous Roman.

"That was a moment of weakness. I promise it won't happen again." Strangely, after this morning, I've come to the conclusion that I'm not afraid of him. Seeing the beast in broad daylight seems to have helped me gain a clearer perspective of him. Or maybe it was the full-frontal nudity this morning that did the trick. He certainly didn't look so threatening completely naked. Except for that *thing* between his legs. I'll never get that image out of my mind. It fills me with both curiosity and doubt, because surely it won't fit...down there. It's impossible, isn't it?

Do all virgins have the same thought, or is this a result of my sheltered upbringing? Ginevra once broke Papa's rule and hid a toy in her room. She showed it to Arianna and me, but even that dildo wasn't as large as what Roman's packing in those tailored trousers.

Do all men look like that? Or is Roman unique in that area?

"Penny for your thoughts," he breaks through my musings.

My cheeks instantly flush and I avert my gaze from the general direction of his crotch. My new fiancé literally caught me thinking about his dick over dinner. White-hot horror sweeps through me. I feel his yellow-hazel gaze bore into the side of my averted face.

He clicks his tongue. "Well, that's an interesting reaction to such a simple question."

I'm going to curl up under the table and die from embarrassment.

"Bright red cheeks, rapid pulse, dilated pupils. Tell me, principessa, are you thinking naughty thoughts?"

God strike me down now and take me away.

Roman rises from his seat. He circles around the table, keeping his gaze locked on me. I try to avoid making eye contact, but as he comes closer we're like magnets, unable to resist each other. He lifts me up, sits in my chair, and sets me in his lap.

Immediately his whiskey-vanilla scent swims up my nose and straight to my brain. His muscles are hard beneath my butt and at my back. He loops his arms around my waist, caging me against him. With one hand, he tilts my chin up until our gazes collide.

"You clearly stated how you're no longer afraid of me, so your pounding heartbeat must be from some other emotion than fear. Is it anger...or lust?" He skims his thumb across my lips and they part, catching his attention. "I see."

Without warning, he lifts me up like I weigh nothing at all, and repositions me so that I'm straddling his waist, my legs dangling, my hot pussy—that's what Ginevra said it's called when it gets wet and tingly—presses against his erection.

He's hard. Again.

Fascinating.

This version of Roman is what I call *hot Roman.* He's neither good nor evil. Though I swear he's hell-bent on driving me crazy with his touch. I never know how long it's going to last until *cold Roman* takes over again. All I can do is hang on for the ride and see where it takes me.

So far this is what I've learned about the man who's taken me captive. From his behavior in the kitchen last night, to this morning when I literally kicked him out of his own bed, and later as he threatened me in front of my family.

I'm not sure what to expect next, all I know is that I'm curious.

"That's better," he breathes against my lips, holding me to him. "Now I'm going to taste you."

What?

His mouth moves over mine. Gently at first, as if waiting to see how I'll react, if I'll push him away or not.

Oh. He means kiss me.

Tentatively, I reach up and thread my fingers through his short, silky hair, smash my breasts against his chest, and tug him closer. That's all it takes to snap his control.

He nips at my lips. His mouth covers mine, tongue demanding entry, which I give him. He tastes me and explores my mouth, and I do the same in return.

Nik kissed me once, brief and chaste, and seemed to find it underwhelming. That was nothing like this. This is an entirely different thing.

Roman's fingers tangle in my hair. He devours me like a man starved, need and desperation communicated clearly in each sweep of his tongue. The heady taste of his wine mingles with his natural scent. Yesterday I hated him—I still might—but right now I crave everything that he's willing to give me. *Hot Roman* makes me feel like I've never felt before.

Seen. Wanted. Powerful. I want more.

He trails kisses along my jaw and down my throat. I tilt my head back to give him better access. A wanton moan escapes me when he sucks on the side of my neck.

"Roman," his name sounds like a plea on my lips. What I'm begging for, I haven't a clue. Besides, *more.*

He groans into my neck. One hand firmly grasping my hair, his other slides down to grab my ass. He rocks me roughly forward onto his dick. We both moan from the pleasure. I hold onto his broad shoulders as he does it again, and again. Rocking my hips, I meet his rhythm, my pussy growing wetter and throbbing with need.

Roman slightly adjusts his angle, and I gasp. Through my panties and his trousers, with each roll of our hips, he presses against my clit.

I've never— Oh my God.

Before long, I'm a writhing mess. I'm pretty sure this is called dry humping and I've never experienced anything more divine. He slides me along his thick length, faster and harder, until I see stars.

My body quakes. All I can do is moan his name and collapse against his solid chest. My breath comes in shallow pants, sweat trickles down my spine, and I've never felt anything this intense in my life.

He roars into my ear, his hips jerking wildly.

We take a moment to catch our breaths. I think my head clears more quickly than his, because I'm the first to sit up straight and pull slightly away.

His eyes are closed, his cruel lips parted, and he looks like a god brought to his knees by the power of ecstasy. My heart skips a beat at this brief, unguarded glimpse at him.

Infatuation, that's what I'm feeling. I've become

enthralled by my captor, my savior. The man who kidnapped me, then risked his own life by diving into a frozen lake to save mine.

I should probably stay away from him, but I can't. In truth, I don't want to. Everything about him either infuriates or fascinates me–sometimes both.

He's gorgeous as he catches his breath. I'm tempted to run my tongue up his neck and lick his Adam's apple, then trail it along his sharp jawline. But I don't. I've taken too many risks already tonight.

This unguarded moment doesn't last long.

He catches me gazing at him and a steel door slams down over his features. Every ounce of warmth and lust is gone. The man staring back at me is *cold Roman*, and possibly the villain. I'll know as soon as he opens that cruel mouth.

Yep, my suspicions are confirmed when the hand in my hair tightens. He draws my head backward, then lowers his face until our noses are almost touching.

"Did Kozlov do this with you, too? Did he kiss you? Did he let you ride his cock like a good girl?"

My brow furrows in confusion. Why on earth is he bringing up Nik right now?

"Answer. Me."

My scalp stings from the hold he has on my hair.

"No. No, I never did this with Nik."

"Don't lie to me!" He's livid, practically feral, and I haven't the slightest idea why. Why right now? Did I do something wrong? He's ruining a beautiful moment.

His accusation makes me angry.

"I'm not lying to you. I swear."

"How far did you go with him? How much of your body did you let him touch?"

"Not that it's any of your business, but he chastely kissed me. Once. Now let me go, you're hurting me."

That seems to snap him out of this sudden rage. His fingers loosen, and he frowns as if he finally realizes what he's doing. Remorse briefly flits through his eyes.

His next question surprises me. "Why did you agree to marry Kozlov?"

I carefully consider my answer. Why did I agree to the arrangement?

"I did it for my family. Mama's always told us that we would have to marry to strengthen our family's ties with others. Papa needed us to join with the Russians, I'm the eldest daughter, so it's my duty to make the alliance."

Roman searches my face with his dark gaze. I'm sure he's trying to figure out if I'm lying or not. Since I have nothing to hide, I stare openly back at him. I have nothing to hide. If he wants me to bare my soul to him, I will.

After a few seconds have ticked by, he nods, silently accepting my explanation. He lifts me from his lap. "Go to bed."

"Oh, are you done interrogating me for tonight?" I fold my arms under my breasts and stare him down. It's not easy because, even seated, he's almost as tall as I am. Even so, I do my best.

He pinches the bridge of his nose. "I said, go to bed. That's an order."

"You're not the boss of me, so don't give me orders. I'm going to finish dinner, and then I might think about going to bed. Or I might stay up and watch a movie. I haven't decided—"

His sharp glance cuts me off. "If you don't get your ass upstairs and locked in your room this minute, I swear I'll bend you over this table and fuck you to within an inch of your life."

Heat pools low in my stomach, but I scoff at his threat. His brows lower and I can tell he's not bluffing. I'm not sure why he wants me out of the room this instant, but he does. Thus, the threat.

Deciding this is a losing battle, I drop my arms to my sides, and say, "Yes, *sir*."

"Don't take that tone with me, principessa." Roman's features darken further. His intentions are clearly written across his face. He lunges, grabbing for me with his long arms. I retreat with a startled squeal. Turning on my heel, I dart from the dining room and up the stairs. If I let Roman catch me, I'm sure I'll do something stupider than have an orgasm in his lap. Like let him fuck me on the dining room table.

Once I get to my room, I lock the door.

My heart batters my ribcage. Is he going to come after me? Why am I excited by that thought?

I know I shouldn't poke the bear, but with Roman I can't help it. I like seeing him lose control. It makes me smile when his impenetrable mask slips and I spot the emotions he hides behind it. And there are plenty of them. He's a man of many emotions, some shallow, while others run deep.

My lips are still swollen from his kiss. That kind of pure, raw primal energy I find seductive. The fact that all of that, and more, is bottled up inside one man drives me to want to uncover more.

I'm sure it's a dangerous game. One that we've just begun to play. Roman won't back down, and neither will I. Even if it breaks us, we'll see this through to its end. Whatever that end may be.

Minutes turn to a quarter of an hour, then half an hour and I know he's not coming for me tonight. Sighing, I sulk in my room.

The fact that I'm moping about my captor pushing me away so that he *won't* steal my virtue disturbs me. Greatly. As it should. Obviously, I have some deeply buried issues, which I'm not willing to unpack at the moment.

Besides, he didn't let me finish that delicious dinner. While he ate grilled chicken over greens, the cook, Luis, had made me chicken Alfredo and garlic breadsticks. Absolutely delicious.

A knock sounds on my door, followed by, "Miss Sophia, it's Diana."

Slightly disappointed—what's wrong with me?—I open the door for her. "Yes?"

"Mr. De Luca had me rewarm your dinner and bring it up. I'll put it on the table and collect the dishes in the morning."

"Thank you." A smile curves my lips. The divine aroma makes my stomach gurgle.

This deed gets slotted under the hero category. *Roman, you're my white knight.* I'm going to prove it to both of us. You'll see.

Roman

I'd avoid the girl if I thought it would do any good. Over the past few days, she's settled into the house as if it were her home. Her voice and Diana's float along the hallway. Her honey scent lingers, telling me when she recently left a room. The house is livelier with her presence here, and the staff seem more at ease. I make what necessary trips I need to into the city, but other than that I work from my home office.

Work holds a slightly different meaning to what it did before her arrival. I keep catching myself staring into space, out the floor to ceiling windows that over-look the garden, the sound of her moans replaying clearly in my memory. And my dick gets hard multiple times a day. It's distracting as hell.

She's supposed to be my pawn. Not the woman turning my world upside down by simply existing in it.

When I'm not fantasizing about her coming apart

in my arms, I hear the echo of her words in my thoughts.

You're lonely.

Lonely.

I haven't been with a woman in six years, of course I'm fucking lonely. That explains why my mind wanders back to the girl every five minutes. What I really need to do is fuck her out of my system. A good hour spent with her in my bed will surely be enough to satisfy my craving for her sweet pussy.

Why do I resist the idea, then? Going into this, I had set my mind to using her and ruining her innocence. Once my mind is made up about something, I tend to see it through. What's giving me pause now?

Lonely is different from *horny*.

I'm horny as hell, but my loneliness is what wants her close. I want her company, to hear her voice ring through the halls, to see her smile at me when our paths cross.

What the actual fuck?

If I'm not careful, that girl is going to burrow her way deep under my flesh, all the way to my cold, dead heart—perhaps to find that it still has a pulse.

That's the most ridiculous thought I've had since thinking I'm *lonely*.

I'm fine. I enjoy my secluded, simple life. She's not going to change that.

I bring up the spreadsheet I've been staring at for the past fifteen minutes, once again trying to make sense of the numbers. Maybe I should go to my office in the city. I might get more work done there.

Instead I call Eve, my assistant, and have her set up a dinner reservation for tonight. I'm taking the girl out. It's probably a terrible idea and I'm sure I'll come to regret it. But it's time that I show her off and publicly stake my claim on her. Plus, we have business to discuss.

After I hang up, I go in search of the girl. I find her in the kitchen with Luis. The scene before me makes me come to a sudden stop. My Italian cook has his hands on Sophia's while he shows her how to knead dough. She's smiling as she warmly chats with him.

My fingers ball into fists.

Like a fog of menace, I step into the kitchen and silence descends. They both glance up, freezing in place. The grin fades from the girl's lips. Luis takes one long look at my expression, then decides to do the smart thing by quickly removing his hands from hers and backing away from the girl. His face drains of color.

"*Signore*, I was simply—"

"I don't care for your excuses," I snap, looking my cook up and down. He's in his mid-fifties, balding, and carries his weight around his middle. Am I really worried he'll steal Sophia away from me? I must be insane. Though stranger things have happened. Once upon a time, I overlooked another man as a threat, and that mistake cost me more than I'm willing to admit.

Plus, Luis's temperament is much more palatable than mine. Average looks aside, a woman could find him charming, easy to talk to, a brilliant chef.

My eyes narrow on him. He begins to sweat in earnest.

The girl catches on to the context of our awkward exchange and rolls her eyes. My palms itch with the desire to spank the sass right out of her.

"You can't be serious." She turns to my cook. "I'm sorry your boss is such an asshole."

Luis's eyes bulge, panic flashes across his features.

Sophia continues, "You're an excellent chef and anyone—besides him—would be grateful to have you. Honestly, I'm surprised you haven't poisoned him by now. I know I would have."

Oh, would she? I don't know why I find that idea amusing. It's not.

"Never!" Luis's panic turns to dread. "I would never think of doing such a thing, *Signore*."

"Well, you're a better person than I am." She pats him on the shoulder, and my attention latches on to where she's touching him. Then shoots me a honey sweet smile. The sassy little minx. "Can't you see you're interrupting? What do you want anyway?"

Never mind spanking her, I'm going to fuck the sass out of her instead. If she can't think straight, then she won't be able to make smart remarks. Or maybe I'll shut her up with my cock in her mouth. At that thought, my cock begins to grow hard. Goddamn it.

"Well?" She places her hands on her hips and impatiently taps one foot. At *me*. I never let such insolence go unpunished. If I did, my rivals would have prevailed by now.

I glance at Luis. "Out!"

That's all the encouragement he needs to scurry from the room, leaving me alone with this creature who has no idea how close she is to being hauled across my lap and spanked.

"That was rude," she remarks, still having no idea the kind of danger she's in.

I prowl closer, slowly, until I have her pinned between my body and the massive island. Only then does worry appear in her wide brown eyes. Her honey scent drifts up my nose as I lean in and murmur, "I want to make something very clear, principessa, if you ever let a man touch you like that again, I will kill him. If you ever touch another man, I will kill him. If another man touches you for any reason, I will kill him. Do you understand?"

Her breath hitches. "Yes."

"Good. Now—"

Her phone chimes with a text, then a moment later, two more. I ease back to stare down at her.

"Who is so desperate to communicate with you?"

"Um." She retrieves her phone from her pocket. Her cheeks flush pink as she reads the text, making my stomach drop. "It's Nik. He's angry about me leaving him. He's also warning me about you. He says you're a snake."

Sophia must think I've lost my mind when she glances up to find me smiling. Nik's fallen right into my trap. I knew taking away his toy would get his attention. He can't stand the fact that I now have what was once his.

"Are you feeling okay?" she asks with genuine concern.

"Never better. Do not respond to his messages, no matter what they say. In fact, you should block his number."

"But—"

"You don't belong to him any longer. You belong to me." Why is she arguing with me about this? She has absolutely no reason to want to stay in contact with that piece of shit. "Block his number. Now."

That should rile him up even more. Will he come looking for his precious ex-fiancée? I hope so.

"You can't have everything you want all the time."

"Yes, I can." I take her by the waist and pick her up —she squeaks—planting her ass on the countertop so she's closer to eye level. My palms land on her thighs. "Block his number."

"No."

My gaze narrows. "Are you arguing with me just to be difficult?"

"Maybe." Her lips twitch.

"Why?"

"Because no one in your life sets any boundaries for you. You boss everyone around, or worse threaten them for nothing, just like you did with poor Luis." She folds her arms in the small space left between our bodies. "I've been told what to do, and done it without question, my whole life. I'm over it. I'm not going to do whatever you say just because you said it. You don't own me."

My grip tightens around her thighs, and I drag her

ass to the edge of the countertop, positioning myself between her legs. "That's where you're wrong, principessa. I do own you. I own all of you. One day you'll realize you're mine."

She swallows hard. "And when that happens, will I own all of you, too?"

All I can do is stare back at her for a long moment.

"I'll freely give you my body, even my money. But you don't want my frozen heart or my tainted soul."

"I might."

Her penetrating gaze bores into mine, showing me the honesty behind her words. Instead of dwelling on what she could mean, or the strange sensation in my chest that might be something akin to hope, I close the distance between us and claim her lips with my own. Her hot mouth opens. She's eager and willing to be claimed, no matter what she says.

The fact that she's a prisoner in my house barely seems to affect her mood. If anything, she's taken my home, my refuge, and turned it into her own. She's more the lady of the house than my captive. I'm not entirely sure how she turned her situation around so quickly and efficiently.

My hands slide over her hips, up her ribcage, to her breasts. She gasps into my mouth when I tease her nipples with my thumbs. Her body is so responsive that I can feel the shudder of pleasure that rolls through her because of my touch.

She wants this. She wants *me*. How is that possible?

That realization has me spinning. I'm beginning to

suspect this girl is no mere mortal, she's a siren, and I am doomed.

Since I'm already hell-bound, what difference does it make if I perish in the arms of this vixen as she drags me down to the underworld? I might even enjoy my demise.

Temporarily staking my claim on this woman is not going to suffice. I want to own her, all of her, until I've had my fill of Sophia Pontrelli.

At that moment, I make the decision to claim her as mine. Really mine. All *mine*.

I'm taking her for myself. I'll see this charade all the way through to its conclusion by marrying her, and binding her to me as completely as possible before man and God. The entire world will know who she belongs to by the time I'm done.

A possessive, animalistic growl rumbles in my chest.

It will be the ultimate insult to Kozlov to see his ex-fiancée as my wife.

Nipping at her bottom lip, I drop my arms to my sides and step back. "We're going out to dinner tonight. Meet me in the foyer at seven sharp." My gaze takes in her swollen lips and shallow breaths. She's fucking gorgeous. "I need to get some more work done."

With that, I turn away, resisting the urge to glance over my shoulder as I leave the kitchen. Tonight is important. It has to be perfect. I'm going to make her an offer she can't possibly refuse.

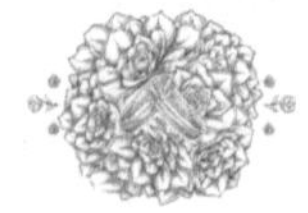

When work eludes me, I decide to meet up with Baron at the Leonidas Gentleman's Club where we're both members. I trudge up the stone steps to a building that embraces ancient Greek architecture.

As I approach the front, my gaze lifts to the words stamped into the stone above the four columns.

Only the sons of lions shall enter.

Reading that phrase never grows old. Every time I walk under those words, my chest inflates with a sense of pride, because behind these doors is an entirely different world. Exclusive, decadent, and private. A world made especially for those who've earned their place to dwell in it.

I enter through the massive double doors into a marble foyer. The club's concierge inclines his head in acknowledgment as I stride past him on my way to the poker den.

My footsteps are softened by the plush red carpeting in the wide hallway. Marble statues occupy lit alcoves, and original artwork hangs in front of the dark wood paneling.

I keep my gaze averted from the paintings, ignoring their presence. The statues I don't mind, but the artwork I detest.

"De Luca!" Baron waves me over as soon as I enter the den. "I took the liberty of ordering your usual."

I take the seat opposite of him and glance at the fifty-year-old Macallan, before picking up the glass and taking a sip. "How generous of you. The next round's on me."

"No need. I bought the bottle, so enjoy it." He puffs absently on a cigar, the smoke curling upwards to the high ceiling.

I eye him. "How's the wicked step-family?"

"The ultimate pain in my ass, as usual." He sneers into his own glass. "Can you believe my step-monster proposed the idea of wedding her daughter to me?"

"What did you say to that?" I can tell by the dangerous energy hovering around him that he's more agitated than usual.

"I told her that would be incest."

I shrug. "You're not related by blood."

That earns me a scowl. "You never have been funny De Luca, don't try to start now."

"It's simply an observation. Let me guess, she's nagging you to marry your step-sister?"

"Nagging is an understatement, she's practically feral. That woman is worse than a starving mutt with a bone when she sets her mind to a particular outcome. I'd rather chew off my own arm than marry her daughter."

"Let me know if there's anything I can do to help." I swish the Macallan around in my mouth, savoring the smooth honey-peat flavor.

Baron groans. "You know I've considered getting

rid of her, countless times, and I'd do it except that my father gets in my way every damn time. It's almost as though he knew how my mind works and thought of every way to keep his wife in control, and alive, long after his death."

"That's because you think exactly the same way as he did," I point out.

"Not true. I'm nothing like that bastard." He nods to someone at the door. "Look who finally made it through the club's doors."

I swivel around in my chair, seeking out who he's referring to, and find three Bane brothers casually assessing the place.

"Well, if it isn't the bane of our existence," I mutter.

"It's probably been a while since they've heard that one." Baron watches them as they watch us from a distance. "Niall is fine, why can't they all be like him?"

"Good question. I'm going to have to file a complaint with the owner if he keeps letting the riffraff become members." Baron and I attended college with Eoin and Malachy Bane. Both are insufferable assholes. But the real driving force behind their family is the eldest, Alistair Bane.

Eoin and Malachy saunter over to us, their eyes gleaming with mischief. I glance at Baron. "Do you think the no fighting policy extends to us?"

"Do not get us thrown out," he replies through gritted teeth. "We're civilized, let's act like it."

I snort. "Speak for yourself."

"Gentleman," Baron says in greeting to the two Bane brothers.

"Hey, look here, it's the Black Baron and the King of the Sea." Malachy scoffs. "Where do you two think you're from, some sort of Disney movie?"

"At least we have memorable reputations." I sip my Scotch. "Unlike... Wait, what are your names again? Aren't you new around here?"

"Yes, we are." Eoin shoots us a rabid grin. "We didn't have our spot waiting for us because of Daddy. We actually had to earn our way into Leonidas."

Baron's tone is dry when he says, "What an accomplishment, if only you knew what to do with yourselves now that you're where you don't belong."

"Say that again, Baron." Malachy narrows his eyes. "We can take this outside and I'll make you eat your words."

Eoin looks just as eager to beat our asses. Of course, they'd be the ones bloody and broken at the end—if not dead. Unfortunately, the club also has a rule against murdering other members, which is a pity.

Alistair comes up behind his brothers and places a hand on each of their shoulders. "I think we've seen enough of the poker den, let's check out the rest of this place."

The Banes throw us dirty glances as they exit the room, and the atmosphere returns to normal, everyone focused on the game in front of them. Or in our case, on our drinks.

"Well, that was a delight." Baron puffs on his cigar. "Why did you want to meet up today?"

"I needed to get out of the house and clear my mind for a while." I avoid looking him in the eyes, for fear he'll read more into my explanation.

Baron leans forward. "This wouldn't have anything to do with you carrying a certain young woman over your shoulder and out of her engagement party, would it?"

My gaze snaps to him. Dammit.

"No. Not a damn thing," I lie.

Tonight is going to be important. I needed to get out of the house for a while so I can clearly think about how I'm going to bait the girl and lure her in. So far, I've come up with a couple of different approaches.

The problem is my desire to claim her for myself. The visceral urge to make her my own is messing with my cool head for business. And tonight is supposed to be all about business.

"I see." The rare grin that appears on Baron's face is too knowing for my comfort.

Why did I think it was a good idea to meet up with him under these circumstances?

Right, I remember.

Because he's the only man I consider a friend.

CHAPTER 10

Sophia

Adress arrived for me in the late afternoon. Diana brought it up and told me I was supposed to wear it to dinner that night. I thought it was a sweet, if not domineering, gesture from Roman. Then when I opened the box, my heart nearly stopped. Crimson silk lay before me.

I stand in front of the double wide full-length mirror in my bedroom, dressed, hair and makeup done, and ready to leave. The silk hugs my curves from the hips up, the skirt falling in several layers of airy fabric to the floor. It's beautiful.

Nik hated it when I wore red. He said it made me look like a cheap whore.

Apparently, Roman disagrees.

I've always loved the way I look in red. The rich color brings out the highlights in my dark hair, and seems to make my tan skin glow. I smile at myself in the mirror. Which does little to calm my jumbled nerves.

I'm going out tonight with Roman De Luca. On a date, our first date—at least I think this is a date. People will see us together.

For the past few days I've been living in a kind of limbo. Just me, Roman, and the household staff, existing in our own little world. Here, I'm free to be myself. To push Roman's buttons with no real consequence other than his hands on my body and his sultry voice in my ear. My skin heats at the memory of this morning in the kitchen.

But out there, everything is different. The world will eat us alive if we're not careful. Outside of these walls, I have to be the perfect mafia wife: Respectful and demure. Out there, I *am* his property.

Slipping on my heels, I make my way downstairs to meet Roman at exactly seven o'clock. He's already waiting when I descend the staircase. He looks like a dream in a tailored dark suit and tie. His hair is perfectly styled, face clean shaven, posture deceptively casual.

His gaze finds me, and for a moment the impenetrable wall in his eyes falls away. Past it I see his thoughts and emotions. He looks at me with awe, a hint of lust, and what I can only describe as hope. Then sadness and pain war for dominance before he pushes them aside. By the time I reach the bottom step, all I see is pride in his eyes before that barrier is firmly back in place.

"You look perfect...except for one thing. You're not wearing any jewelry."

I'd hoped he wouldn't notice. "Whoever Papa had pack up my things didn't include any of my jewelry. I don't have anything here, and with the short notice about going out tonight, there wasn't time to make a trip into the city."

The trip itself wouldn't have taken too much time. Facing my father and mother is another story. A quick stop by their place to grab more of my belongings is out of the question. I know Papa was coerced, but the haste in which he had me thrown out still stings. I need more time before I can face him.

"I have just the thing." Roman snaps his fingers, and Diana appears, carrying a black velvet box. "This will go perfectly with that dress."

She stops beside us and pops it open. Inside is a dazzling ruby and diamond necklace with matching earrings. It's absolutely stunning. I've never seen anything quite like it.

Only after gaping at it for several thundering heartbeats, do my eyes land on the logo in the middle.

Maçon.

I'm familiar enough with wealth. Mama insists my sisters and I wear designer clothing, and I have some very nice pieces of jewelry from *Tiffany*'s and even *Cartier*. But *Maçon Jewelers* is next level. They are the most exclusive jewelry designers in the world. So exclusive that most people haven't ever heard of them. This piece alone had to have cost millions, *plural*.

I glance up at Roman with a sudden realization,

because *Maçon* only works with diamonds. "Those aren't rubies, are they?"

"No, they're red diamonds. I see you're familiar with *Maçon*." He lifts the necklace from its case and drapes it across my neck, clasping it in the back. Done, his fingertips trail down my shoulders, making me shiver. "This belonged to my great-grandmother, so it's been in the family for a while. It looks exquisite on you, principessa."

Butterflies erupt in my stomach every time he calls me by that endearment. I cast him a shy smile. Another thoughtful gesture from him to add to my White Knight list.

"Thank you," I say, reaching for the matching earrings and putting them on.

I stand before the foyer mirror. He's right, the diamonds go perfectly with this dress. Roman seems to have had this all planned out, but what are his intentions?

I eye him. "You know you can't buy me, right?"

"What do you mean?"

"I mean I don't have a price. I'm not for sale."

He smirks. "We'll see about that. Let's go." He offers his arm and I take it.

The limousine waits for us outside. We sit next to each other for the ride into the city. Roman's presence eats up all the oxygen in the space and presses against me from all sides until I'm hyper aware of his every subtle move, every small shift and flex of his fingers. The way his knee touches mine.

I try to relax by gazing out the window, noticing

how the snow has melted to dirty slush beside the road. Soon I'm lost in my own thoughts.

My goal is to break through Roman's barriers, to see beneath his mask, but I'm starting to worry that in the process, I'm crumbling too. Each time he kisses me, I want more. I drift to sleep each night thinking of his hands on my body, and his possessive words in my ears.

I'd think, knowing a man for less than a week, it would be impossible to have the beginnings of feelings for him. But every single day has felt like an entire week. His presence in the house, having dinner with him, the inability to ever fully escape him, is wearing me down.

I'm just unsure where it's all leading. I knew this was a dangerous game, but am I willing to pay whatever price is owed?

Roman's large hand covers both of mine. I glance at him, surprised.

"You're fidgeting. Care to tell me what's on your mind?"

I study him for a full ten seconds. "Do you actually care, or are you asking out of politeness? Never mind, I know the answer to that question, since you do absolutely nothing out of politeness."

Although *caring* isn't exactly one of his personality traits either.

A rare chuckle escapes him. "You're quite observant."

How can I not be, when everything about him demands my attention. He's impossible to ignore.

Especially since we've been cooped up in the same, albeit massive, house for days. Avoiding each other should be easier. It's not.

"Why do you care what I'm thinking about?"

"Because half the time, I'm sure you're plotting my demise," he drawls.

"And the other half of the time?" As soon as I ask the question, I know exactly what his answer will be. Heat creeps up my neck and washes across my face, all the way to my hairline.

"You and I both know the answer to that, principessa." His gaze darkens and the air around us grows thick with lust.

I clear my throat—twice. "I was thinking about how much time we spend in the house together. I feel like I've gotten to know you somewhat well in a relatively short amount of time."

"Hm. I suppose we've moved beyond being mere acquaintances." His hand squeezes mine in my lap.

I scrutinize him for a moment. "What are you thinking?"

"I'm wondering what it is that you want?"

"What do you mean?"

"You said before that you grew up with the expectation of an arranged marriage. If that weren't the case, what would you have done with your life? Did you ever have any dreams or desires of a different future?" His intense gaze holds mine. "If you could do anything, what would it be?"

I swallow thickly, turning my head to gaze out the window again, as I consider his question. Once, I had dreamed of a different life. But people like me don't get to make those types of choices. Our lives are not our own, they're part of a legacy. We don't think in terms of individuals. We think in terms of generations.

It's all about what we leave behind for those who come after. Wealth. Connections. Alliances. A solid foundation in which to flourish.

"When I was twelve, we went to The Metropolitan Museum of Art and I fell in love instantly. I wanted to do something in the art world. Either work at a museum, one day become a curator, or even open my own art gallery. I was kind of obsessed for a while."

Before reality kicked in. Mama had to put it to me bluntly for the first time: I would never have a career. My future was as a wife and mother, to be at my husband's beck and call, and that was it.

I spent two days in my room crying over my shattered dreams. That was the last time I dared to reach outside of the world I was born into.

Roman's thumb caresses my wrist. "I can see you working in that field."

I glance over at him, completely taken off guard. "You can?"

"Sure. You're a people person, you have a strong personality, and I'm beginning to suspect you have a sharp mind."

I laugh. That's probably Roman's idea of a compliment. Then something occurs to me. "You have a huge house, but no art on the walls. Why?"

His thumb stills. "Because I don't particularly like art. It's too emotional for my tastes, and a distraction."

"That's exactly why I love it."

"That's why I hate it." He angles away, and our conversation dies a miserable death.

Who hates art? The obvious answer is Roman De Luca. I guess the real question is: Why?

CHAPTER 11

Roman

Offering the girl my hand, I help her out of the limo. I chose an appropriate two-Michelin-starred restaurant for us tonight, where we can be seen together. The rumor mill will start, and by tomorrow morning, we'll be the talk of the city. Everyone will know that Sophia Pontrelli is mine. That I intend to marry again. If she'll truly have me. Which is a deal I plan to seal tonight.

So far the evening's not off to the best start. I shouldn't have shut her down over our discussion of art. The truth is, I was about to confess to her exactly why I don't like art and the emotions that it summons.

I almost slipped up and let her in. It can't happen again. Emotion is a sign of weakness, and in this world, the weak are destroyed. Someday, even this girl will learn that lesson.

With a possessive hand resting on her hip, I steer us into the restaurant where we're seated at a table overlooking Central Park. Already I feel the burn of people's eyes on us. Excellent, I want them to look their fill.

From the fake smile plastered on Sophia's face, I can tell she's familiar with this game, too. Good. Her parents really did train her well.

I order for us: A bottle of their best wine and a four-course meal that will keep us here for several hours. Once the server leaves, I scan the room, noting the whispers have already begun.

Roman De Luca doesn't date.

Who is that woman?

Why is she with him?

They haven't seen a woman on my arm since...my wife. Six and a half years ago. Back in a time when I didn't know how cruel this world could be, even to a man like me. *Especially* to a man like me.

I gaze across at my companion. She sits ramrod straight in her chair, excellent posture, dressed to kill, and stunningly beautiful. She's the epitome of a mafia princess, and soon to be my perfect wife.

"This may seem like a social occasion," I tell her, "but we're here for business tonight."

She quirks a brow. "Oh? What business do we have to discuss?"

"Our future, of course."

"I thought that was set in stone."

"And what does your version of that look like? Give me the details." I'm curious where she sees us going after having known each other for so short a time.

"Okay." Our wine arrives, and she takes a sip before continuing. "You'll spend the next two and a half months parading me around like a show dog—"

I choke on my wine.

"—then, when the day arrives, you'll drag me to the altar where we'll be married. A simple honeymoon somewhere tropical, where you'll claim your spoils, then you'll deposit me in your formidable house where I'll produce numerous heirs for you while I die of boredom. At some point, we'll grow to resent each other, but that resentment will morph into bored acceptance as we grow old."

I stare across the table at her. She's fucking serious.

"I'm glad we have the same vision for our marriage." I lean slightly forward.

She rolls her eyes. "Is that really what you want?"

"Is that what you want?" I counter.

"What I want doesn't matter."

"What if it did?"

She pauses, scrutinizing me. "Stop talking in riddles and get to the point, Mr. De Luca."

I smirk at her bossy tone. "What if instead of being forced into this union with me, you actually chose it for yourself?"

"That will never happen."

The smile slides from my lips. "I can be very persuasive. In the last decade I've managed to double the profits of my father's company. Believe me, when it comes to business, I know exactly what I'm doing."

"We're talking about marriage, not business."

"Marriage *is* business. It's a contract. Anyone who

tells you otherwise is a fool." And anyone who thinks they're marrying for love is doubly foolish.

"Fine. Dazzle me with your powers of persuasion." She sips her wine. I can tell from her mild expression that she's humoring me. She has no intention of changing her mind about our arrangement. Luckily, I've cracked tougher nuts than her.

"I want a willing wife—in every department." I rake my gaze down her body just to see her flush. Gorgeous. "You'll need to produce at least one heir. You'll also have to accompany me to numerous social events every year. We'll share a bed, and no other man will touch you. Ever."

She leans forward, giving me a clear view of her cleavage. "This is the most *romantic* proposal I've ever heard."

I swear I'm going to fuck the sarcasm out of her, sooner rather than later.

Ignoring her sassy comment, I continue, "In return, you will have everything money can buy, a comfortable home, and my protection." I watch her carefully while I deliver the real gold. "And a college degree, as long as the university you attend is local. After that, if you choose, you may find a job at a museum."

Her entire body stiffens. Slowly, deliberately, she sets down her wine glass.

"Can you repeat that last part, please?"

I grin, knowing I've caught her, now I just have to reel her in. "You may go to college and work in any field you desire. I'll pay for all of it."

"You'd do that for me? Why?"

"I'm not doing it for you." I chuckle at her exasperated glare. "A business arrangement should be mutually beneficial for all parties involved."

"Right. But what if... I don't know. What if I can't have children? You need an heir. What happens then?"

"Simple. I'll kick you out and take a new wife."

She glowers at me. "You're horrible."

I laugh, drawing attention from those around us, and a startled glance from my soon-to-be wife. Reaching across the table, I squeeze her hand. "If we run into any fertility issues, we'll work through them together. You have my word."

Surprisingly, I mean it. Yes, I need an heir. Am I willing to give up Sophia if she can't provide one? Absolutely not. She's *mine*.

It occurs to me that I should ask the question: "Do you want children?"

She nods. "Two max. I'd like to be a mother, but I also want a career. A real career, not spending my days organizing and volunteering at charity events." She cocks her head to one side. "You do realize I could be in college for six years. I don't want to go to college and have children at the same time."

"I'm a patient man. You're young, so we'll wait until you're ready."

Sophia's eyes narrow again. "Who are you and what have you done with that overbearing brute I've spent the past week with?"

"When force doesn't work, I resort to wish fulfillment. It's a simple, but effective, strategy."

"Ah, there he is. I was getting worried that all this talk of marital bliss had done him in."

Another laugh bursts from my chest. She smiles at me this time, and I hide my answering grin behind my glass. Sophia is a breath of fresh air. I haven't enjoyed being around another person this much in a very long time, maybe ever.

She's smart and funny. Even if her jokes are mostly at my expense. Every day she shows me more of herself and the ground beneath my feet unexpectedly shifts. I never know what she's going to say next, only that she has my full, undivided attention as I wait for her to speak. Knowing whatever she says will be at least blunt, if not also insightful.

This woman may be my undoing.

I'm marrying her, with our own negotiated terms. This is not my original plan. In fact, it's far from it.

However, what's most alarming is the fact that I haven't thought about Kozlov since we sat down. I'm doing this because I want her, not because I want to punish him. Kozlov doesn't factor into this. I'll still ruin him, but not by ruining her too.

She's mine. Forever.

Now I have to finalize this deal.

Reaching into my pocket, I pull out a small velvet box and open the hinged lid.

"Sophia, will you marry me?"

This is the second time I've been blinded by the brilliance of a one-of-a-kind *Maçon* this evening. Except this piece of jewelry comes with a question that I never expected to hear from Roman's mouth.

He's *asking*, instead of demanding. In fact, he has asked a few questions this evening and actually listened to my responses. And he's laughed—twice. Maybe there's hope for this man yet.

Even so, I can't give him a simple answer. I want to go to college more than anything, but he knows that and he's using it as leverage so that I'll willingly be his wife. I shouldn't have told him my secret desire if I didn't want him to use it against me.

Would marrying Roman really be so bad? I can't escape him. I still don't actually have a choice, unless...

"What if I say *no*?"

I'm acutely aware of the attention we've drawn.

Strangers' eyes bore into the back of my head. Roman's face remains impassive, as if he's unaffected by their blatant stares.

"If you don't want this, I will send you back to your father, under one condition: You may not marry Kozlov. However, your father will be free to marry you to anyone else of his choosing."

I purse my lips, thinking that over. Basically, I'd be back to square one. No Roman, no Nik, and available for Papa to marry me off to some other man all for the sake of an alliance. Would it be a different Russian? Or perhaps an Irishman?

Whoever they'd be, they're an unknown quantity. I don't like that.

Another problem is I can't see myself being shoved back into that box. I've changed in the last week. I don't want to be some man's pawn any longer. At least Roman is giving me a choice, which is far more than I ever expected from him.

In truth, I'm astonished that we're having this conversation. I pegged Roman as the type of man to drag me to the altar while hurling threats. Instead, he's a businessman through and through. And a damned good one.

Papa would never negotiate with me or give me a choice, not really. If I go against my family's wishes, I know the guilt will eat away at me. Plus, that direction doesn't include college.

I've made my bargain with Roman. It's as good as I'm going to get. Which is far better than I ever thought possible, so I'll take it.

"Yes. I will marry you, Roman De Luca."

I swear that surprise and relief flash behind his eyes for a moment before those two reactions are gone, wiped clean by the knowing smirk on his cruel lips. Did he really think I'd reject him?

Is Roman De Luca, God of the Seas, not as self-assured as he pretends?

An even crazier thought pops to mind. Does he actually *want* me to be his wife? I thought this was a business transaction and desire played no part in it. Am I wrong?

I keep my questions to myself. Only time will tell what Roman's true motivations are, or if I'm simply overthinking the matter.

Roman takes the diamond ring and slides it onto my finger, as the dining room explodes with applause. A grin splits my face and butterflies flutter around my stomach. Strangely, my joy in this moment feels genuine.

Finally, I've found a way to go to college. I'm no longer stuck on the predictable path that was my life before meeting Roman. For the first time in a long time, I'm excited about my future.

The butterflies go wild when Roman leans in and kisses me. This kiss is somehow different from the ones before it. His mouth claims mine with such passion and possessiveness that I feel his brand on every inch of my skin. I'm his now. And I have a suspicion that he's never going to let me go.

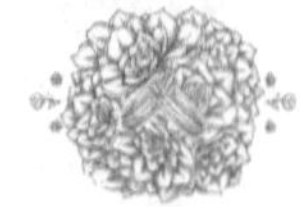

After dinner we step outside, where Roman continues to surprise me by having a horse-drawn carriage waiting for us in Central Park. The top is drawn up to protect against the elements. Roman helps me inside, sits beside me, and arranges a thick blanket around us like we're a normal couple on a real date. Once we're settled in, the driver starts the carriage rolling.

Lamplight illuminates the wide path. All around us the city glows and twinkles.

I'd been on four dates with Nik and none of them were like this one. He spent his time nitpicking my food selection, talking about his expectations from his future wife, and never bothered to officially propose. In fact, he had a courier drop the engagement ring at my house with a note that ordered me to be wearing it the next time he saw me.

This date... Roman...

I'm practically speechless.

This is a side of Roman that I hoped was there, and have dared to suspect as much, but seeing it come out all in the span of a single night has my heart doing somersaults.

"What do you think?" Roman asks, broadly gesturing with one hand at our surroundings.

"This is actually... *romantic*."

"Is that such a bad thing?" He quirks a brow.

"Well, no. It's just downright shocking to be honest."

He chuckles, the sounds deep and warm. "Give me some credit, principessa, I can be charming when the occasion calls for it."

I shoot him a doubtful glance, which he sees, making him laugh again. I've never heard him laugh as much as he has tonight. It's a pleasant sound: Deep, throaty, and a little rough. I could get used to hearing his amusement.

"I'm glad you view this occasion as one that calls for your charm." I relax, sinking further into the seat, quite aware of Roman's body heat pressing flush against my side.

"It seems only right to woo my future wife." He stretches one arm across the back of the bench seat, letting his fingers rest on my shoulder. His light touch sends a shiver through my body. I've never been so aware of a man's presence before him.

Future wife.

I'm actually doing this. Not only that, but for the first time in my life, I actually agreed to it. My arranged marriage has somehow turned into something I want, with perks I never saw coming.

Roman's right, he is very good at business dealings. When he sees something he wants, he knows exactly how to get it. That alone should make me wary. Except that I think he's good for his word. He won't change the terms of our agreement, he'll fulfill them to the letter. I will do the same.

I can't wait to tell my sisters and cousins I'm going to college. They're going to freak out.

We ride in companionable silence for a few minutes, enjoying the scenery. When we round a corner, a large body of water comes into view, city lights reflecting on its inky surface.

Roman notices me staring at it. "Do you want to walk for a bit?"

"Can we?"

"Of course. We can do anything we want." He calls for the driver to stop and wait here for us.

This time, instead of taking my hand in his, he wraps his large hands around my waist, lifts me up, then slowly sets me on the ground. Even through my wool coat, his palms heat my skin. We linger there for a moment, our gazes locked on each other.

My stomach dips and twists as I stare at his handsome face. If I didn't know any better, I'd mistake him for a gentleman right now. His White Knight colors are showing again.

"Kiss me," I blurt, surprising myself.

Without hesitation, he pulls me closer, leans down, and captures my lips. His tongue plunges into my mouth, licking and tangling with my own. Then one of his hands splays across my back while the other finds my neck. His hold is possessive, demanding.

A whimper crawls up my throat. Now that we've struck our deal, and Roman has promised to fulfill my dreams, I crave him even more. I want to know more about not only his body, but his own dreams, his past, and what he desires most. I want to know *him*. My future husband.

Roman ends our make-out session way too soon.

"Let's walk for a while." He offers me his arm, and I take it, attempting to regain my balance. Why does kissing him always leave me light-headed?

We stroll along the edge of the pond, quiet, neither of us in a hurry. It's nice. I wonder if we'll have more moments of peace like this, or if Roman's intentions are to win me over tonight then go back to our usual strained dynamic. I hope this is a turning point for us.

We cross a small bridge, entering an area with dense foliage, and lose sight of the carriage. I don't want to go too far in my heels and risk getting blisters on the walk back.

I stop, and turn toward Roman. "We can start back now if—"

The shaking of a shrub behind me is all the warning I get before a strong hand painfully grips my arm, yanks me backward, and cold steel is pressed to my neck. I gasp, holding my breath. Even so, the scent of cheap, cloying cologne invades my nostrils. My heartbeat pounds in my ears, nearly drowning out all other sounds.

"Give me your wallet and that watch," demands the man who's holding me at knife point. "Don't worry, rich bitch, once he hands over his things, you can give me your jewelry too. I like this necklace. Looks like it's worth a lot." He runs his blade over the diamonds.

The momentary distraction is his death warrant.

Roman cocks his gun. "Get your hands off my

fiancée." His tone is cold enough to make my blood freeze, and I'm not his intended target.

The man behind me stills, his breath catching in his lungs. "Hey man, let's not get crazy. Okay? Looks like I brought a knife to a gunfight." His chuckle sounds forced. If I were him, I'd be shitting my pants about now.

"Don't make me repeat myself." Roman bites out.

"Yeah, yeah. Okay." His hold on me loosens enough that I slip out of his grasp, and stumble straight to Roman.

Roman slides a possessive hand around my waist, shoving me behind him, so that his body is shielding mine.

I peer around his arm at my assailant. The man is holding up both hands and slowly backing away. His calculating glance darts between Roman's face and his gun. He must see something he doesn't like in Roman's expression because suddenly he spins around and makes a run for it.

Roman shoots him in the back—twice.

The gunfire causes my ears to ring. I stand there, watching, as Roman casually strides over to the man on the ground, turns him over with the toe of his shoe, and shoots him point blank in the head. Unfiltered malice rolls off him in waves.

I stare at the dead man on the ground. Maybe I should be horrified, or at least scared, but I feel nothing at all.

From the moment he yanked me away and held a knife to my throat, I knew he was a dead man, just as surely as I know the sun will rise in the morning. He attacked the wrong couple tonight. It cost him his pathetic life.

Roman appears at my side, startling me. He puts away his gun and peers into my face. His knuckles scrape along my jaw as he searches my gaze, for what, I don't know.

"Are you hurt?" he demands.

I shake my head. My voice comes out slightly hollow and distant. "You shot him in the back."

It's more of an observation than an accusation.

Roman's fingers curl around the back of my neck in a dominating hold. "I told you before, if any man touches you, he's dead. I keep my word, principessa." He leans down, his nose brushing against mine. "If he'd drawn a single drop of your blood, I would have tortured him for days. He should count himself lucky to receive a quick death."

His words send a shiver down my spine. My lips part, and his gaze drops to my mouth.

Then he lifts me in his arms. "Let's go home."

CHAPTER 13

Roman

We ride home in silence, my girl tucked under my arm, and violent rage simmering in my veins. I should have seen the fucking mugger before he got his filthy hands on her. I should have been paying more attention to our surroundings. It's my fault her life was put in danger.

I was distracted, flying high on the triumph of winning her over when she was so clearly set against ever agreeing to be mine. Then that damn kiss in the park put my head straight in the clouds, and all the blood in my body rushed to my cock.

Fucking stupid.

I need to do better. I can't let my enjoyment of Sophia's company be a constant distraction. Tonight was a wake-up call. If I don't get my head on straight, both of our lives will be in danger.

When we arrive home, I put Sophia to bed. She's

quiet, exhausted after her ordeal. Or perhaps in shock. Me shooting that miscreant right in front of her may have been the wrong move, but I had no other option than to let him flee. That wasn't happening.

It's too late for regrets now.

I head downstairs to my study, pour a large brandy, and bring up Baron's contact on my phone.

ROMAN DE LUCA

Any news?

BLAKE BARON

I told you I'd keep you up to date on my progress.

ROMAN DE LUCA

I'm not a patient man. It's been a week.

BLAKE BARON

Obviously. I've been working behind the scenes. First piece will fall next week and should be in the papers.

ROMAN DE LUCA

I'll look for it.

As soon as I've finished my text exchange with Baron, my phone rings. I mutter a curse at the name that appears on the screen. What does *she* want?

"Hello, Mother," I say in a clipped tone.

"Don't '*hello, mother*' me. I was enjoying a nice evening out with my friends, when the gossips invaded the wine bar like a swarm of bees." She's always overly dramatic. "Do you know what I learned tonight, Roman? Do you?"

"I—"

She steam rolls right over me. "I learned that my son, my only child, proposed to a woman. In a public restaurant. And she said yes. That's right, my son is engaged. The very same son who hasn't bothered to tell his own mother that he's been dating, that he's met someone, or that he intended to propose to her."

I inwardly groan at her dramatics. "Mother, stop. It's not what you think."

"So, you're *not* engaged to be married?"

I suppress a sigh. "I am engaged. But it's an arrangement. I'm not marrying for love."

"Who is it? And why? You don't need anything from anybody else enough to warrant locking yourself into a loveless marriage. I didn't even know you were considering the option of marrying again. If I'd known, there are plenty of young ladies I could have introduced you to, sweetheart."

The last thing I need is my mother involved in my love life. Or any of my business dealings. Both would lead to complete, irreparable devastation.

"Mother, it's fine. I have my reasons for marrying her, that's all you need to know."

"I thought your father, God rest his soul, was the most stubborn man I'd ever met, but now I think you take first place with that particular character flaw. So, who is she? When am I going to meet her? When is the wedding? Did you knock her up, is that why you're doing this out of the blue?"

I pinch the bridge of my nose, feeling a headache coming on. "Her name is Sophia Pontrelli. You'll meet her soon enough. The wedding is set for the beginning of May. No, she's not pregnant."

"Damn straight I'll meet her soon. You haven't forgotten about my charity ball next month, have you? Bring her so we can be properly introduced."

Right, that damn ball. How had I let it slip my mind?

"We will be there." I grudgingly promise.

"Good. Now be a good boy and go to bed, it's after midnight." The call ends.

Shaking my head, I toss my phone on the desk. How does she always manage to get the last word in?

I swallow the rest of my brandy in one go. That woman is enough to drive even the most patient man to drink. And patience is not one of my virtues. If I had it my way, I'd drag Sophia to the courthouse tomorrow, now that she's agreed to be my wife. But this is a long-game, and I need to let it unfold at a reasonable pace. Rushing could ruin everything. I can't appear desperate to marry Sophia.

Waking my computer, I shoot an email off to my assistant, Eve. Sophia will need an appropriate ball gown for my mother's event. As well as everything that goes with it. Hair and makeup for sure.

A red dress, I specify. I enjoy seeing Sophia in that color, it's as bold and beautiful as she is, fiery and alluring. She should always wear crimson.

With that in mind, I add a note to include under garments in that color as well, then press send.

The thought alone of Sophia in crimson lingerie is enough to make my cock grow. I can picture her beneath my desk, on her knees, those chocolate eyes on mine as she sucks me off. Her pouty lips wrapped around my dick.

Fuck. I adjust my trousers, and shift in the chair.

It's late, I really should go to bed. However, due to the adrenaline from shooting a man earlier, and my current arousal, sleep is the last thing on my mind.

Shrugging out of my jacket, I pull my tie free, and unfasten the buttons on my dress shirt. Immediately, I feel more relaxed. After only a moment's hesitation, I unbutton my trousers too, releasing my cock into my hand, and give it a stroke.

Fuck yes. My hips jerk. It's been too long since I've handled myself like this.

I close my eyes, and my mind conjures more naughty images of Sophia while I jerk off like a horny fucking teenager. Each picture is filthier than the last.

Ramming my cock down Sophia's tight throat.

Sophia licking my balls.

My cum spurting all over her face and tits.

I've tasted her sweet mouth, but that's only the beginning of my cravings. I want to eat her pussy, her breasts, and taste myself on her lips. I'm going to fuck her bare and fill her with my cum.

She'll have to get on birth control if she doesn't want to become pregnant yet. Because once I have her, I already know I'm not going to be able to get enough. She's mine. I'm going to fuck her like I own her.

I groan. My balls tighten, and I'm so close to release.

A soft gasp in my doorway makes me open my eyes. At first, I wonder if my fantasies have bled into reality, because Sophia is standing in the entrance. Her soft lips are parted, cheeks flushed, and her gaze glued to my fisted, veiny cock. She's wearing a slinky silk nightgown, her nipples peaked through the thin fabric.

When her pink tongue darts out to lick her lips, my hips buck and I lose control. Ropes of cum land on my dress slacks and shirt. My head falls back, mouth open, as the force of the release wracks my body.

The grunt that leaves my throat is raw and primal.

After a few moments, my breathing evens out and I release my dick.

"Roman?"

My head snaps up to find that Sophia really is standing on the threshold of my office, temptation incarnate, and she did witness me...jerking off.

"What are you doing down here?" I demand, quickly cleaning myself up. She stayed and watched. Did she like what she saw? Is she embarrassed? Does she think I sit around in my office all day stroking myself off?

Christ.

"I couldn't sleep. I knocked on your door, but you weren't in your room, so I figured you'd be here."

My gaze snaps up to meet hers. She came looking for me? Why?

"You've found me, so what is it you want?"

She sighs at my abrupt tone. "Your hot and cold switch has a hair trigger, you know that?"

"Does it?"

She cocks her head. "You know it does."

"And which version do you like better? Hot or cold?" Fuck, why am I baiting her? Or am I *flirting*? For fuck's sake, what's gotten into me tonight?

She answers without hesitation. "Hot."

"Are you sure?"

"I'm positive." Sophia steps further into the room, head held high, shoulders back. I clearly read the challenge in her posture.

"How about we test that theory?" I beckon her forward with two fingers. "You agreed to marry me, so I think it's about time that I sample the goods."

Her pulse flutters in the hollow at the base of her throat. The blush in her cheeks and dilated pupils tell me how much she wants me. Somehow, miraculously, this gorgeous creature craves my touch.

Does she truly know what she's asking for? I doubt it. Because behind my civil mask is a brutal beast who has lain dormant for far too long.

One that wants to ravage.

To unapologetically claim.

If she opens his cage, I don't know if I can control him.

Roman invites me behind his desk. His impressive cock is tucked away in his trousers, but his shirt is open, showcasing an expanse of smooth skin and lean muscle. Plus, a trail of black hair from his navel that disappears beneath his waistband. Seeing him naked once, briefly, is not nearly enough to satisfy my curiosity.

Once I'm within arm's reach, Roman lifts me by the waist and sets my butt on his desk. Still seated, he wedges his body between my legs, and rests my heels on the arms of his chair. His palms land on my knees. I sharply inhale at the contact.

Slowly, in agonizing measures, he slides his hands up my thighs toward the hem of my short silk night-gown. I reach back, bracing myself on his desk.

My breath hitches when his thumbs brush the insides of my thighs. As his hands move, his yellow-hazel eyes remain fixed on mine. He's watching my every subtle reaction.

Unfortunately, his impenetrable mask is securely in place. He's hiding something behind it, but right now I don't know what he's thinking or feeling. I wish I could see past it. Just a glimpse would be enough for now.

I know I'm dealing with *hot Roman*, but is this going to be a punishment or a reward? I guess I'll find out soon enough.

I reach for him, skimming my hands over his warm skin. My engagement ring's massive diamond sparkles in the faint light, reminding me that the dynamic between us has truly shifted. I'm his, and he's mine. Soon we'll be each other's forever. For better or worse.

"Thank you," I say to him. He cocks a questioning brow. "You shot that man in the park, and you saved my life."

His instant reply is predictable. "I didn't do it for—"

I grab a fistful of his hair and crush my lips against his to shut him up. I don't want to hear him deny what he did for me—again. He saved my life and he knows it. And he *did* do it for me.

Because he may be unwilling to admit it, but there's something going on between us. An undeniable pull. A yearning that must be satisfied before it implodes.

When he lets his guard down around me, he laughs, he relaxes. I am also happier in his company when we seem to be aligned. It's all a mystery to me still, but I can't pretend to ignore it any longer.

He deepens our kiss. His tongue slips into my mouth, tangling with mine, just as he rips my panties off with his bare hands. I startle at the sudden sting. My surprised squeak is muffled by his mouth.

Pulling away, he ducks his head down, between my legs. His hot tongue finds my wet pussy and he feasts. Roman licks and sucks.

"Oh my *God*." I had no idea this would feel so amazing. It's my new favorite thing.

When I thread my fingers through his hair and pull his head closer, he utters an encouraging sound, and the sensations reach new heights.

I moan, writhing on his desk where his large, rough hands pin my hips, preventing me from riding his face.

Roman shocks me by flinging my legs fully over his shoulders, grabbing my waist, and standing up straight. I cling to his head as he carries me—while continuing to eat me out—to the long vertical windows that over-look the garden.

My back hits the cool glass. It's such a stark contrast to his hot mouth that I gasp.

He pins me there. I'm at his complete mercy, high up in the air with my feet dangling over his shoulders, sandwiched between him and the window. All I can do is hold onto his head and grind my pussy against his face.

Again, he grunts his approval.

Roman sucks on my clit, then teases it between his teeth. *Holy Christ!* My legs begin to shake. My back arches off the glass as I'm hit with an orgasm that's much more powerful than the last one.

I cry out. Stars burst behind my eyelids.

I'm certain Roman won't survive my thighs crushing his head, but I also don't care. This is the most amazing experience I've ever had. It's totally worth his demise.

As I come down from my out-of-body experience, Roman is lapping at my pussy, smooth and languid, making me squirm. His gaze finds mine and he smiles like a cat who caught the canary. That expression on his ruthlessly gorgeous face makes my pulse stutter.

"Oh, you lived," I say in my blissed-out state.

His brow pinches with confusion.

"You didn't die from suffocation," I elaborate.

His grin widens. "You taste so good, I'd gladly spend hours between your thighs deprived of oxygen."

A fresh rush of arousal shoots through me all the way from my head to my toes.

Roman steps away from the window, taking me with him. He lifts me up, briefly tosses me in the air as if I weigh nothing at all, and catches my hips before my feet can touch the floor. Instinctively, my legs wrap around his waist.

"What are you doing? You can't just toss me around." My protest is weak as I cling to him like a monkey.

He chuckles. "I can and I will."

Some of his mask has fallen away. He gazes back at me, the amusement plain in his eyes.

Leaning forward, I claim his lips in a kiss. He jerks,

startled. I'm not quite sure why until I taste myself on him. It's slightly sweet and musky, but I don't shy away from it.

Roman groans into my mouth. I feel his cock stiffen between us, and I rock my hips into him. I want him inside me. If his mouth feels that good, I can only imagine how his cock might feel buried deep inside my pussy.

Abruptly, he pulls me away, nearly dropping me to the floor. I manage to land on my feet but stumble, my head spins and hurt wraps around my chest.

Really? He decides to reject me now?

"You should go to bed," he says, raking his fingers through his disheveled hair.

"Why are you pushing me away?"

"I'm not." He sighs. "I'm not usually a patient man, but you're a virgin and I'm not going to take all of you at once. I want you to remember each experience along the way to popping your cherry. Which I will do one day. Not tonight."

I wrap my arms around myself and frown. When he puts it like that, it sounds like he actually cares about my pleasure.

He mistakes my confused frown for one of disappointment. "Don't worry, principessa, one day I'll have all of you: Your body, your heart, and your soul."

Stunned into silence, I stare at him.

We agreed on my body being part of our bargain, but I didn't think my heart and soul were also included.

What does Roman De Luca really want from me?

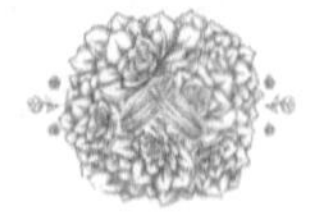

Years ago, when I erroneously thought college was an option, I'd done some studying. Columbia University in New York City is where I've always wanted to go, but it is not the easiest to get into. With only a four percent acceptance rate, I have to wow the acceptance committee.

So, I spend the next few days researching the process. Turns out I have to take the SAT, submit an application to the college, and then wait until the summer to know if I've been accepted or not.

First, I have to study for the test. Which I spend almost all of my waking hours doing.

Roman spends his time working from his office in the city, which means I rarely see him. Left to my own devices, and now that I'm not a flight risk, I'm able to go out whenever I like, as long as Enzo takes me in the car.

On a day when my brain simply can't absorb any more information, I decide to get together with my sisters for an afternoon coffee out on the town. We meet at a coffee house in my old neighborhood. The area is protected by the Italians, so we don't have to bring any extra security.

Ginevra takes one look at my engagement ring and her eyes bulge out of her head. "Holy shit, Sophia, I'm surprised you can hold your own hand up. That rock must weigh a ton and a half!"

Arianna pulls her back into her chair. "Don't make a scene, Ginevra."

Our youngest sister is unfazed by Arianna's chiding. She sits in her seat and winks at me.

"It's so good to finally see you both again." I hug Arianna, then Ginevra, before taking my seat. "Tell me about everything I've missed. How's Mama?"

I've only been away from my family for a couple of weeks, but it feels like a lifetime.

"She's fine." Arianna slides my usual order, a hazelnut latte, across to me. "Papa and her have been at odds with each other ever since Roman basically kidnapped you. He's getting the cold shoulder treatment lately. It's been a bit tense over dinner, but other than that it's fine. We still don't know what Roman is holding over Papa. Papa swears it's not blackmail."

"Roman hasn't said anything about it. He seems more focused on Nik than on Papa." I shrug. "I'm not sure which one of them was originally his real target."

"Was?" Arianna frowns. "Has something changed?"

My cheeks heat. "It has. At first, Roman only seemed to want this arrangement for business purposes, but now, I'm pretty sure, he actually wants me. We've come to our own agreement that suits both of us. And," I sip my latte, "he's going to pay my way through college."

Ginevra smacks the table in her excitement.

"That's great! You've always wanted to get your degree."

Arianna's frown deepens. "But, is he going to let you find a job afterward? Or is it a trophy degree?"

"He's going to let me work. He promised." I smile at my doubting sister. "It's fine, Arianna, we've worked it all out."

"Okay. I just don't want to see your dreams dangled in front of you and then crushed. People play some twisted mind games at times. I don't think most men are to be trusted."

"Since when have you become so pessimistic?"

She tilts her head to one side. "You've obviously been away so long that you don't remember me. I've always been this way."

Ginevra giggles. "Yeah, without you around, Sophia, the household is miserable. Arianna casts her negative energy over all of us." She dramatically sighs. "Most days, I wish to be kidnapped just like you were, so I can escape this black cloud that I call my sister."

Arianna glares at Ginevra, who remains unaffected, as always. I smile behind my coffee cup. I've always been the blunt, but relatively even-tempered one. Ginevra and Arianna are such opposites in so many ways that I'm surprised they haven't killed each other yet without me acting as a daily buffer between them.

"I missed you two."

"Aww, that's sweet." Ginevra leans her elbows on the table. "Now tell us the truth. Have you had sex yet?"

I choke on air.

"Ginevra, that's inappropriate," Arianna grumbles.

Gin shrugs. "What? No, it's not. We're sisters, we should be open with each other about our sex lives. No one else is going to share any information with us. And I'm not going into my marriage bed unprepared."

Out of all of us, Ginevra is the most prepared. Never mind the fact that she's the youngest and still a virgin. At least I'm pretty sure she is untouched, like the rest of us.

"We haven't gone all the way yet, but we've done some other things that felt really good," I confess, my cheeks blazing.

Arianna turns her glare on me. "Don't encourage her. You know what she's like. We'll find her in a back alley with some poor boy she coerced, even though he knows if they're caught, he'll be dead."

"Ah, rude." Ginevra swats at Arianna. "I wouldn't do *that* in a filthy alley. I have more class than that."

"Not much."

I laugh. "Mama must be tearing her hair out dealing with you two."

"Yep," they say in unison, then shoot each other glares before erupting into giggles.

I shake my head at them. "So Roman's throwing us an engagement party. To my utmost astonishment, he's agreed to let you two, and Ravenna, plan my bachelorette party. So, you better start planning."

"Hell yes!" Gin wins another narrow-eyed glance from Arianna.

Our conversation settles into party details, venue

options, and reining in Gin's wild ideas. It's an absolutely perfect afternoon spent with my sisters.

As I'm leaving, I check my phone's voicemail. There's a missed call and a message from an unknown number. Just in case it's important, I press play.

Nik's voice comes out of the speaker. "You're going to regret this, you stupid filthy slut," he slurs. "You think you can agree to marry me and then drop me for another man? You can't. And I know you're behind that shit leaked to my cousin. You're trying to drive a wedge between me and Dimitri. I know it's you, because that's the kind of game harlots like to play. You manipulative slut."

The voicemail cuts out.

I swallow hard, staring down at my phone as I slide into the backseat of the town car. I've never heard Nik so belligerent before. He's clearly lost his mind.

"Everything okay, Miss?" Enzo asks from the driver's seat. He's a mild-mannered man in his late sixties who's worked as Roman's driver for decades.

"Yes. Fine. Let's go home, please."

He gives me an easy salute.

I didn't think Nik would be this upset about losing me as his fiancée. Though to a man like him, it's not so much about me, as it is about his wounded pride. A man who's been crossed like he has is dangerous.

Unease twists around my gut and solidifies. I have a feeling I haven't seen the last of Nik Kozlov.

CHAPTER 15

Sophia

"This arrived for you, Miss Sophia." Diana places an enormous box on my bed, and I uncurl from the window seat where I'm studying for the SAT. "Here's the note that came with it."

I take the envelope from her and read the card.

Meet me in the foyer at eight sharp. ~ Roman

Glancing up at Diana, I ask, "Do you know where he's taking me tonight?"

The box delivery and instruction to meet him in the foyer remind me of our very first date. I can't believe that was only two weeks ago. Since then, we've both been so busy that I've lost track of the time. I'm glad Roman is taking me out again.

Diana shoots me a sly smile. "I'm sure you'll find a partial answer to your question in this box. Open it. Let's see what's inside."

With an amused huff at her secrecy, I lift the top

from the box to discover another red dress—no, not a dress, a ballgown. My breath catches as the intricate beading shimmers in the light. It's gorgeous. Obviously, we're going somewhere really fancy, and potentially quite significant.

Lifting out the gown, I find a pair of matching satin heels, and a smaller box of jewelry. At the bottom, there's a matching, blood red set of bra and panties. Roman has planned my outfit down to the tiniest detail. Heat creeps across my face at the thought of him seeing me in these underwear.

The heat further warms at the realization this is exactly what he *wants* to see me wear.

Diana claps her hands twice. "Let's start getting you ready."

Two women enter my room. After brief introductions, they get to work on my hair and makeup. I place myself in their capable hands, listening to their ongoing chatter, as they transform me from simply Sophia, into a masterpiece.

Once they're done, Diana helps me dress and put on the jewelry. By the time we're finished, it's a quarter to eight, and I'm restless with nerves. At least I look amazing. I barely recognize myself in the full-length mirror.

Triple checking everything, I finally decide to go downstairs early and wait for Roman.

A few minutes later, he emerges from the shadowy hallway. He's striking in a perfectly tailored black tuxedo that emphasizes his broad shoulders and impressive height.

He stops short, his yellowish gaze lingers over me as heavily as a touch. My skin flushes where his eyes wander. The dress is cut low enough in the front to reveal an alluring amount of cleavage. A laced bodice cinches the waist, then the skirt flares out, falling in spills of silk to sweep the floor.

"You are stunning." His tone holds reverence, awe, like I've never heard from him before. He offers his arm and I gratefully take it.

"Thank you. You clean up pretty nicely yourself." That gets a rumbly chuckle out of him as we duck into the car. "Are you going to tell me where we're going tonight?"

Roman drops a possessive hand on my knee. "We're going to a charity ball. Attendance is mandatory, but we don't need to stay too long."

"How is attendance mandatory? I thought you were your own boss and no one could tell you what to do," I tease.

His lips form a thin line. "This ball is hosted by my mother. You'll understand when you meet her that she doesn't take *no* for an answer."

"Wait," I fully face him, "you're taking me to meet *your mother?*"

He dips his chin in an affirmative.

"Holy crap." I glance down at myself. "Is this dress too revealing? Oh my God, I should have bought her a gift—or at least flowers." I frown up at Roman. "You should have told me I was going to meet your mother tonight. I'm completely unprepared."

He gives my knee a squeeze. "It's fine. Relax. She's

not expecting anything from you other than to meet you face-to-face. Everything is going to be fine."

I sit back in the seat. It's too late now for further preparation. All I can hope for is to make a decent first impression.

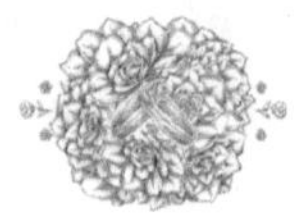

Roman places my hand on his arm as we enter the ballroom. All eyes turn to us and linger, a hush coming over the crowd, and I'm pretty sure it has little to do with the sinful crimson dress I'm wearing, and everything to do with Roman. He's striking to behold.

"Why are they staring at you?" I whisper. Maybe I'm missing something important.

"They're not. They're staring at you."

"What?" I sharply glance at him. "Why?"

"Because no one has seen a woman on my arm in six years. They're not used to such a sight." He glances over at me. "And because you're a vision."

Ignoring the blatant stares and shocked whispers, Roman leads us into the crowd. No one dares to point out the fact that he brought a date. They politely nod as he introduces me to his acquaintances and business associates. Most of them are names I recognize from overhearing my father at times.

These people here tonight rule this city—either legally, or as part of its illegal underground. Being rich, powerful, and influential, they all have enough in common to socialize with each other.

I would expect several less than savory business dealings going on this evening under the innocent umbrella of this charity function. That's the way our world works.

"Roman, darling, I'm so glad to see you." A beautiful woman swoops in and kisses him on both cheeks. "You've kept me waiting for far too long."

I bristle at her public display of affection. The emotion catches me off guard. I'm jealous. When did I become so possessive of Roman's affections?

Roman turns to me and says, "Sophia, I'd like you to meet my mother, Isabella. Mother, this is Sophia Pontrelli, my fiancée."

Momentarily stunned, I blink at her like an owl. *This* is Roman's mother? I mean, I guess she's old enough to have birthed him—barely. Either that or she has found the best skin care routine in the world, and somehow looks fifteen years younger than her chronological age.

Roman gazes down at me with an inquisitive look that seems to say: *Why are you acting so weird?*

Mrs. De Luca gives me an appraising once-over before embracing me in a tight hug. Holding my shoulders, she kisses me on both cheeks.

"You are gorgeous, my dear. And to think that Roman has been hiding you away, keeping you a secret from me." She leans close. "I know he says your arrangement is strictly business, but now that I've seen you, I know he's lying. How could he possibly resist falling in love with a girl as lovely as you?"

Flustered, I have no idea how to respond to her. Instead, I say, "It's very nice to finally meet you, Mrs. De Luca."

"Please, call me Isabella. You'll be my daughter-in-law soon enough." She grins at me again, then sweeps off to greet her other guests.

The woman is a force of nature. No wonder Roman accommodated her request to make an appearance here.

He places his hand on my low back. "I apologize. She can be overly zealous at times. Now that I think about it, she's pretty much like that all the time."

"How are you so reserved, when you have a mother who is the exact opposite?"

"By choice," he grunts. "If I were as whimsical as her, I'd have lost the family fortune a long time ago."

I glance around the place, suddenly seeing it through new eyes. "Wait. This is your mother's house, isn't it?"

Roman nods. "Yes. As well as my childhood home."

I become completely fascinated with this palatial house, trying to imagine a little Roman running around its halls. Did the staff play with him? Did they celebrate holidays in this room?

Seeing my expression, he chuckles. "I'll give you a tour."

How does he know what I'm thinking without me saying a word? Am I that easy to read?

"I'd like that."

"Good. But first, we'll dance." He leads me out to the dance floor. The music switches to a waltz, and ignoring the curious glances and murmurs, Roman glides me around with such grace that I feel like I'm floating.

This monster of a man can dance? He never ceases to amaze me.

I glance up at the ceiling mural. It's obviously hand painted. The herringbone laid floors beneath us are solid wood. The amount of detail put into the crown molding points to excellent craftsmanship. They're all signs of extreme wealth of a bygone era.

I knew the De Lucas were a rich family, but this is old money, generational wealth. In comparison, my family is newer money, having only been here for a couple of generations. Papa's still climbing up the social ladder, still trying to establish the Pontrelli name in this city.

All of that is beneath Roman. He grew up with a guaranteed spot in society. A society where gentlemen are expected to know how to dance, taught proper manners, and though they may appear old-fashioned at times, they are the class who rule the rest of us. Empires are born and fall, even among their own people, while the rest of them just continue to accumulate wealth and status.

That insight casts Roman in a new light. He might be ruthless, but he's also as well-bred as they come. And he chose me to be his wife.

As we glide across the floor, the world around us

seems to fall away until all I know is Roman. His hand on my waist, the heat of his body, those blazing eyes boring into mine. He gazes at me like I'm the center of his universe.

He is, in a word, perfect. I didn't see it before, but now I do.

And that thought scares me. I'm in danger of catching feelings for this dark knight. If I fall down that rabbit hole, will he fall with me, or will I find myself all alone?

I've always figured a loveless marriage is the only version I can have. Not necessarily because I'm undeserving of love, but because duty to my family comes first. Now, with Roman, I'm not so sure what my future holds.

The waltz ends, and for a long moment we simply stare at each other. His gaze caresses my face. My lips part and I sway closer to him, seeking anything he's willing to give me. So many unspoken words sit in the crackling electricity between us.

Roman finally breaks the spell. "Now for that tour." He takes my hand in his.

Before we make it far, we're held up by another of Roman's associates. He introduces us.

"Sophia, I'd like you to meet Blake Baron, my oldest friend and colleague."

Hesitantly, I shake the man's hand. So, this is the Black Baron that everyone whispers about in shadowed corners. He's not at all what I expected.

He's a similar height and build to Roman—formidable—but that is where their commonality ends.

Mr. Baron has wavy blond hair and brilliant blue eyes. His lips are fixed in a sneer, as if he's perpetually displeased with everyone and everything around him.

"It's a pleasure to meet you." He sounds downright bored.

"Same." I cast him a thin smile.

Mr. Baron turns his attention to Roman. "I'm on my way out. I'll be in touch about you know what. I told you it would be in the newspaper, didn't I?" Without waiting for a reply, he strides away.

What a strange man. I stare at his retreating back, while trying to make sense of his cryptic message. What was in the newspaper?

"What was that all about?" I glance up at Roman, who shrugs. I don't believe his denial for an instant. But I let it go.

"Come." He takes my hand again.

We stroll through the expansive halls, Roman shows me the library, recreation room, living and dining rooms, theater, pool, then we end up in his childhood bedroom. His mother keeps his things out. The room seems untouched from when he must have lived here, that of a teenage boy's room, except that it's clean. Though I doubt Roman has ever been untidy in his life.

I take it all in. It smells faintly of vanilla. The space is sophisticated and decorated in whites, navy and soft blues. A few nicknacks decorate his shelves that are loaded with books. The only real personal touch is a collection of framed pictures of him with his family over the years.

I do a double-take at one of them. Surely that smiling, optimistic youth isn't *this* Roman De Luca? Even in his college graduation photo he looks...different. Happier, full of life, and more relaxed.

Then I finally pin down what it is I'm seeing. His eyes. In these pictures his emotions shine through them, open and inviting. Unlike the man I know today, who is mostly unreadable, shielding his thoughts and feelings from others.

What happened to Roman in the past decade? Why the dramatic change in him?

He closely studies me as I explore his room. I'm keenly aware of his gaze following my every movement, everything I touch, the spots where I linger.

I pick up the graduation photo, the only one where he's alone in the picture. He's handsome, around my age, and mirth dances in his eyes. This version of himself is buried somewhere deep inside of my future husband.

Turning to Roman, I say, "Who changed you? Was it my father or Nik?"

His muscles tense and he becomes unnaturally still. The air between us hums with tension. Suddenly he springs at me like a tiger.

He snatches the frame from my hands, then grabs me by the waist and presses my back up against the wall. I gasp and my heart flutters—with fear or excitement, I'm not sure. His body is flush against mine, pressing me into the hard wall at my back.

His lips move lightly across mine as he speaks. "I never want to hear Kozlov's name come out of your mouth again. Never speak it. Don't even *think* it. He's not worthy of his name upon your lips. Do you understand me?"

"Yes," I say breathily. My every cell is aflame from the perfect way his strong body fits against mine. Pure dominance radiates from him, brushing against my skin.

He pins my wrists above my head. "Good girl."

So Nik is the one who's wronged him, not Papa. I wonder how. What is the bad blood between them?

"You're thinking about him again, aren't you?" He nips at my earlobe.

My sensitive nipples rub against his hard chest. "I was just..."

"No lying." He sucks at my neck, and I moan.

"I'm not going to lie. Yes, I was thinking about both you and him." I can barely think straight as he plants seductive kisses along my collarbone.

"And what did I tell you about that, principessa?" He murmurs against my skin.

I inhale a shaky breath. "You told me not to."

"And you disobeyed." He grinds his erection against my stomach as he leaves another love bite on my neck. My pussy throbs, needing more. I wrap one leg around his knee, pressing us closer together.

"I can hardly control my own thoughts. Sometimes things show up in my mind before I can stop them." I'm rambling. I have no idea if my defense makes any sense at all.

"Then you'll learn to control yourself. Or you'll be punished." He kisses me, his tongue parting my lips.

I kiss him back. We devour each other with fevered desperation, until his words fully sink into my lust-clouded mind.

I break away. "What do you mean by 'you'll punish me'?"

"I'll bend you over my knee and spank your gorgeous ass." His steady gaze holds mine, showing no remorse or shame at his threat.

I roll my eyes at him. "You wouldn't dare—"

Abruptly, he scoops me up, and tosses me onto his bed.

"What the hell?" I bounce on the mattress and glare at him.

"On all fours. Right here. Now." He takes off his jacket and rolls up his sleeves, exposing muscular fore-arms. Heat burns through me at the sight of him, at his bossy words, and his lustful gaze.

Hesitantly, I comply.

He arranges me so that I'm aligned with the edge of the bed, and he stands beside me. Slowly, he lifts my dress up to my waist, exposing my ass. I suck in a gasp at the cold touch of metal a moment before my thong is cut away. The thong he bought for me. Roman balls up my underwear and shoves them in his pocket along with the knife.

His fingers shallowly enter me from behind, finding me wet. I press back against his hand, demanding more, but he leaves me wanting, teasing my clit instead. He's never touched me like this before and it's exquisite.

Pressure builds low in my belly as he works me up

to an orgasm. But before I can come, Roman withdraws and smacks my ass—*hard*.

I yelp at the sharp pain. Then moan as his fingers find my clit again. He's rough, quickly working me up again, only to spank me right before I can come.

My frustration quickly builds as I experience two very different types of pleasure. His fingers circling my clit, and the hot pain of his palm across my butt cheeks, which only seems to heighten my arousal. I moan, whimper, and gasp as he punishes me in the most amazing way— one I never imagined I would enjoy.

He's spanking me, but it's more than that. He's also denying me release.

"Do you know why I'm punishing you?" He speaks in a strained voice, his palm rubbing circles on my burning ass.

"Yes," I gasp.

"Tell me why?"

"Because I thought about Nik," I say before thinking.

Smack! I shudder at the sting. Only to moan when his fingers slide inside my pussy, finding my wetness, and spreading it to my clit.

"That's only half of the reason. Do you know why else?"

I try to think through the haze of frustration, pain, and pleasure. "Because I tried to run away?"

"That too." This time he continues pleasuring me, and slaps my ass with his free hand. My body jolts, my inner muscles clench. "But there's one more reason. Name it."

"I don't know." I writhe against his touch. I'm so close, yet know my orgasm is unattainable until we're done playing this game. "Please," I whisper.

"Do you think I'm the kind of man who will take pity on you, principessa?"

I shake my head. "No."

"That's right." He spanks me again—one, two, three—and my orgasm builds, ready to burst forth. His fingers slow, teasing my entrance again. I'm so slick he slides easily up and down my pussy.

Turning my head, I glare up at him. "What do you want from me?"

He takes a moment to consider my question, all the while slipping his fingers through my wetness. "*Everything*. I want everything from you, Sophia. More than you'll ever be willing to give. Mark my words, I'll take everything from you and more."

Roman shoves his hand down the front of my dress and pinches my nipples while his fingers pinch my clit. When he leans over and bites my butt cheek, I tip right over the edge into the most explosive orgasm I've ever had. Stars burst in my vision, and I scream his name so loudly the guests downstairs can probably hear me. But I don't care.

"Good girl," he says as I collapse, trying to catch my breath. "Fuck me, Sophia, you're glorious." He peers down at me with lust-soaked admiration. "Just don't roll your eyes at me again, or I'll have to spank you."

I stop myself, turning my would-be eye roll into a sigh. "*That's* your third reason for punishing me?"

"It's as good a reason as any other."

I eye him. "You're sadistic."

"You always say I'm a monster. What did you expect?" A wicked smirk slides across his lips.

My gaze drops to the bulge in his trousers, and I reach for him. I want to taste him. He's had plenty of fun with me, now it's my turn.

He catches my wrist. "No."

"Why not?" I practically pout, sitting up on the bed.

That smirk flashes across his face again. "You're showing how much you want me, principessa."

"Why shouldn't I?"

"Because I doubt you fathom what your desire does to me." He kisses the back of my hand. "Come on. We've made our appearance, now we should get going before my mother comes looking for us."

I shudder at that possibility. I'm trying to make a good first impression on Mrs. De Luca, not get caught doing naughty things in her son's old bedroom.

"Um." I walk over to the mirror and cringe at the damage. My hair is wild, lipstick smeared, mascara streaking down my face, and my cheeks and neck are flushed. Plus, I'm missing my panties.

I turn to Roman. "I can't go out like this. I'm not even sure how we're going to slip out of this party without being seen."

"You look perfect." Roman's grin is possessive and devious. "Like you've been thoroughly satisfied—for now."

"Roman—" I chide him.

"I'll help you fix your hair."

Ten minutes later, I look passable. My body aches in the most amazing way, and Roman left a multitude of little red marks on my neck, but besides that I'm presentable enough.

Roman slides his hand up my throat and grips the back of my neck. I shiver at his commanding touch. The hold is purely possessive, staking his claim to everyone who glances our way as we weave our way downstairs, through the ballroom, and out the front door.

Roman

"**W**hat do you mean by a *delay* in shipment?" I speak into the phone, elbows resting on my desk, jaw clenched when all I get in response are excuses. "I don't care what it takes to get it where it needs to be on time, Ricardo. If you need to hire more labor, then hire them. That paperwork should have been done weeks ago. If you can't do your fucking job, then I'll replace you with someone who can. Get. It. Done."

I hang up. There's no point in discussing the matter further. Ricardo will either get the job done, or face the consequences when Don Casella doesn't receive his goods. Because ultimately, this will come down on my head and that shit rolls downhill. If my man's fuck ups put me in poor standing with Casella, there's going to be hell to pay. And he knows it.

Fucking hell, the past couple of weeks I have been dealing with one issue after another. I'm beginning to think I'm cursed. When I know the truth is I've been horribly distracted, and that's why my business dealings are causing chaos.

At all times, there must be a captain at the helm, or it all goes to shit.

I lounge back in my chair and drag my hand over my face. Weary exhaustion settles deep in my bones.

A rap on my door has me barking, "What?"

My assistant, Eve, pokes her head inside, unruffled by my ill temper. Fuck knows she's seen enough of it lately.

"Sir, your fiancée is here to see you."

I stand, pacing the space behind my desk. Sophia is here. She's never come to my office in the city before. Unfortunately, this is a bad time. Since claiming her for myself, I've put minimal effort in with my business. I need to stay focused and ensure everything runs smoothly from now on.

Sophia is a distraction that I don't need right now.

I've said some really stupid, and dangerous, things since proposing to her. I've given into temptation and tasted her, I showed her my childhood bedroom—which no one else has set foot in since I left for college, and I've killed for her.

What was that nonsense I'd stated about wanting her body, heart, and soul? I must have been out of my fucking mind.

She'll make a good wife. I'll come to her when I need an heir, but that's as much as I can give her. She's too adept at clouding my mind and then I forget about what's important—my business. Sophia has a knack for making me lose all perspective. I can't risk it again.

I might make an exception for our honeymoon. But that's it.

"I'm busy. Send her away." I wave off Eve, expecting her to bow out and close the door.

Instead, the door bursts the rest of the way open and my future wife strides into my office like she owns the place. She ditches her coat on a chair, and places a large to-go bag on top of my desk.

I fold my arms. "I'm busy right now."

"I brought us lunch. I know you haven't eaten yet today because I called Eve, and she told me you haven't come out of your office since this morning." She checks her watch. "It's three in the afternoon, Roman."

I shoot my narrowed gaze at Eve. Who was smart enough to disappear as soon as Sophia shouldered her way in here. I'll deal with her later. *I'm* Eve's boss, and she shouldn't be telling Sophia about my eating habits, or anything else for that matter.

"I'm not hungry." Though the scents wafting from the bag smell divine, and my traitorous stomach rumbles. "Now take your food and leave. I'm not in the mood for your sass today."

She rolls her eyes. "Don't be rude."

Did she roll her eyes at me? I stare at her, the warning clearly written across my face.

She stares back, wide-eyed, realizing what she just did.

Only the desk separates us. I push a button beside

one drawer to turn the windows opaque. No one needs to see what's going to happen in here. That's private, between myself and my naughty wife-to-be.

Straightening, I wait for the windows to complete their transformation. Tension builds and crackles in the air, holding us both rooted in our places. By design, my office is also soundproof. I have no reason to hold back on Sophia.

Finally, I lunge.

Sophia lets out a surprised squeal. It's so fucking adorable that my chest swells with fleeting delight. She backs up as I advance on her with long strides, until her ass hits the credenza against the far wall. My fingers curl around her delicate neck and gently squeeze.

"What did I say about rolling your eyes at me, principessa?"

Her lips part, and her pretty tongue darting out to moisten them.

"You said you'd punish me for it." She's practically panting, but I don't see fear in her eyes, all I see is excitement.

I momentarily freeze, several realizations dawning on me at once. She likes what I did to her the other night during the ball. She wants to be punished. She wants *me*, and she's not pretending.

As if to prove my epiphany, Sophia pulls on the tie keeping her wrap dress closed. The fabric falls open, revealing a crimson lace bra, matching panties and a garter belt attached to sheer black hosiery that end in sky high, fuck-me heels.

My mouth goes dry.

"Do you like what you see, sir?" She breathes those words, ever so slightly arching her back, thrusting those perfect tits towards me, tempting me with her siren song.

I have another realization: I'm no match for this creature's seductions.

I'm fucking doomed, and I'm not even a little bit mad about it.

If anyone else had barged into my office in the middle of the workday, and refused to leave, I'd have put a bullet in their head and called my cleanup crew. But for this woman, I'll happily say to hell with my business empire. One afternoon won't make a difference in whether it sinks or survives.

Fucking hell, she's more dangerous to me than she realizes.

I pull her toward me by her neck. "If I didn't know any better, I'd think you wanted to be bent over my desk and fucked like a good girl."

"Yes, please, sir." She's breathless, her entire focus is on me.

Fuck. There goes my workday—and I can't even find it in myself to give a damn.

The idea of showing up to Roman's office in lingerie and seducing him has lingered in my head for the past couple of days. This morning I managed to get up the nerve to see it through. So here I am, bared before my future husband, who looks like he either wants to strangle me or fuck me into the next century.

I can tell he hasn't yet decided.

We're not married. By my family's standards what I'm doing is wrong. I'm not his wife, we're not bound before man and God, so at this moment I am nothing more than his slut, a wanton woman begging to be disgraced.

But I don't care. I'm done playing by everyone else's rules. I want to have sex with my fiancé, and that's exactly what I'm going to do. I want to be his good girl. That's my choice to make.

Roman caresses my cheek with his thumb, his

expression pained. "Sophia, you don't want your first time to be on top of a hard desk."

"Don't tell me what I do and don't want. I'm on the pill. I want this." I grab a fistful of his shirt and tug. He leans down so I can reach up and kiss him. I pour everything I have into this kiss. Sucking, licking, showing him how much I want him. Right here, right now.

I rub against him like a cat in heat, and moan into his mouth.

He snaps.

Roman's mouth devours mine, feasting like a glutton. He effortlessly lifts me off the floor, and I wrap my legs around his waist as he carries me across the room.

He clears half his desk with the swipe of one arm, the contents crashing to the floor, then sits me on top. We're both breathing hard, hands and fingers fumble to undress each other, as our kiss turns sloppy. I expose Roman's glorious chest, ripping the buttons from his shirt in the process. They roll across the floor and beneath furniture, never to be seen again. In turn, he tears off my thong, brutal and unforgiving.

"Is this what you want?" he asks in a husky voice, popping the front closure on my bra.

"Yes." I lean back on the desk.

"Tell me. Tell me what you want." His tone is low and raspy. "Say it."

I reach for him. "I want you inside me. I want you to make me come."

"Are you saying you want me to take your virginity, principessa?"

I nod. "Yes. Take me."

Without another word, Roman releases his cock. It's thick and veiny, precum oozes from the end as he strokes it up and down. The sight makes my mouth water.

"You have a decision to make now. Do you want this an inch at a time or all at once?"

I stare at his massive dick. I know it's going to hurt, but I don't care, this is what I want. After this first time, it should feel good. Right? Maybe. It is huge.

"All at once." I meet his eyes. I'd sooner get this part over with so we can move on to more enjoyable things. Apparently, Roman's of the same mind, because without further ado, he grabs my hips and shoves his cock all the way into my soaked pussy.

I draw in a sharp breath at the uncomfortable invasion. A dull ache and discomfort follows the initial sharp pain. He's so big that I feel like, at any moment, my insides are going to burst apart.

Roman groans. "Relax, principessa. Eyes on me, and relax your muscles." His thumb circles my clit, sending shivers of pleasure through my taut body, and I slowly begin to loosen my muscles around him. As soon as I do, that minor pleasure turns to ecstasy, and the pain begins to fade.

His cock remains fully seated in me as his fingers circle my clit. I arch my back, and he hisses, pinning my hips down with his free hand. He keeps me still while he works me up. His hooded eyes give little away, though I can tell he's struggling to remain in control. He wants to let loose, and I want that too. Why won't he let go?

Leaning down, Roman sucks and rolls my nipples between his teeth—my fingers spear into his hair—adding another layer of stimulation to my already overwhelmed nerves. I try to buck my hips but he keeps me pinned. His thumb moves faster, flicking my clit, until liquid heat pools low in my belly. The pressure builds and builds.

When I'm afraid I'm going to implode from the intensity, my orgasm crests over me all at once.

"Roman!" I cry out. Wave after wave of blinding, white hot euphoria washes through me, seizing my body.

"*Fuck.*"

Suddenly I'm empty. Roman fists his cock, pumping thick spurts of cum over my stomach and tits. The sight is erotic, but a strange disappointment hits me hard in the chest. I feel like something is missing from this experience. Why didn't he come inside me?

He must see the emotion in my expression. "Don't worry. One day I'm going to ruin your sweet little pussy, but first you're going to beg me to do it. You're going to tell me exactly what you want. That you want me to fuck you and come inside your sweet cunt. Only then will I fuck you until you forget your own name, and fill you up with so much cum that you'll know who owns you."

To drive home his point, using his index finger, he scrawls his name in the semen coating my stomach. A satisfied, possessive smirk appears on his lips.

I gape up at him. I told him I wanted him inside me and for him to make me come. He'd done just that. Only that. Nothing less and nothing more—except mark me with his cum.

I swear *hot Roman* and *cold Roman* are merging to become *filthy Roman*. Who is both hot and cold at the same time. He says the naughtiest things, satisfying me only enough that I want more, with the cold calculation of a predator on the hunt.

As usual, I'm never indifferent around Roman. Irritation, edging on fury, pulses through my bloodstream at his tricks. Why does he have to be so difficult all the time? Why does he hold me at arm's length when we both know we want more of each other?

One day, I'm going to strip him of his cool, calculating control. Then we'll see who's begging and for what.

I set down my pencil and glance up at the wall clock. Ten minutes until the end of this SAT section. Glancing round the classroom, I notice that several others look bored or worried as they also wait for the timer to sound.

At this point, I *think* I'm doing well enough. God knows I've studied my ass off this month. If I don't score high enough to have a shot at Columbia University, then I don't know what I'm going to do besides try again. But time is running out. I need to get my application in before the wedding and the university's deadline.

My other worry is that I don't have a formal GPA. I've had private tutors since the age of thirteen and have my GED, I just hope that it's enough.

The timer dings and we take a ten-minute break before diving back into the test. Over three hours total. By the time it's over, I'm mentally and emotionally exhausted, but there's no rest to come, not today.

Enzo drives me home, where I lie down for a power nap, then get ready for my engagement party.

Most people, especially in arranged marriages, don't have two engagement parties—to two different men—within two months of each other. But I guess I'm not *most people*.

We were planning to skip this part of the celebrations, but after Mrs. De Luca met me, she insisted we do everything properly—including another engagement party.

We travel to the venue, Roman and I both lost in our own thoughts for the drive, him on his phone and me staring out the window. When we arrive and enter the space, I immediately realize this party is completely different from the first one.

This time, instead of being at my parents' house, we're at a riverside venue that exudes elegance. Mrs. De Luca chose the location and had a hand in the arrangements. I'm pretty sure she has magical powers because somehow this party makes the one before it pale in comparison, even with less time to plan. It's probably just that touch of what old money can bring: Vital connections and understated perfection.

The guest list that previously was a tacky display of wealth, power, and who-knows-who, is pared down to friends and family. This gathering feels more intimate—more real, somehow, too.

Yet, *this time,* I'm not on edge. Standing beside Roman, his palm resting on my lower back, strikes me as natural, even comfortable. We look like a real couple tonight—a couple who wants to be here instead of one forced together. Ironic, given how we met.

My parents approach us. It's the first time I've seen them since Roman literally tossed me over his shoulder and carried me from my childhood home.

Mama flings her arms around me, squeezing me in a tight hold. "Sophia, my beautiful daughter, you are glowing tonight."

Warmth heats my cheeks. Even though my sexual experience with Roman in his office was not entirely what I expected, I feel different now that I've lost my virginity and became a woman. It's a subtle shift, but it's noticeable.

Can Mama tell? Is that why I'm glowing tonight?

Drawing back, she kisses my cheeks and I return the gesture. "Thank you, Mama."

Her gaze hardens when she glances up at Roman, then over at Papa, who appears more tired than is normal. Dark circles haunt his eyes, his lips pull down at the corners, and his full head of salt and pepper hair appears limp.

Concern draws my brows together, until I remind

myself that Papa would have handed me over to anybody. I consider myself lucky that it turned out to be Roman instead of someone worse. Even so, Papa is not in my good graces right now. I don't know if he'll ever be again.

Mama returns her gaze to Roman. "You better be treating my daughter well, Mr. De Luca. While you may have succeeded in intimidating my husband into giving you our daughter, I'm not so easy to break. If you give her less than everything she desires, I'll show up on your doorstep, and, believe me, you won't like the consequences."

"Mama!" I gasp, never have I heard her speak to anyone outside the family like this before. Though I guess...Roman is part of the family now. Or, at least near enough.

I glance up at Roman, who's yellow-hazel eyes give away no hint at his thoughts. He's not the type of man most people threaten and live to tell about it. What is Mama thinking?

Roman reaches out and takes Mama's hand in his. "I promise to give your daughter everything she desires and more." He places a chaste kiss on the back of her hand before releasing it. "You have my word."

Mama seems slightly in shock, and more than a little flustered. I'm not surprised. Roman can be charming as the devil himself when he wants to be. He uses it like a weapon in his arsenal. I should know.

His gaze lands on me and my stomach flutters. I have a love-hate relationship with my body's reaction to him. One look from him and I'm all but giddy. That, paired with him making promises to my Mama, and my heart opens to him a little further.

Damn it, what if I'm falling in love with my fiancé? Is that so bad?

Yes, it's bad, because our marriage is a business arrangement and nothing more. There's no room for feelings between us. Roman has made it perfectly clear that he doesn't believe in love, so if I don't want to end up hurt, I need to start doing a better job of protecting my heart.

It's simply difficult when he turns on that charm and starts spouting romantic notions. We both tend to get swept up in the moment. But I can tell by the way he shuts down afterwards and I don't see him for days at a time that he regrets the sweet things he says to me.

Marriage is a business transaction, nothing more. I'd be wise to remember that around him.

"I see my son is laying on the charm." Mrs. De Luca glides up to our small group, and Roman makes the introductions. This is the first time our two families have met face-to-face.

"A pleasure to meet you both," she says. "I'm sure we'll get to know each other much better in the next couple of months."

"I do hope so." Mama beams at her. "You did a wonderful job pulling this together for tonight. We may have to reconsider where we're doing the rehearsal dinner."

"Of course. I can certainly help with that." Mrs. De Luca takes Mama's arm and they drift into a quieter corner as they continue to chat about wedding plans. Those two are so alike, with their strong personalities, that they'll either hate each other or become fast friends. So far, it's appearing to be the latter.

"God help us," Roman murmurs, his gaze on our mothers.

"Mmm, my thoughts exactly."

"Sophia, dearest?" Papa draws my attention to him. "I know you're angry with me right now. I just want you to understand—"

I shake my head. "Save it."

He gasps, rearing his head back as if I'd slapped him. True, I've never spoken so bluntly to him before, so it would come as a surprise.

"What you did was wrong, Papa. I have nothing to say to you."

He scowls. "Yet, you don't seem to be blaming *him*." He tips his head toward Roman, who's standing beside me as still as a statue.

"Roman and I have come to an understanding and struck a bargain between ourselves. No thanks to you, Papa."

At least he finally has the sense to look remorseful. With a curt nod, he hesitantly moves away from us, rejoining the greater crowd.

I hate being angry with my father, but I don't know how else to deal with him. Our family has always put the good of the whole above that of an individual member. However, I can't believe he let me go so easily. He sent a staff member to pack my things before he even had time to break the news to me. It hurts.

I turn to Roman. "What did you threaten him with that night?"

He catches on to my meaning quickly enough. "Ruin. Complete and absolute ruin to his entire family if he didn't turn you over to me immediately."

Of course. Roman's the kind of man who doesn't do things by halves. It's all or nothing—until it comes to me, then he only does things by halves.

"You're horrible," I tell him. Why can't I summon up the same level of anger, or even hatred, for Roman that I currently hold for my father? I did hate Roman in the beginning. Hell, I loathed him.

I can't seem to recall exactly when that changed. All of those times that he's rescued me must have worn me down.

"You keep saying that. But your actions indicate that you like that I'm horrible." His thumb caresses my back. "Tell me it's true."

I ignore his demand. "It's unfair of me to hold a grudge against my father when you gave him no choice in the matter."

"Oh, he had a choice." Roman spins us around until my back is to the wall and he's standing in front of me, blocking my view of the room. "He had to choose between his standing in this entire city and you. He chose his fortune and reputation. It's as simple as that."

I scowl at him. "Any man would make that same choice given those two options. He made the right choice. I shouldn't fault him for that."

"I disagree." Roman's fingers wrap around my

upper arms. "There are people in our lives worth fighting for, worth risking it all for. Perhaps it's time you reconsider your own worth."

I scoff. "My *worth*? My own father handed me over to you without a fight at all. After he promised me to a brute so we could strengthen our ties with the Russians. What *worth* should I think I have?"

Roman leans in, his breath tickling my ear when he speaks, "You're mine now, and I will never let you go without a fight."

My stupid heart skips a beat.

I remind myself that to Roman I'm no more than a possession, a necessity. He needs a wife, an heir, and there's nothing about me that makes me worthy other than having a womb.

Why on earth would he think I see any worth in myself at all, other than what everyone else wants from me?

He doesn't.

Papa doesn't.

And I... I don't know what to think.

CHAPTER 18

Roman

We arrive home from the engagement party that felt much too real. Too intimate. I made promises to her mother of my own free will, without seeking an advantage or getting anything in return other than the woman's blessing.

Why would I do such a thing?

The more time I spend around Sophia, the more strangely I act. I barely recognize myself.

Right now, I'm teetering on the edge of two options. One, I give in, let myself loose, and fuck her out of my system once and for all. It could take weeks, or even months to get enough of her. But then I could regain control of myself and only see her when she needs to fulfill her duty of giving me an heir.

Option two is much safer. I can keep hold of myself and not let her burrow any further under my skin. I will resist temptation. I will avoid her at all costs.

I glance down at her as we walk through the front door. She's the sweet goddess of sin and ruin. My own special kind of temptation. I'm afraid of becoming addicted, so the safer choice is to distance myself from her siren's call.

"Goodnight, Roman," she says, immediately heading upstairs to her room.

I pause in the foyer. That was too easy. Something is wrong, she seems off tonight, and I'm afraid it's because of what I confessed earlier. Her father did have a choice and he took the easy route by giving her to me. Though I suppose it was unnecessary for me to rub that in her face.

That, I'll admit, was an asshole move.

Though this may be a blessing in disguise. If she's angry with me, and keeps her distance, then I don't have to put forth the effort. All my problems are solved.

"Goodnight," I call after her, though she's disappeared from view.

Instead of going upstairs, I head into my office. I haven't touched Sophia since we had sex on my desk at HQ. I've been busy and she hasn't come to seduce me again. Does she regret what we did that afternoon? Is she waiting for me to come to her?

Either way, it doesn't matter, I remind myself. Avoiding each other is for the best. We're both safer this way. She has her life, and I have mine.

Simple. Straightforward.

Dropping into my chair, I heave a sigh. Why the fuck are women so complicated?

Why do I care? I don't care.

I'm keeping her for purely selfish reasons. For business reasons. It's not like I'm in danger of developing feelings for her, for fuck's sake. My heart froze over a long time ago. I could fuck her without feeling a thing toward her if I wanted.

The lie tastes like acid in the back of my throat.

Fuck. Somewhere along the way, I've started to care about her. First for her physical safety, and now for her feelings, her wants, her needs. I hurt her feelings tonight—and I fucking *care*.

The promise I made to her mother haunts me. What possessed me to make such a vow? Do I really intend to give Sophia everything she desires?

I'm afraid to answer that question, so I wake my computer and open my email application. There's an unread message that helps put my head on straight and keep me focused.

De Luca, did you see yesterday's newspaper? More good news today: Word on the street is his cousin is distancing himself from the situation. Others are following his lead. The FBI investigation will tear them apart. ~B.B.

I did see yesterday's article about the FBI cracking down on the Russian mob after receiving an anonymous tip about some of their more unsavory business pursuits. No doubt that has caused quite a stir among the Kozlov Bratva. They'll soon realize the leaked information leads back to Nikolai Kozlov and if they want off that sinking ship, they'd better jump now.

The fact that the cousin, Dimitri Kozlov, already understands the significance of the situation is a good sign. His uncle runs the Bratva, which puts him second in command, and Nikolai Kozlov third. That third leg is about to be torn out from under them, if they don't kick it out first.

I delete the email, removing all traces of it from the server. Once this is over, I want no lingering reminders of Kozlov.

Sophia stays in her room for three days. Three. Whole. Days.

I work late in the city and don't see her in the mornings before I leave or at dinner when I return. The dining table is once again a place of solitude and loneliness. That sense is somehow more disturbing now than before Sophia's arrival. Another sign that she's trying to infiltrate my psyche. Perhaps succeeding, too.

On the third evening, I finally break.

Normally, I'm made of stronger stuff. I might not be patient, but I will meticulously plan and wait out a rival. It seems all of that falls apart when it comes to Sophia.

After sitting through yet another lonely dinner, I

bring a full, warm plate up to Sophia's room. I'd hoped that forbidding Diana and Luis from delivering the meal to her room would force her to come downstairs and join me. But she never appeared. And I won't starve her. If anything, I bring the food as a peace offering—extra garlic breadsticks included.

My knock goes unanswered, so I press my ear to the door. At first, all I hear is silence on the other side, then a distant smothered wail and sniffle. She's crying.

Deja vu slams into my chest with enough force to make me stumble backwards. Dread twists and coils in my gut, and my lungs struggle to draw in a full breath of air. Memories of a different room, a different woman, on a different night invade my mind.

Before I know what I'm doing, I've wrenched open the door and rushed inside. A panicked scan of the room shows it's empty.

I drop the plate on the first horizontal surface that I pass, and continue further into her bedroom, frantically seeking Sophia. Another sniffle draws my attention to the dimly lit bathroom.

I catch sight of her in the illuminated mirror. She cradles a handful of pills in one palm, tosses them in her mouth, and gulps half a glass of water to swallow them down.

My stomach drops to the floor.

No.

A cold sweat breaks out on the back of my neck, as I storm into the bathroom and grab her arms. Her eyes are red-rimmed. Her face, pale.

"What did you *do*?" I demand.

Her eyebrows pinch. "I don't know—"

"Which pills did you take? Answer me!" Releasing her, I open the medicine cabinet, searching for a bottle of sleeping pills, prescription painkillers, anything harmful in large doses. "*What the fuck did you take?*" I bellow.

"Roman."

All I find are bottles of herbal supplements and vitamins. Can a person die from a Vitamin C overdose?

"*Roman.*" She wedges herself between me and the vanity cabinet. "Look at me."

I glance down at her and pause, quickly scanning her features for any sign of lethargy.

She reaches up and palms my cheek. "I take supplements nightly. You know, herbs that are good for my hair and nails, my skin, my brain. All those things."

I freeze, staring down at her as her words gradually begin to make sense. Vitamins? Nightly?

I glance up at the cabinet's contents and the bottles all over the countertop. There's nothing harmful here.

She didn't— She's not trying to—

Eventually, the vice clenching my intestines loosens.

I catch sight of myself in the mirror. Wide, wild eyes stare back at me. I look like a deranged killer out for blood.

"You thought I was trying to kill myself, didn't you? Why?" Sophia's voice drags my attention back to her, and I lower my forehead to rest against hers. Our breaths mingle. Her honey scent further soothes my frayed nerves. Normally I'd suck it up, push these embarrassing feelings back into the box where they belong, and shrug off this whole situation.

But right now, I just can't. Or maybe I don't want to. I'm not sure.

Sophia's arms wrap around my neck. She holds me close, not saying another word. I hug her waist, drinking in the comfort she offers, as the seconds tick by, and my thundering heartbeat slowly returns to normal.

Her presence, her touch, her warmth is a balm to my aching soul. She feels so good in my arms, so I give myself this moment to silently open up and let her in. For a few seconds, I allow her to hold on to all my broken pieces. To let myself fall apart in her arms.

I neither shed a tear nor make a sound during this process. I don't even know if she realizes how vulnerable I am in this moment, before I pick myself up and don my inner cloak of armor.

Dropping my arms to my sides, I straighten and she lets me go.

"I'm sorry," I murmur.

"For what?"

I skim my thumb across her cheek. "For telling you the other night that your father had a choice and didn't choose you. For hurting your feelings. That is why you're sad, is it not?"

She gives a curt nod, her expression closed and distant. "Partly."

I sweep a strand of hair behind her ear. "Penny for your thoughts, principessa. Is it the SAT scores?"

"No, not that. I haven't heard back yet. It's just... What you said did hurt, but it was also true." Her chocolate brown eyes lift to mine. "I also realized that I have very little self-worth. I've spent my whole life knowing, and accepting, that my life is not my own. My value is in what I can give to others. Without that, I'm nothing." Her eyes shimmer with unshed tears, and my cold, frozen heart cracks open. Too bad there's nothing inside except an endless void.

I hold her face between my hands. "That's not true. You're worth far more than that."

"No, I'm not." She shakes her head. "The only reason you want me is because you need a wife. But we both know that you could easily replace me with any other woman. It's all the same to you."

Guilt collides with my outrage on her behalf. Because in theory, she's right. Whoever was engaged to Kozlov would now be mine, no matter who she was or what she looked like. No matter her personality or family name. I didn't care. At the time, my sole agenda was to steal away his fiancée.

That's no longer true.

Now, I care.

And I don't want just any woman, I want *her*. However, admitting that leads to dangerous territory.

"That's not true," I say again, with more conviction this time. "You're irreplaceable, Sophia. I'm sorry I've made you feel otherwise." I'm also angry at her family for raising her to see herself as worthless on her own. "I promise you that you're going to do great things with your life. You'll find your sense of self. College is only the beginning."

Her lips quirk up in a sad smile. "Aren't you afraid I'll spend your money on college, then leave you?"

"No." *Terrified.* "As you'll soon learn, for a De Luca, divorce is not an option."

"How romantic. Of course, it's not. So that means that you're confident enough to have a wife who rules her own life, who won't be at your beck and call all the time as I go off to college and do great things?" Her gaze searches mine for the truth.

"I am. I don't want to hold you down, principessa. I want to bind you to me in every way possible. I want to own you, possess you. I want your every lustful thought to be of me. But I don't want to hold you back." My lips brush against hers. "No one could ever take your place."

"Is that why you panicked when you thought I was trying to kill myself?"

I release her as if I've been burned, and step away. "Let's not talk about that."

I never want to think of it again.

"Is that what happened to your late wife?" she whispers, not knowing when to let it go.

"I said leave it," I snarl, leaning against the far wall.

She folds her arms. "You want to possess my every thought, but you won't tell me anything about yourself. How is that fair?"

"The past is the past. Leave it buried where it belongs."

"Is it though? Because you seem to have some kind of grudge against Nik that has me wondering—"

I charge at her. "What did I tell you about saying his name?"

"You and all your rules." Her cheeks are flushed and anger flashes in her beautiful brown eyes. "You know what I think? I think you put all these rules in place to protect yourself. Because you don't want to face any of your issues. You're a sad, angry, lonely man who keeps the world at a distance to protect yourself. What you don't realize is that's not the solution, you're only making it worse. You're wasting your life and one day you'll come to regret it."

"You don't know a damn thing about me or my life!" I crowd her, pinning her against the bathroom cabinet. "I know you have some fantasy running through your head about being able to fix me. Give it up. It'll never happen. I'm not worth the fucking effort."

Sophia stands her ground, unafraid of me and my rising temper. She caresses my face. "That's where you're wrong. You're worth every effort, because when I look into your eyes, I see a broken man desperately crying out for help."

I slam my fist down on the countertop, and snarl, "I don't need your goddamn help."

Then I storm out of the bathroom, out of her bedroom and into mine, where I slam the door closed. Bracing my back against the solid wood, I close my eyes.

How can she possibly see so easily into my soul?

I curse myself for always being so blunt with Roman. I don't know what's wrong with me. Every time he's around I speak my mind, as if I have no filter at all. I've never been this careless with my words before. He just makes me so angry.

Angry, confused, and passionate in my need to help him.

I'm determined to break through his barriers, and terrified of what I'll find on the other side. He's so closed off, so *hurt*, his emotions are like a festering wound. If he doesn't ease the pressure, one day he's going to explode and destroy his entire life. It's going to kill him.

Who hurt him so badly? Since he refuses to speak of his wife, I assume it's her. Though he could simply be mourning her loss. I don't know because he won't tell me anything.

It's so frustrating. *He's* frustrating.

Even so, I realize that I shouldn't push him to the edge every time. He's allowed to keep his relationship with his late wife private. It's none of my business. I'm simply concerned. I've poked around every inch of this giant house and there's not a single trace of her. No photos, no mementos, nothing to clue me into her past existence at all.

It's chilling.

I have no idea who she was. It's like she never existed. Her memory has been wiped from every surface. Perhaps Roman loved her so much that he can't bear to be reminded of her even in the smallest way.

My skin prickles with jealousy. I know Roman once had a heart, I saw that in those old photos of him in his childhood home. Maybe he gave it to her and that's why there's nothing left for me. It's not that he doesn't want to develop feelings for me, it's that he can't. He has nothing left to give.

I calm down in my room, feeling twice as guilty about riling up and driving Roman away when I spot the dinner plate piled high with a massive side of my favorite breadsticks. He brought me a peace offering and I ruined it with my big mouth.

Apparently too much honesty can backfire. Everything I told him is true, about my feelings of inadequacy and what I think of him. Was I too harsh? Did I overstep?

My intention is not to hurt him. Quite the opposite, I want to help him. But I don't know how.

I mull that over.

The least I can do is apologize.

With my mind made up, I slip out of my room and across the hallway to his door, where I knock twice. No answer. He could be in his office downstairs, but before deciding to search for him, I knock again, and then try the handle. It turns easily in my hand and the door swings open to reveal a dark, quiet room.

Even so, I swear I can sense his presence within. It dominates the space, refusing to be ignored, and draws me in like a moth to a flame.

"Roman?" I whisper into the dark. "Are you awake?"

My question is met with silence. The darkness is so thick that I can barely make out the placement of the furniture. Though I've been in his room once before and generally remember his bed's location.

"Roman?" A floorboard creaks beneath my footstep, and the brief rustle of bedsheets is the only warning I have before a hand clamps over my mouth and a gun barrel's cold metal presses against my temple.

I hold my breath, squeezing my eyes shut. My heartbeat hammers against my ribcage, attempting to flee the scene. A chill races up and down my spine.

I wait, for what feels like an eternity, but in reality is no more than a handful of seconds, for Roman to either kill me or let me go. I know he's made up his mind when his palm falls away from my face, the gun disappears, and the bedside lamp clicks on.

He spins me around to face him. "*Fuck!* What are

you doing sneaking into my room in the middle of the night, principessa? I could have killed you."

"I-I came to apologize," I squeak.

Releasing me, he drags his hand over his short hair, steps away and sighs. Only then do I notice that he's completely naked. Does he always sleep in the nude?

"You have nothing to apologize for, Sophia." He seems more rattled than I am from having his gun pointed at my head. Stupidly, perhaps, I have this deeply rooted confidence that Roman will never hurt me—on purpose or by accident—especially now that the danger has passed.

I cross my arms, keeping my gaze fixed on his face. "You stormed out of my room an hour ago. I assume that means I offended you in some way."

"You simply like to tell me things I don't want to hear. Truth or not." His fingers thread into my hair as he comes in close. He draws circles with his thumbs over my temples, then he pulls me into his arms, resting my head against his bare chest. "I'm sorry for losing my temper."

Instead of hassling him, I decide to let the subject drop. I loop my arms around his waist and press my body into his, seeking both his warmth and comfort.

A truce. I can deal with that for now.

"You're right," he whispers into my hair. "It's unfair of me to demand everything from you when I won't meet you halfway. To answer your questions... My past haunts me every day and night. My wife did try to commit suicide by taking pills on multiple occasions. I am sad, angry, and lonely. And I most certainly don't deserve you." He takes my face between his palms and leans down to make eye contact. "You are innocence. You're a breath of fresh air, a lifeline for a drowning man like me. I will do nothing but ruin you, taint you, and take from you until you're no more than an empty shell. I should let you go, but I can't. Not now, not ever."

My heart breaks for him. He may not give me the details, but this is the most open he's ever been. Now I at least know something about him, about his past, from his own admission instead of rumors. Obviously, there's a lot of trauma that he hasn't healed from yet. But I don't believe for one instant that he's as irredeemable as he thinks.

"Thank you." I brush his lips with mine. "But there's one major point you've missed."

He nips at my bottom lip. "What's that?"

"I want you to ruin me, Roman."

"You don't know what you're saying," his voice is raw with dangerous yearning.

"Yes, I do. Let me in. Take all of me."

He keeps his thoughts and feelings tightly reined in, and his urges too. I want him to give all of himself to me. If I can't yet have his every thought and feeling, then I'll take his body.

He tilts my chin up, his blazing gaze meets mine. "Beg me." His voice is rough, deep, and commanding. "Beg me to ruin your sweet little pussy."

"Please, Roman. *Please.*" I lift my nightgown over my head and stand naked before him.

"*Fuck.* You're perfect." His fingers dip between my wet thighs. "And so fucking responsive."

He picks me up and tosses me on his bed, as I let out a startled squeal. Then he's on me, his massive body covering mine, his mouth claiming my lips. He settles between my legs and stretches my arms above my head.

His raspy voice speaks into my ear, "I'm going to fill your sweet little cunt with my cum and claim it as mine. I'm going to fuck the sass out of you, and you'll never speak back to me again. Hell, you'll have forgotten your own name by the time I'm done with you, but you'll remember mine. I want to hear my name on your lips when I make you come."

I swallow hard and spread my legs wider for him in clear invitation.

Roman fists his cock and pushes the head to my entrance. "Now you're going to take this like a good girl."

In a single thrust, he fills me up, and the air whooshes from my lungs. This time there's no sharp pain, only pressure. And *this* time he doesn't stop once he's buried to the hilt, he doesn't hold back. He withdraws, nearly leaving me empty, before pushing inside over and over again.

One of his hands rests on my hip while the other pins my wrists. I circle my legs around his waist to help steady myself as his cock plunders my pussy. He fucks me hard, deep, and fast.

His fingers find my clit, his hot mouth sucks my

nipples, and my back arches off the bed. The stimulation overload is short circuiting my brain. All I can do is feel every sensation, from the throbbing of my clit to the desperation in which Roman fucks me into the bed.

My orgasm explodes out of nowhere, rocking my entire world. My pussy squeezes Roman's cock so hard that his relentless driving has me gasping for breath. He pinches my clit and I fall apart all over again, harder this time.

"Roman!"

With an appreciative grunt his hips jerk and he slams into me with wild abandon. Pulsating warmth floods my insides as I feel him come, filling me with his semen.

Roman pulls out, flips me on my side, captures my leg and rests my heel on his shoulder. At this new angle, he slides his still hard cock into my pussy, slowly this time.

"Such a good girl. Did you like that?"

"Hm-hm." I watch him through my lashes, my body limp and tingly.

With both hands free, he explores every inch of by body as he leisurely fucks my cunt.

"You're going to come for me again, principessa." He smacks my ass.

I moan. "I don't know if I can."

"You can and you will." He plucks my nipples until they pebble, then his fingers skim over my stomach to my pussy. His thumb presses in alongside his dick.

"Roman!" I gasp. "I can't–"

"Shh, you can take it." To prove his point, he removes his thumb, and he slips two fingers in, curling them. They hit yet another sensitive spot that makes my toes curl.

"That's my girl," Roman purrs.

He spanks my ass while finger fucking me alongside his cock. My fingertips dig into the bedding and my eyes roll back in my head. All I can do is hang on as another orgasm builds, then sweeps me away in its ecstasy.

Roman's guttural cry finally brings me back to earth. His features contort as he pumps cum inside my pussy, his muscles rigid with strain, until finally he collapses on top of me, still buried deep.

Our rapid breaths mingle, our sweaty skin is slick between us, and my entire body aches in the most delicious way.

This? *This* is sex. This is what I've wanted.

Roman's body flinches, as if he's suddenly remembering where he is, and he eases off, letting his forearms take his weight.

"Did I hurt you?" He scans my face.

I offer him a shy smile. "No. I've never been better."

He grunts. "You say that now."

Roman rolls to the side and his fingers fill my pussy.

I gasp. "What are you doing?"

"I'm feeling all my cum in your sweet cunt." He groans. "It's leaking out of you. Fuck that's hot."

Is it? I spread my legs wider, giving him a better

view. He watches his fingers slide in and out of me for a couple of minutes, with growing possessiveness and desire shining in his unguarded eyes.

"Such a good girl, you did so well." His heated gaze flicks up to my face. "But you're going to be very sore. Let's get you in a warm Epsom salt bath." He scoops me into his arms and carries me to the bathroom.

I love the way he handles my body. Like I weigh nothing and I'm his to toss around as he pleases.

Then it dawns on me: I just gave myself to Roman before marriage. Technically, this is the second time we've had sex, but it feels different with him having come inside me. This time the sex feels real, complete, in a way it didn't in his office.

Given my upbringing, I should be ashamed. Even though I decided to cast aside my family's morals in this area, that's easier said than done. Those beliefs are imbedded deep in my psyche.

Yet... This feels right, like I'm meant to be in Roman's bed, his body in mine, and maybe one day I'll find my way into his heart as well.

I only hope I don't come to regret it.

"Another round of drinks!" Ginevra calls out to our server where we sit in the VIP section of the club. My sisters and cousin brought me here for my bachelorette party tonight. The place is loud and crowded, even in the VIP section.

"Three is the limit, Gin," Arianna warns her over the din. "This is your last one."

Gin laughs. "This is Sophia's bachelorette party. Live a little. It's bad enough that you all vetoed the custom T-shirts I ordered for us."

Shaking my head, I hide a grin behind my cocktail glass. Yeah, the shirts that read: *Kiss me, it's my last night of freedom.* That one was for me. I can only imagine what kind of punishment Roman would have in store for me if I wore the thing. On that note, maybe I should have put it on.

No. Bad idea. I'm still sore from last night.

Taking a sip of my Appletini, I shove that thought aside, and regain my original train of thought.

Arianna's shirt was the worst: *Uptight bitch. Needs a good dicking.*

What kind of person gets her sister something like that? I mean did Gin seriously think we'd wear those out tonight?

Knowing Gin. Yes, yes she did. Which is why she's been grousing about it for the past two hours.

Our third round of fruity cocktails arrive and I'm feeling fantastic, apart from my traumatized vagina. For the past week Roman and I haven't been able to get enough of each other. The man has stamina. Last night we went for four rounds before finally falling asleep—in his bed, again. At this point, I should move into his room. I'm hardly ever in mine anymore.

Ravenna leans over and murmurs in my ear. "You're staring off into space again."

A blush heats my cheeks. Yeah, I've been doing that a lot lately. Daydreaming. About not only my future, but what my life could look like with Roman. I should try to stop myself, because what we have is mostly physical—it's not love—but I can't stop daydreaming about the possibilities. What if Roman falls in love with me and I with him? Is that really so impossible? What if we can be truly happy together?

"Come on," she says, taking my arm. "Let's hit the dance floor."

"Wait. Not yet. I have something to tell you all."

Gin gasps. "You're pregnant!"

"No." I kick her under the table. "I got my SAT score and submitted my application to Columbia University!"

Their faces light up.

Gin claps, then lifts her cocktail in the air. "Congrats! Sophia, that's amazing."

"I'm so proud of you." Ravenna clinks her glass with mine.

Arianna offers her congratulations too, but I can see the calculations in her eyes, she's worrying about all the ways my college dreams could go sideways.

I down my drink, knowing I won't dare finish it if it's left unattended on the table. I'm not as concerned as Arianna, because I know something that I haven't told anyone but Roman. I scored a 1570 on the SAT. Which, from what I looked up, is excellent.

Unless the university absolutely hates the rest of

my application and essay, I have a strong feeling they'll accept me for the fall term.

I'm so excited, I might burst. Instead, I allow Ravenna to drag me into the crowd. Arianna and Ginevra follow us and we form a tight circle, then let loose. The four of us haven't hung out like this in ages. Too bad our fifth isn't here tonight. Ravenna's twin sister is currently traveling back from Italy to be here in time for my wedding.

But tonight still reminds me of when we used to have our own dance parties in the pool house. Just the five of us, our bodies pumped with too much sugar in the form of soda and candy, and blaring music. We were too young for the clubs at the time—not that our parents would have let us go.

As it is, Arianna and Ginevra got into this place with fake IDs. I would have been fine going anywhere, but they insisted, even Arianna. Which surprised the hell out of me. Arianna *wanting* to go to a club? Shocking.

The beat drops and we get slow and slinky with each other. All the other people around me fade into the background. Roman insisted on upping my security for tonight, so I know we're well protected.

Which is why I'm stunned speechless when someone roughly yanks my arm, turning me toward them. My confused gaze collides with furious blue eyes. *Nik.*

He hauls me closer. White hot fury radiates from him. "No one steals what's mine, you stupid whore."

CHAPTER 20

Roman

Baron refills our glasses from the scotch bottle. We're in a private booth on the third level of the club, looking down on the VIP section, and the main floor further below.

Tonight is Sophia's time to celebrate with her sisters and cousin, but hell will freeze over before I let my wife-to-be out of my sight. Especially in a crowded club where predators of the human variety lurk in the shadows, preying on innocent girls like them.

The irony of being one of those myself is not lost on me. However, my intentions tonight are to watch over what's mine and not interfere with her fun.

Baron sniffs at his scotch before taking a swallow. "The last part of your plan has fallen into place. Kozlov is both under investigation by the FBI and accused of being an informant on the Bratva. His personal and professional life are in tatters. It's only a matter of time before he's either in prison or silenced by one of his own." He sets his glass on the table. "How's it going with stealing away his fiancée?"

At the mention of Sophia, my gaze dislodges from where she's dancing and meets Baron's knowing smirk.

"Why would you think she's part of my revenge plan?"

Baron waves away my question. "You're completely transparent, De Luca. Even now. Do you know what I see?"

"No. And I don't want to know either."

He continues anyway. "You thought you'd steal her away from him, enjoy her for a while, then toss her back after she watched his destruction. Instead, you've fallen for her. She has you so firmly wrapped around her finger that you literally cannot spend a minute away from her. So, you're up here, spying on her, like some kind of love-sick fool."

"Watch it, Baron," I rumble in warning. "I'll only stomach so much of you for old time's sake. Besides, you know absolutely nothing about love. You wouldn't recognize it if it shot you in the face."

He sneers. "Thank fuck for that. After watching everything you went through with Olivia, I'd rather kill myself than ever fall in love."

My mood turns sour at the mention of my first wife. "Don't ever speak her name to me."

Baron studies me for a couple of seconds before he nods, once, then returns his attention to the dance floor. "I will say that the blond is pretty enough. Which one is she?"

I glance down. "Ginevra Pontrelli. She's the youngest sister, barely eighteen, and the wild one."

"Is that so?" His interest is piqued. "I'd fuck her for a night."

"No, you won't. I'm marrying into that family, which puts Sophia's sisters under my protection."

"You're such a hero, De Luca." He fakes a yawn. "How boring."

"Fuck you."

"Thanks, but you're not my type." He leans slightly forward. "Though the red-head with them, she looks a few years older, is also quite fuckable."

I grunt. "She's married to the Beast."

"Right." He snaps his fingers. "I remember that now. Such a scandal. Twins are always troublesome. Wasn't he promised the other one, and then surprise, it's the wrong twin?"

"For someone whose business is information, you're certainly lacking in some areas. That happened over a year ago."

Baron sighs, settling back into his seat. "You can't expect me to stay up to date on who is arranged to marry whom and how their match turns out. I'd rather eat a can of nails." He raises his glass to his lips. "Do you see what I see?"

I pull my attention from Sophia again and scan the club. Following Baron's line of sight, I spot Dimitri Kozlov, Nikolai's cousin, two booths over. My teeth clench. At least he's alone, as far as I can tell.

"What the fuck is he doing here?" I say more to myself than to Baron.

"Strangely, I don't know. Business, perhaps? Oh, no, things are about to get interesting. Motherfucking *idiot.*"

I glance at him, momentarily confused. "What the—?"

Below us, Nikolai Kozlov has his hands on Sophia. He's hauling her through the crowd toward the emergency exit. She's struggling but his grip is relentless as iron.

Rage, unlike I've ever experienced before, thrums through my veins. I'm on my feet, shoving people out of my way to get to Sophia. None of them matter. I only care about her.

The urgency to get to her is all-consuming.

Kozlov is going to fucking die for laying his hands on her. I'm going to make that beating I gave him in the library seem like a bit of rough fun between friends. He'll be begging me to pull the trigger by the time I'm done with him.

I charge through the crowd to the door leading to a staircase and head down toward the exit sign. Baron is hot on my heels.

When I reach the bottom of the stairs, I exit into a back alley. There, two of Kozlov's goons block my path while he drags Sophia toward a waiting car. That's when she finally sees me.

"Roman!" Her scream pummels my gut. She thrashes harder against Kozlov, momentarily slipping from his grip until he catches her again and carries her toward the car.

I don't have time to fuck around. The first goon to

step in my way, I throat punch. He stumbles backward and drops to the ground, allowing me to advance on Kozlov. I catch up with him as he's opening the car door and trying to toss Sophia inside, but she's giving him hell.

That's my good girl.

With a clear shot to his face, I deliver my wicked right hook. He drops Sophia, who immediately scrambles to my side, and I wrap her in my arms where she's protected, safe.

Kozlov, the coward, dives into the backseat as the tires screech in their haste to leave the scene. He knows he's a dead man, whether I ended his life tonight or it waits for another time, makes no difference. He tried to steal my principessa and he's going to pay the ultimate price for that attempt.

I cradle Sophia's face between my palms. "Are you okay? Did he hurt you?"

"I'm fine. Just a little shaken up." She covers my hands with her own. "Where is my security? How did Nik get to me?"

Good fucking question.

I hold her against my chest, taking a moment to look around. Baron has the other goon on his knees, a knife held to his throat. Without any hesitation, Baron draws the blade across his neck, a clean, deep cut. Blood flows freely down the man's chest and onto the grimy pavement.

I can always count on him to have my back. We've been there for each other since college.

The exit door bursts open. Ginevra, Arianna, and

Ravenna come pouring into the night air. They take one look at Baron's impassive expression and the dead man at his feet, and abruptly come to a halt. Their eyes are wide with horror.

Finally, the door opens again, and one of the bodyguards I assigned to Sophia emerges.

"Fuck, fuck," he says, taking us all in. "They're all dead, boss. These fuckers got the jump on us all at once."

"I don't care for your fucking excuses. Get this cleaned up. Now." My harsh tone snaps him out of his shock and into action.

"Yes, sir."

The girls step around the two dead goons and rush up to Sophia. She dislodges herself from my hold to embrace them.

While they're checking in with each other, I approach Baron. "Cut off all of his resources. I want him to have to go all the way to Russia to find a single soul for hire. Fuck it, make sure no one from his home country will work with him either. He's a dead man walking."

If our wedding wasn't in two days' time, I'd hunt down Kozlov myself. But I don't know how long it will take to find him, and I need to be there for Sophia. A pathetic piece of shit like Kozlov is not going to get in the way of my plans with my new wife.

Baron gives a curt nod. "Consider it done. Whenever you want him found, just say the word."

"Very good. When the time comes, I'll hunt him down myself." I uncurl my fists and sigh. Kozlov will be my first order of business once we return home from our honeymoon. I don't give a shit about his suffering anymore, the next time I see him, I'm going to gut him. "I'm taking Sophia home. I'll have my driver—"

The door slams open for a third time, banging against the brick building. A man so broad and tall that he has to duck into the opening, steps forward. I immediately recognize him by the scars across his surly face and his blond hair pulled into a ponytail at the nape of his neck.

Cian "The Beast" O'Rourke.

"Ravenna," he snarls at his wife.

"Cian? What are you doing here?" She goes to him, not at all afraid of the enormous, pissed off man.

"You didn't actually think I'd let you out of my sight, did you?" He palms the back of her neck and draws Ravenna in for a heated, possessive kiss.

Hm, he seems like a man who shares my sentiments. I only know him by his reputation, having never met in person until now.

Holding Ravenna to his side, he addresses me. "I'll take the women home. We'll go around the side of the building because it's a madhouse in there."

"Very well." I send a text to my driver, then wait while Sophia says her goodbyes for the night. Standing slightly away from them, along with O'Rourke and Baron, I study the man.

The Beast's massive stature makes Baron and myself look slight in comparison, which is no easy feat. The man is imposing, rough enough around the edges that even I wouldn't want to meet him in a dark alley. Yet, here we are.

"Goodnight. See you soon." Sophia joins me as our car pulls up, and my arm automatically snakes around her waist.

I nod a farewell to the two men. Both of whom I'll be seeing again at the wedding.

As soon as we're seated inside, she turns to me. "I know Nik doesn't care about me at all. We were never in love, and he was hardly even affectionate toward me. So what's going on? Why does he want me back enough to kidnap me? Is it his pride?"

"Is that what he told you? That he wants you back?" My teeth clench, my fingers form fists.

"Yes. When I told him *no*, he tried to kidnap me. I feel like I'm in the middle of a pissing contest between you two. What's going on, Roman?"

Guilt slams into my chest so hard it rattles my ribcage. I put Sophia in this position. In danger. My original intention was to use her as a pawn, a thing to be torn apart by Kozlov and myself. So much has changed since I first walked into the Pontrelli house that night to set my plan into action.

I don't want Kozlov anywhere near Sophia. She's mine in every way and I'll abandon my entire plan for revenge to keep her safe. Not that it will go that far, but I'm willing to sacrifice whatever is needed to protect what's mine.

"Roman?" she prompts.

"Kozlov apparently can't take rejection." The flippant response burns like acid in my mouth. I can't tell her the truth of how I put her in this situation, or she'll loathe me forever. Once I deal with him, I'll never have to lie to her again.

I hold her to me. "This will all be over soon. We'll be wed, then he won't dare touch you. I promise."

Especially since he'll be dead soon.

CHAPTER 21

Sophia

Originally, my wedding was supposed to be a grand affair at our church. But on my wedding day, I find myself getting ready in a suite at The Plaza on Fifth Avenue. It's the most coveted wedding venue in the city and often booked out years in advance. I have no idea how Roman's mother managed this, but it's beyond amazing, like a real-life fairytale.

The suite is a swarm of activity. Hair and makeup artists attend to my four bridesmaids and me. My cousin Elena arrived yesterday from Italy, joining her twin Ravenna, and my two sisters as a bridesmaid. We've spent the entire morning being pampered and primped within an inch of our lives. I don't think I've ever looked this perfect in my entire life.

The only negative energy hanging over me today is the memory of my horrifying bachelorette party a couple days ago. What was Nik going to do with me once he got me away from Roman?

I inwardly shiver at the possibilities.

Nik screamed at me and hit me at our engagement party because I wore a red dress and he didn't like it. What would he do to me for being with Roman.

In the beginning, he might have forgiven me since I was technically kidnapped, but not now. I've freely given my body to Roman, we're getting married, and I want this. Nik would have no mercy.

The other horror that night was Blake Baron. He'd sliced that man's throat open while looking extremely bored, like he's killed a hundred times. What kind of psycho can't summon up a single emotion while they murder another person? Even seeing a hint of hatred or disgust on his face would have made me feel better —but nothing. Absolutely no emotion sparked in his eyes.

Today he's Roman's best man.

My mother and Mrs. De Luca enter the suite together. They've become good friends over the past few weeks.

Mama sees me and gasps. "You are breathtaking, Sophia."

"Thanks, Mama." I turn toward the wide, floor to ceiling mirror one last time. The gown is one of a kind, custom made for me by a much sought after Italian designer. It's the epitome of elegance. All white silk edged in silver lace, a million tiny beads that catch the light and sparkle like dappled moonlight on the surface of a lake, with a train that goes on for miles. The veil is attached to a tiara that glitters with diamonds.

I feel like royalty. And I certainly look the part.

"It's almost time," my wedding planner announces. "Please everyone find your seats and take your places. We'll start the procession in five minutes."

Mama gently squeezes my shoulders. "I know today isn't what we originally planned, including your groom, but I hope this is better. I hope *he* is better."

"It is." I grace her with a reassuring smile. "He is, too. Roman is complicated, but he's a good man. I'm proud to become his wife."

"Good. As you know, I love your Papa, even if I hate him a little right now. But that wasn't always the case. Arranged marriages are hard in the beginning. I hope you'll be blessed like we were and fall in love with your new husband one day."

I nod, stepping away from her to take my place in the procession line behind my sisters and cousins. My heart warms, thinking of how I'm pretty sure I'm already in love with my husband-to-be and falling deeper every single day.

My bridesmaids proceed to the dais as music floats through the air. Papa appears by my side, then the time finally arrives.

In what feels more like a dream than reality, I walk down the aisle on my Papa's arm toward Roman. As soon as I see his bright yellow-hazel gaze on me, all I can focus on is him. He's ridiculously handsome in his tuxedo. I keep thinking I'll get used to his masculine beauty one day, but if that day is ever coming, it's not today.

In fact, I don't think I ever fully realized how gorgeous he is until this moment. His rugged good looks render me breathless as I stand in front of him.

The ceremony, the vows, and the exchange of rings goes by in a blur. Then suddenly, Roman and I are kissing to a roar of applause and cheers. He presses me into his body, his tongue slips past my lips in a kiss that's meant to not only conquer but claim.

It says I'm his.

He's mine.

We're one before man and God.

Even the Devil can't ignore our union.

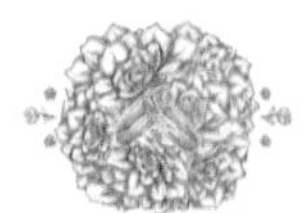

After the longest afternoon of receiving congratulations from what must have been half of Manhattan, we finally have time for a dance. My cheeks ache from smiling so much. The butterflies who've escaped their cage in my stomach continue to flutter around, drunk on happiness.

Just like the first time we danced, as soon as Roman sweeps me onto the floor, the rest of the world melts away. Everything around us disappears, until it's only me and him, our bodies moving as one, every touch, breath, and glance demands my full attention.

"You're happy," he notes with an edge of wonder.

"Why wouldn't I be? I'm living in a fairytale today."

"Not only for today, principessa. From this day forth, you're my wife. You, Mrs. De Luca, shall have everything your heart desires. If you want to spend the rest of our lives renting elegant ballrooms, dancing in ball gowns, and eating catered food and drinking champagne, then you shall have it. Hell, I'll buy you this place if you want it."

My stomach does another flip. I have no doubt he means every word.

"I love you," I blurt.

His steps falter. Surprise, and something darker flickers in his eyes before that damn impenetrable mask slides back into place. My gut reverses directions, plummeting.

Did I say something wrong?

Shouts draw our attention to the entrance. Glass shatters on the marble floor, and everyone quiets as they stare at the security guards who are wrestling a man to keep him from entering.

Not just any man: Nik.

He sees me and hollers, "No! You've married the Devil himself! He's the Devil!"

Nik's insane ranting dies down as he's escorted away. Hushed murmurs sweep through our guests and a heavy cloud of uncertainty hangs over the ballroom. The moment is broken when the orchestra starts a new piece, one meant to distract from the unpleasant episode.

But the moment between Roman and I is also shattered.

"I think it's time we leave," he says. "The jet is waiting for us."

"The jet? Where are we going?" As far as I know, the plan is to have a brief honeymoon in the Hamptons, then go home. There's no reason to do anything too elaborate when celebrating an arranged marriage. Though so far, we've not held to the original plan at all.

"Since you seem to enjoy elegant historical venues, I've booked up the honeymoon suite at *Airelles Château de Versailles*, then we're on to Paris for three weeks."

"Wait. We're going to *France*? Right now?"

He takes my hand in his. "Yes. Unless there's another Versailles and Paris that I'm unaware of in Europe."

"Oh my God, Roman, that's too much."

He frowns down at me. "Don't be ridiculous. Nothing is too much where you're concerned. Now, allow me to sweep you off your feet."

And he does. Literally. Carrying me bridal style, we exit our wedding reception to a chorus of cheers.

France, here we come.

After a private jet ride to Paris, then a helicopter to Versailles, we arrive in the early hours of the morning. But I'm wide awake, having napped through a good portion of our travels.

I change for the night, slipping into a silk nightgown, before finding Roman in the living room of our honeymoon suite.

He beckons me closer to where he's seated with his index finger. "I have something for you."

"Oh yeah?" I sway my hips, capturing his attention. "What is it?"

"This." He holds out what looks like a black credit card. "I had this issued for you before we left so that you can purchase anything you want from now on. Paris is a good place to break it in. There are plenty of places to shop."

Tentatively, I reach for it. "Is this what I think it is? I didn't realize these actually existed."

"They do. And that one is all yours, *wife*."

My insides warm when he calls me his wife. It's better than any other endearment.

"Thank you." This piece of matte black metal is yet another reminder of Roman's legacy. I suck in a harsh breath, as a thought hits me. "Oh my God, we never signed a prenup before the wedding."

"Why would we?" He takes my hips and plants a kiss on my stomach through the slinky fabric. "Everything that is mine, is yours."

"But—"

"Shh, I didn't forget, Sophia. I don't want a piece of paper hanging between us."

I climb into his lap, my brows furrowed in confusion. "But you're the one who said marriage is a business agreement, a contract. Yet we don't have one in writing."

"I did say that, didn't I?" He places an open mouth kiss between my breasts, his strong hands groping my ass. "Maybe I was wrong."

It's official. Roman De Luca has lost his goddamn mind. Who is this man I'm straddling? Certainly not the ruthless businessman who negotiated terms of our marriage over dinner.

All those thoughts flee my head when he grinds his growing erection against my needy pussy and teases my nipples through the silky fabric. I arch my back, demanding more.

"I don't want to talk about contracts," he says, dragging his tongue up my neck. "I want to fuck my wife."

My gaze drops to the noticeable bulge in his trousers, and I place both palms on his chest. This time I'm going to have a taste of him.

I crawl out of his lap and drop to my knees, then reach for his fly.

He catches my wrist. "What are you doing?"

"Isn't it obvious? I want to taste you, *husband.* Don't you dare try to stop me this time." I lick my lips and his gaze darkens, but he releases my hand and sits back.

He groans as I undo the top button then the zipper to free his cock. It's heavy in my hand, smooth, hard and hot. I lick the head, and Roman lets out a curse.

He tangles his fingers in my hair, and I open my mouth to take him in.

"So fucking beautiful." He thrusts in, an inch at a time, until his cock hits the back of my throat. My eyes tear up, and I gag. "Relax your throat, principessa. That's right. Take all of me. Just like that. That's a good girl. Fuck."

I suck him as he leisurely fucks my face, enjoying every second of it, but especially the way he keeps moaning and cursing. His fingers tugging and flexing in my hair.

Following my instincts, I palm his balls, and with a guttural cry he spurts hot cum into my mouth. Greedily, I swallow it all.

Pulling out, he drops to his knees and kisses me thoroughly, tasting himself on my tongue. Roman rests his forehead against mine while he catches his breath.

I grin. The idea that I can bring this man to his knees fills me with an unexpected sense of satisfaction.

"Now it's your turn," he rumbles, picking me up and tossing me over his shoulder. He smacks my ass as he walks into the bedroom. There he tears away the silk, and lays me on the bed like a sacrificial virgin, his hungry eyes eating me up.

My nipples peak and skin tingles under his heavy gaze. He licks his lips and I can see the filthy beast within him rise to the surface, ready to claim me for himself. *Filthy Roman* is my new favorite person.

Stalking closer, he undresses, then climbs onto the bed. He grips my hips, lifting them until my pussy meets his mouth. Then he feasts.

I'm completely at his mercy as he fucks me with his tongue, his fingers, nipping and licking my clit. Tension builds in my lower belly.

I begin to orgasm, when Roman pulls away. A second later, he slams his cock into me, and I tip over the edge once more. He fucks me through my first orgasm and into a second, then a third. I cling to his shoulders, meeting him thrust for thrust. Our bodies grow slick with sweat.

Roman curls his fingers around my throat, staring deep into my eyes. "You're my wife. *Mine.*"

His back arches, hips jerk, and he pumps my pussy full of cum. I scream as I come with him.

"I love you," I tell him in my dazed state. I mean it, I can feel the truth in my words all the way down in my soul. I'm in love with Roman De Luca, my husband, the man who stole me from another.

Roman buries his face where my neck meets my shoulder. "I don't deserve you," he mutters.

I frown. That's not exactly the declaration of love I'm seeking.

What if, after everything, Roman really is incapable of love?

CHAPTER 22

Roman

We spent three days in Versailles before heading to Paris for the rest of our honeymoon. I've taken Sophia out to dine at the Eiffel Tower, shopping along the Champs Élysées, treated her to a spa day, and fucked her so many times I've lost count.

I haven't been this relaxed and happy in so long, I'd forgotten what it feels like. Maybe I never truly knew. Sophia makes me come alive in ways I didn't realize I was missing. Making her laugh, seeing her smile, watching her eyes light up with wonder brings me way more satisfaction than it should. I live to make her happy. I thrive on her enjoyment.

So much so that I can't wait to tell her where we're going today. I want to see her face light up, the adoration in her eyes when she looks at me, and be the one who puts that smile on her gorgeous face.

"Breakfast arrived," I tell her when she exits the

bathroom, her hair already dried, her body clad in a silk robe that leaves little to the imagination. "Come sit on my lap, wife."

Her chocolate brown eyes shimmer with lust as he sashays over to me and perches across my thighs. Securing her on my lap, I tear off a piece of croissant, hover the offering in front of her lips, and wait for her to open up. When she obeys the silent command, I feed her the buttery morsel.

"Good girl," I murmur.

The lust in her eyes intensifies and her pupils dilate. I'm half tempted to ditch my plan and spend the day in bed with her instead. We've done that twice so far—spent the entire day and night locked in our room, worshiping each other's bodies, only taking breaks to eat and shower.

We have five days left and I think we've seen enough of Paris. Tomorrow we'll stay in. I'm going to fuck her so good she can't walk, and the very idea of leaving this hotel room never enters her mind for the rest of our stay.

But today's plan is a must.

I feed her another piece of pastry, then say, "We're going to the Louvre."

Her eyes widen. She chews and swallows before replying. "*We?* But you hate art. And that's all you'll find at the Louvre. I can go on my own, it's okay."

"That's not going to happen," I growl. "I'm taking my wife to the Louvre. Don't argue with me."

"Okay," she gives in. A shy grin forming on her lips. "Thank you!"

With a much too chaste kiss on my lips, she bounds from my lap and into our room to get ready.

Satisfaction and excitement grow like a tumor in my gut. I love pleasing my wife.

"Where is everyone?" Sophia asks as we enter the Louvre Museum. Normally this place is crawling with tourists, screaming children, and other distractions. But not today.

"Elsewhere." I chuckle at her bewildered expression.

"Roman, this place looks closed. Are they under construction or something?"

"No. They are closed to everyone except for us. We have the Louvre all to ourselves for the day."

She stops me with a hand on my arm. "Wait. You booked the *entire museum* for us? How? It's a public venue."

My grin turns devilish. "Today it's ours and ours alone. We'll have a private tour followed by a catered lunch in front of any piece of art that you wish."

Finally, she gets over her shock and squeals with excitement—music to my ears. "You, husband, are the most wonderful man in the world."

Her praise makes my chest feel like it's about to explode. I live for these moments.

"Come, let's meet our tour guide." I steer her through the entrance.

"Hello and welcome, Mr. and Mrs. De Luca. My name is Elise and I'll be your guide today." The woman approaching us speaks with French-accented English, and she's around my own age, tall, slender, and professional. "Come right this way."

We spend the next three hours touring the quiet, peaceful museum. Once Elise realizes Sophia's level of interest and her self-studies so far in Art History, she becomes much more animated. The two of them speak in depth about all kinds of things from the art itself, to history to politics in those times.

I tag along. For once, not the center of attention as the women are swept away by their conversation and the tour. Elise was the perfect choice of tour guide.

I mostly glance at the paintings, sometimes tuning into what our tour guide has to say, and other times reading the plaques. Until I find myself in front of... I check the title. *La Mélancolie.* The lone woman in the painting looks miserable, but also completely unreachable. She's off in her own world of sorrow, depression has sunk its claws so deeply into her heart that the world around her simply no longer exists, it can no longer touch her soul.

When Sophia notices me lingering, she doubles back. She stares at the painting for a long moment, her arm snaking around my waist. At first, I don't let her in. It's not that I don't want her silent comfort, it's that I know I don't deserve it.

But soon enough, my willpower falters and I wrap

her in my embrace. I can only imagine what she must think of me, that out of the entire museum, this is the painting that captures and holds my attention.

It shouldn't be. I owe my past nothing.

Simply gazing at this piece of art and letting it conjure up hidden emotions of sorrow and guilt is a betrayal to Sophia.

"We should keep going," I murmur.

"No. Let's stay for as long as you want."

I glance down at her. "Even if this painting makes me think of another woman?"

A long, strained pause floats in the space between us.

"Yes. Especially because it does. Roman, you'll never break free of the past until you confront it. *She* will always have power over you until you face your feelings and choose to let them go. I'm right here by your side and I'm not going anywhere. I promise."

Her insight and understanding has me reeling.

It's my turn to be consumed by wonder. Sophia is simply amazing. I know deep down in the darkest corner of my soul that she's too good for me. She's too good to be true, yet here she is by my side allowing me to face the demons of my past without judgment. Without being jealous and making this moment about her instead.

I fucking love this woman.

If only the words didn't stick in the back of my throat every time I thought to utter them.

Honeymooning with Roman in France was incredible. I don't even have the words to describe the full experience. Memorable. Mind-blowing. The experience of a lifetime. I mean, we ate a lavish, private lunch in front of the *Mona Lisa*. Who else can say they've done that?

Since we've been back, I've been more motivated than ever before in my life. I've been reading all the Art and Art History books I can get my hands on. I officially moved into Roman's bedroom. The entire mood in the house has shifted, it feels lighter, happier since our return.

We're just beginning to settle into a new routine. Life is good.

I'm lounging by the pool in the June sunshine, eating fresh mini pizzas that Luis made and sipping lemonade, when Diana comes out with today's mail.

The poorly suppressed excitement in her expression has me immediately sitting up. I reach out for the envelope, my fingers trembling. Is this the news I've been waiting for? Only one way to find out.

The return address in the corner indicates it's from Columbia University.

Like ripping off a band-aid, I tear into the envelope and pull out the single sheet of premium paper. My eyes skim the top couple of lines, once, twice, and my pulse races enough to make me light-headed. I let the words sink in.

"Well?" Diana prompts.

I glance over at her. "I've been accepted." My voice sounds hollow even to my own ears.

She beams, and I smile back at her. That's when the news fully hits me.

"I've been accepted!" I scream, and hug her. "I'm going to Columbia University in the fall!"

Roman appears over Diana's shoulder. He leans casually against a pillar, pride shining in his eyes as he watches me. When I release the housekeeper, he wanders over.

I leap into his arms. He catches me, with an easy chuckle, and crushes me to his chest.

"Congratulations. I knew you could do it, principessa."

"You did?"

"Of course. When you're determined, nothing in this world can stand in your way." He takes in my dubious expression. "Have some faith in yourself, I have plenty in you."

I'm beginning to believe that's true. He seems to

think I can take on the world and it will bow before me, opening any door that I decide to knock upon.

My gaze narrows. "You didn't influence my acceptance, did you?"

Roman clicks his tongue in mock offense.

"Absolutely not." He sets me on my feet. "This was something you had to do for yourself, on your own merits, and you did it. I've never been more proud of you."

Relief washes over me like a tropical waterfall. I did this. On my own. Without help from Roman, or my father, or anyone or anything else. I studied hard and it paid off. I've been accepted into the college of my dreams.

I smile at Roman. "I'm going to Columbia!"

He pulls me in for a scorching kiss and my toes curl. "We'll celebrate tonight. Be ready by six."

"Where are we going?"

"Dinner on my—*our*—yacht." Another kiss. "Then love-making beneath the stars."

"That sounds amazing."

"Good. Don't be late." After one more kiss, he disappears back inside the house.

I create a group video call with my sisters and cousins. As soon as they're all on, I blurt out the good news.

"Congratulations!" Ravenna and Elena say in unison.

"That's wonderful." Arianna shoots me a reserved grin.

"Ah! I'm so envious." Ginevra pouts. "You get to

experience the world outside of...this. There'll be parties and boys. You lucky bitch!"

I laugh at her reaction, having expected nothing less from Gin. "News flash, I'm married, so there won't be any boys."

Gin pulls a face. "Fine. But are you not going to cheat on your husband because you're afraid of what he'd do or because you're madly in love with him?"

Her question throws me. I blink at the screen like a mute owl.

Gin gasps.

Arianna chides her.

Elena's brows shoot up.

And Ravenna says, "You fell in love. Does he know yet?"

How did this call turn so abruptly away from college and into the murky depths of my relationship?

"Um. I mean, I've said it to him." *Twice.* Now I sound really lame.

Ravenna purses her lips. "But he hasn't said it back to you yet?"

I shake my head, my cheeks flaming. Roman has had so many opportunities to tell me he loves me, but he hasn't. '*I don't deserve you*' is hardly a declaration of love, if anything, it's a brush off. But when I go down that avenue of dark thoughts, I begin to spiral.

What if Roman never loves me?

"Men." Ravenna scowls. "They're so dense."

That catches my attention. "What do you mean? Did you have a similar situation with Cian?"

Elena rolls her eyes. "Don't even get her started on

how much of a fool Cian was for months on end. Then to think he tried to bring himself to kill her when he found out...you know."

"Ooh, spill the gritty details." Ginevra's face fills her screen. "We're all ears."

It's Ravenna's turn to blush and awkwardly lick her lips. "I knew he'd fallen for me way before he was able to say it out loud."

"How could you tell?" I ask.

"There were a lot of indicators, really. The way he looked at me, how he kissed me, the small things that he'd do or say that were just *extra*. And the way we had sex. It changed from carnal pleasure to love-making. I don't know, it's hard to explain."

"No, that makes sense."

The look in Roman's eyes when he watches me these days is different. Less wondering if I'm going to stab him and more like he simply can't believe I'm here with him. And the sex... Yes, that's changed too. It feels more intimate than before. So maybe...he loves me too?

Gin chimes in. "Well? Does he do those things, Sophia?"

"It's none of our business," Arianna tells her in a clipped tone.

"But I want to know. I mean, she's fallen for him so—"

Gin is like a dog with a bone. Once she's set her mind to something there's no shutting her up until she gets what she wants.

I wave at the screen. "I have to go. Bye!"

I end the call before they can dig any deeper into my complicated love life. All I want to do is bask in the excitement of getting accepted to Columbia, not worry about whether my husband loves me or not. That's too damn depressing. Even if there may be a ray of hope.

CHAPTER 24

Roman

The title on one of today's articles reads: *Russian Mobster's Body Found in Hudson. Is Mob Violence Escalating in New York City?* Relief. Disappointment. Both anger at not having been the one to end Kozlov myself, and a sense of closure I never thought I'd experience, crash through me.

It's done. Over. Nikolai Kozlov is burning in Hell.

I should be elated. Strangely, the hollow in my chest remains wide open, a vast empty space of unfulfillment. Maybe if I'd been the one to take his life, to witness the light leave his eyes, I'd be more satisfied.

As it is, I'm glad he's gone.

While we were in the air returning from Paris, I'd employed Baron to hunt down Kozlov and keep him warm until I could deal with him. Since Kozlov's demise showed up in the newspaper, that means someone got to him before Baron.

The end result is the same, however. He'll never

lay a hand on Sophia again. He's no longer out there living in the same world as I am, breathing the same air, haunting my waking hours.

He's dead. Finally.

My phone pings, and I snatch it from the bedside table.

BLAKE BARON

Page six.

ROMAN DE LUCA

I've read it. Who got to him first?

BLAKE BARON

Rumor is that a rival Bratva took him out. But I'm betting it was one of his own. Maybe even his own cousin. Dimitri.

I smile at that thought, of Kozlov being betrayed by those he trusts and holds most dear. Backstabbing hurts, doesn't it? Too bad, for him, the experience was short-lived.

"What's so amusing?" Sophia asks, emerging from the steamy bathroom, her hair wrapped in a towel.

I glance up, caught off guard by her sudden appearance. "Kozlov's dead."

"What? How? When?"

I hand her the newspaper.

Her eyes scan the article, growing round. "You're right, it's Nik. Oh my God, he's dead." She sets the paper on the bed between us and studies me for a long moment. "You never told me why you hate him so much."

Bile burns the back of my throat when I try to speak. I can't tell her the truth, can I? She's too smart, she'll put the pieces together and realize that I took her as a pawn in my revenge game. Even now that it's over, I know she'll start doubting everything we have, every single one of my motivations leading up to this point. I don't want to hurt her like that. I can't bear to see her suffer.

However, I need to give her something. If I shut down, she'll know I'm hiding the truth from her, and then she'll become suspicious and dig deeper. My wife knows me too well. I can't successfully hide anything from her anymore.

"A long time ago, Kozlov stole something very precious from me. We've been enemies ever since." It's a simple statement, and on the surface, the truth.

She ponders my answer. "Did you ever get it back?"

I eye her, wary of how much she sees through my vague response. "I did. But it was returned to me beyond repair. It wasn't worth saving."

"I'm sorry. It must have been something very valuable." The corners of her lips dip downward. "Now that Nik's dead, has your feud ended?"

"Yes. That's all in the past now. Laid to rest forever."

"How long ago did this happen?"

I hesitate. "Six years ago."

"That's a long time to hate someone."

"It is. But now it's over. I promise."

"That's good." She glances at the clock on the

nightstand. "I have to get going. The girls are taking me out to celebrate. Which means a massive shopping spree."

I shoot her an easy smile. "I'll see you at dinner."

Sophia leans forward, planting a sensuous kiss on my lips before she darts into the walk-in closet.

My chest floods with warmth. We've fallen into a beautiful balance of domestic bliss and scorching hot sex. My life is more perfect than it has ever been. Kozlov's death is only the cherry on top. Stealing his fiancée turned out to be the best decision I've ever made.

In the end, I won. Revenge is mine. I also get to keep the girl.

Life is perfect.

Downstairs, I'm about to call for Enzo when I'm struck by a sudden thought. I do a slow turn in the foyer, taking in this massive house and all the rooms I've explored. I swear I've seen every corner of this place, including the basement one time to fetch a bottle of wine from the cellar.

My gaze shifts skyward. A mansion like this must have an attic, right? In one of these rooms there has to be a clue to Roman's past. What did Nik steal from him that's so precious he's spent all these years hating the man?

I have no doubt Roman was involved with Nik's death, even if not directly, he had a hand in bringing it about. Which is fine by me. The world is a better place without a man like Nikolai Kozlov in it.

The question remains: What did Nik steal and then return to Roman? Broken.

I may never find the answer, but I can dig a little

deeper. Where does someone like Roman stash his secrets?

My first thought is... He doesn't, he destroys them. He leaves no trace of any evidence that can later come back to haunt him. Except that his grudge against Nik has held on this long. I wonder if remnants of this object remain. Six years is a long time to hold onto hatred without something as a reminder to continue fueling it.

Could that reminder be in this house? In this country refuge?

The attic. It's the only space I haven't explored. If I don't find anything up there, then I doubt I'll ever know the truth.

Roman says it's over now that Nik's dead. But is it?

Retracing my steps, I ascend the stairs and keep going, up and up. On the third floor, I search around for a while before finding a hidden door set into the paneling. If I wasn't specifically looking for it, I never would have known it was there. Which is probably how I've walked past it a hundred times and never noticed it before.

On the other side is a narrow spiral staircase that leads into an enormous attic. Faint sunlight filters in through high set windows in the vaulted ceiling. Dust particles float in the air. I sneeze.

Purposefully, I take in the entirety of the space. Old furniture and boxes of storage crowd most of the floor. I weave through it, scanning, unsure of what exactly I'm looking for. A clue? To what?

Something out of place perhaps?

In all honesty, this search is probably futile. I doubt there's anything up here other than old and forgotten things. This dusty attic isn't the kind of place one stashes priceless objects.

What was I thinking? My thought to search here was a whim, it can't do any harm.

My footprints form clear outlines in the dust, telling me that no one has been up here in a very long time. Maybe years. So whatever has kept Roman's hatred alive is not here. Otherwise, he or one of the staff would have come through here on occasion. Right?

I reach the opposite end of the space, then pivot, going back the way I came. That's when I spot the picture frames. They're stacked against one wall, behind an enormous armoire that hid them from view when I entered.

So Roman does own artwork. I knew he had to have some art somewhere. What is it doing up here instead of on the walls? Did he take it down for some reason?

I make my way to the framed canvases, dust off the first one, and spin it around to see the front.

I stare, mouth agape, because I certainly wasn't expecting to find this. The painting is the portrait of a handsome man with dark hair and yellow hazel eyes. He's young and mirthful, hope and optimism and... love show clearly on his features.

The painting is so life-like, I reach out and touch it, smoothing my fingertips across his sharp jawline. *Roman.* Again, a much younger, happier Roman.

My gaze falls to the bottom corner where the artist signed the piece with the initials ODL. It's not a self-portrait, so that rules Roman out as the artist. Yet I have no doubt the D and L stand for De Luca. But who is O? His mother's name is Isabella, ruling her out too. His late wife, maybe?

I realize that I don't know her name. Roman has never once uttered her name aloud.

As I stare at his portrait, snippets of information begin to fall into place like pieces of a puzzle. Assuming O is his late wife... She was an artist. Roman doesn't hate *art*, he's hiding from the pain of losing his first wife. Art must remind him of her.

I see why when I dig deeper into the stack of framed canvases and find still life paintings, landscapes, and a couple more portraits. They are absolutely stunning. So realistic that I feel instantly transported to those locations, or like I'm looking through a window to another place. She must have lived and breathed painting to have become this skilled.

He must have loved her very much.

Jealousy claws at my chest. Then I remember how he took me to the *Louvre*. Given what I found, he sacrificed so much to take me there, that must have been incredibly difficult for him to do. To be surrounded by artwork that reminds him of the woman he once loved.

But he did it for me. He suffered through it to be there with me. I can only imagine his pain.

Putting the frames back, I head back downstairs.

I'm really running late now. But I need to get out of here and think. There's so much about Roman that I don't know.

Will he ever fully let me into his life?

My sisters, cousins, and I spend the day shopping, but my heart isn't in it. I should be solely focused on college, on my bright future, and how everything is going wonderfully. But I can't. My thoughts keep slipping to Nik's death and Roman's vague explanation of why they hated each other. I wrack my brain to come up with a stolen artifact that could warrant such hatred.

And then there are the stacks of artwork in his attic. The only sign in the entire house that his late wife once existed. If he can't bear to be reminded of her, then why keep anything of hers at all? Does he visit the attic?

Which leads me to my greatest worry of all.

Roman's inability to tell me the three little words I most want to hear from him. The short phrase that would entirely end my worrying and second guessing about our relationship.

Does he still love her, is that why he won't say it to me? Are his vows to her still sacred to him after all these years? If so, then why marry me?

I don't want to take second place to a dead woman.

I cut our shopping spree short, claiming I have a headache and need to get home. Which is true. All this thinking is making my head hurt.

Though my mind keeps churning over what information I have as Enzo drives through the city streets toward home.

Suddenly, I recall Arianna's accusation of Roman murdering his first wife because he became jealous and possessive when she tried to leave him.

Then that time when Roman thought I tried to kill myself with pills. His late wife had tried to commit suicide, he told me so himself.

Broken beyond repair.

Stolen and returned.

I'm reminded of the painting of that sad woman Roman stood in front of at in the Louvre. The one titled *La Mélancolie.*

I sit up straighter in my seat and slap a palm over my mouth. The question isn't *what* Nik stole from Roman, it's *who.*

Roman's first wife.

Is that even possible? I do the quick calculation in my head. Six years ago, Nik would have been twenty. Roman was twenty-four or so. Assuming his wife was around their age, it's possible that she had an affair with Nik.

But why?

Who would choose Nik over Roman?

BOOM!

A deafening explosion jolts the car forward. I cover my ears and duck down, unsure of where the noise came from or how close we are to the destruction. The flicker of firelight catches my attention through the blacked out rear window. I briefly pop up to see what's going on.

The car behind us is on fire. My security team is in that vehicle.

Now they're obliterated.

Oh my God, what just happened?

"*Fuck!*" Enzo's curse is my only warning before someone crashes into us. My head hits the doorframe—hard. Then we're spinning. Not just my head, the entire car.

Then it stops.

Two shots ring out.

Someone opens my door.

Rough hands hook beneath my arms and drag me into the street. I scream, the sound echoing in my ears. My shriek is muffled as a cloying scent invades my nostrils.

An endless void reaches up and drags me under.

CHAPTER 26

Roman

On speaker phone, I bark, "What do you mean by Ricardo has gone *missing*? Did you check his apartment?" This morning has been a shitshow. Ricardo wasn't at the dock last night to receive and off-load the Casella shipment that finally arrived in port. Now I have to deal with an incompetent underling full of conspiracy theories.

"Um, no, sir. I haven't checked there yet."

"Then go. Check. I doubt he'd up and disappeared."

Ending the call, I buzz for Eve. A moment later she pokes her head into my office. She knows I'm in a terrible mood today, so she patiently waits for instructions. She, unlike Ricardo, is efficient.

If he turns up alive, I'm going to flay him.

"Clear my schedule for the rest of the day. I have to get down to the docks because nobody there can do their fucking job."

Eve nods. "Consider it done."

"And call my wife. Tell her I'll be home late."

"Yes, sir." She waits to be dismissed, then ducks out of my office to fulfill the orders I gave her.

I ring for a car, grab my briefcase, and head out to deal with this bullshit. I'm in the lobby when my cell rings. Fishing it from my pocket, I glance at the caller ID.

Shit. It's Casella.

I consider taking the call, except that I know Don Casella and he's completely unreasonable when anything goes awry. One detail goes wrong and he's absolutely inconsolable. I'd rather get his goods unloaded and to him than admit we have a problem. What he doesn't know won't hurt him.

His call goes to voicemail. The driver opens my door, and I get in right as my phone pings with a series of incoming texts.

DON CASELLA

My shipment has been sitting at the dock overnight?

DON CASELLA

Why isn't it here?

DON CASELLA

Who's in charge?

How the fuck did news of his shipment reach him so quickly? Sighing, I text him back.

ROMAN DE LUCA

I'm in charge and dealing with it. On my way to the docks now to unload. You'll have your goods in a few hours.

DON CASELLA

A few hours?

DON CASELLA

This shipment has already arrived late.

DON CASELLA

You want me to wait a few more hours?

This is exactly what I mean. Completely unreasonable. The cargo has already been waived from inspection. It's safe. A few more hours isn't going to make a huge difference with the given timeline. But I can't tell him that, he'll fucking tear off my head.

The best way to deal with Casella is to send his goods ASAP with an apology, usually in the form of a couple high-end prostitutes. By tomorrow he'll be back to pretending like we're best friends. All of this forgiven and forgotten.

Ping.

Ping.

Ping.

Fuck! He's incessant.

I swipe the screen and put my phone in Do Not Disturb mode. I'll switch it off once the trucks are en route to Casella and we can have a productive conversation.

I'm greeted at the docks by a crew of seven men all milling around two box trucks catching some humid summer sun.

Really? *Really?* I have to come all the way down here for this shit?

"Get that ship unloaded," I bark. "What the fuck are you waiting for, an engraved invitation to do your fucking job?"

They exchange nervous glances, then get to work.

I swear, if no one is here to crack the whip, they'll lounge around all day doing nothing to pad their next paycheck. Except this time, they don't know who they're fucking with. If they don't get that cargo off-loaded in two hours or less, I'm going to shoot every last one of them. How's that for payment?

To hurry the process along, I micromanage the entire, grueling process. Where the fuck did Ricardo get these guys? They act like they've never loaded a goddamn truck in their lives.

Finally, when they realize I'm going to hound them until this job is finished, they pick up the pace, and to my astonishment, show the slightest signs of competency.

After what feels like an eternity, the trucks are dispatched and on their way to Casella. I glance at my watch. One hour and fifty-seven minutes. I guess this crew will live to see another day.

Now I have to deal with Ricardo. I'm firing him and everyone he's hired to work under him.

I switch off the Do Not Disturb mode and mentally prepare myself for the onslaught of notifications. Thumbing through them—Casella too many times to count—I slow the scroll when I see five missed calls from Baron, and seven voicemails from Sophia's sisters.

What the fuck is going on?

First, I call Sophia but her phone goes straight to voicemail. My chest tightens, I know something is wrong. I can feel it in my bones.

I press on Baron's contact.

"Where the fuck have you been?" he answers. "I've been trying—"

"What's going on?"

"It's all over the news. A bomb hit the SUV. The security detail is dead. Then a truck hit the car Sophia was in. I don't think—"

"Sophia was in an accident?" My stomach plummets and the world tilts off its axis. I close my eyes, shake my head to clear it, and focus. "Where is she? Where's Sophia?"

I'm already hustling back to my car and climbing inside, ready to give the hospital's name to the driver.

The driver.

Did Enzo make it out alive? He was the one driving Sophia today, and if they were hit...

Baron's steady voice comes through the line. "They took her, Roman."

No.

"Her driver's dead. Two bullets in the chest. No sign of Sophia, but her purse is in the back seat."

That would explain why she's not answering her phone.

"When did this happen?"

"About two hours ago."

Casella. Motherfucker.

He misjudged me when he thought he could kidnap my wife because of a late delivery. I'm going to burn him, and everything he holds dear, to the ground. No one lays a hand on *my wife*.

CHAPTER 27

Sophia

"Wake up, you little whore." The speaker shakes my shoulders, rattling my small frame. Wait, why does that voice sound familiar? Am I dreaming? Hallucinating? I crack both eyes open.

Christ, my head hurts. One side of my face throbs, but that's in addition to the general overall pounding in my temples. Did I hit my head? On what?

Nausea makes my stomach roil and clench. I lean over, vomit the sandwich I had for lunch all over a grey floor. My entire body breaks into a cold sweat and I start shaking.

Like a runaway semi, the memories surface. Boom. Crash. Chloroform.

Someone pulled me from the car and knocked me out.

Easing upright, I realize I'm tied to a chair in the middle of some abandoned structure. The floor is dirty, cracked concrete, and light filters in through broken windows. The air is still and humid. Water flows nearby, creating an ever-present white noise in the background.

"There she is."

I glance in the voice's direction. My eyes widen, right before the bastard backhands me across the face. The blow sparks glittering stars in my vision.

"I told you, no one steals from me, whore." Nik's features swim before my eyes.

"You're dead," I tell him, even though he's obviously not dead.

He laughs, dragging me in the chair away from the pool of vomit. "These days, all you need to fake your own death is to pay off a cop, a coroner, and threaten a newspaper." He snaps his fingers. "That's it. To the world I'm dead. Which means no one is looking for me."

It must be the blow to my head, or the aftereffects of the drugs, because I'm having a difficult time wrapping my brain around the fact that Nik Kozlov is alive, standing right in front of me.

And I'm his prisoner.

"Why?" I croak. "Let me go, Nik, please."

He squats down so we're eye level. "No, no, no. I have plans for you." His blue gaze feels like ice scraping against my skin. "But first I'm going to tell you a story, and by the end of it, you'll realize exactly how stupid you really are." He chuckles. "You're nothing more than a slut."

I find it difficult to concentrate on what he's saying

with the pain raging through my head. The headache is enough, why did he have to hit me, too?

Strangely, Nik doesn't seem angry. He appears excited, if anything, which has me even more on edge. He's flying high on...something.

Victory? Does he really think he won by faking his death and kidnapping me? Roman will come, and when he does, there will be hell to pay.

Nik straightens up and starts walking in a slow circle around me. "I'm going to tell you all about the monster you married."

"Roman isn't a monster. *You* are." That statement earns me another slap across the face that sends my head reeling. After that, I shut up and listen.

Nik continues walking. "Olivia married De Luca in what was supposedly a love match, except that a year later she fell out of love with him. Or at least that's what she told me when she climbed into my bed and spread her legs for me. Olivia was young and beautiful so I fucked her—countless times. Until she started to get needy."

He continues strolling around my chair, forcing me to swivel my head to mostly keep him in view. "She became overbearing, demanding, and then De Luca found out about us. He started making threats, so I sent Olivia back to him. The only problem is I didn't realize that she was pregnant with my child."

Nik stops in front of me again, grips the chair arms and leans over me. "Do you know what your precious Roman did when he found out his wife was carrying my child? Do you?"

Cringing away, I shake my head.

"He pushed her down the stairs! She survived but my baby didn't. He *murdered* my unborn child!" he screams in my face.

Horror twines around my heart and squeezes. *No.* I don't believe it. Roman wouldn't do that, would he? No, it can't be true.

"If I'd known she was carrying my baby, I never would have sent her back to that jealous, vengeful motherfucker. What he did is unforgivable. But he didn't stop there, oh no, he made sure to further punish her for falling in love with me."

I gaze back at Nik, terrified of what he's going to reveal next.

Could I have been completely wrong about Roman?

Did he murder his wife?

And her baby?

Nik leans in. "He locked her up and threw away the key. No visitors. Her mail is held and searched. Believe me, I tried to get her out. She would have helped me take down De Luca. She would have wanted vengeance as much as I do. Instead, he grows richer and more powerful, while she wastes away in isolation."

Doesn't he mean *wasted* away? Past tense.

My lungs seize, I can't for the life of me draw in a single breath. All the blood in my body freezes. My headache sears white hot agony in my temples, and blurs my vision.

This can't be true.

I don't believe it.

I *can't* believe it.

"Olivia is alive?" My whisper's so faint I can barely make out my own words.

Nik's vicious grin confirms my fear. "She is. Alive and still De Luca's legal wife."

That information swirls in my consciousness, tearing my world to pieces. If that's true, then Roman lied to me from the start.

Oh my God, I'm a fake. An imposter.

Then logic kicks in.

"They could have divorced." I doubt Nik will tell me the truth, but he's the only source of information I have right now. I realize his intentions are to make me suffer with this story, but I need to know more.

Standing upright, he shakes his head. "I've looked, and there's no record of them ever divorcing. Plus, the De Luca's never divorce. Why do you think everyone believes Olivia's dead? It's the only way for Roman to be free to marry again. Now do you see? You're nothing more than a pawn, and his little slut. De Luca has fed you lie after lie. *Nothing* you have with him is real."

I flinch at each accusation.

How could Roman do this to me?

He led me on, married me when he already has a wife.

"Why would he do this to me?" My question slips out.

Nik answers it. "Obviously, he did it to get back at

me. This was never about you, Sophia. You're just a dumb whore."

That's exactly how I feel right now. Foolish. Ashamed. Hurt.

Roman has a wife. He cheated on her to be with me, and lied to me for months. Was he ever going to tell me the truth? Or just throw me away once he was done, knowing full well that I have no rights to anything of his, no legal standing at all.

I can't believe we had a huge wedding, with all our friends and families. A honeymoon, too. All of it was fake.

Nik grabs my chin, forcing me to look at him. "You're exactly like Olivia. History has a funny way of repeating itself, doesn't it? I steal from Roman, so he steals from me. Except this time, he's ruined my life, turned my family against me, and forced me to fake my own death. Now I have nothing. *Nothing*. Soon he'll have nothing too. You'll hate him as much as Olivia does. Maybe you'll finally be the one to kill that bastard."

I cringe backward as his booze infused breath washes over my face, but his grip is too strong to break. The wild, unhinged light in his eyes fills me with fear.

Terror.

The type that sets off one of three reactions: Fight, flight, or freeze and play dead.

Bound to this chair, I have none of those options. All I can do is gaze back at him and beg for mercy.

Mercy that I know I'll never receive when Nik says, "I'm going to start with you. I'll show him what happens to anything he claims as his, when I've fucked you in every hole until you bleed. Then you can go back to your precious *husband* and send him my regards."

He caresses my cheek.

The physical contact makes me sick.

"You're already damaged goods, so if you're a good little whore, I'll share you with my friend." He glances into a shadowy corner. For the first time, I notice the other man in the room. I've seen him before, he's one of Nik's bodyguards, thick necked, vacant eyes, he'll do anything this psycho tells him to do without question.

"You were supposed to be mine, Sophia." Nik draws my attention back to him. "Now I'm going to make an example out of you. And punish you for thinking you could ever leave me."

CHAPTER 28

Roman

"Where the fuck is she?" I demand of Casella, pointing my gun in his face, only to be met with twelve weapons aimed at me in return. That's what I get for barging into his home and interrupting this meeting with all his higher ups.

But I don't give a fuck.

I only care about finding Sophia.

Through gritted teeth, I repeat myself, "Where the fuck is *my wife?*"

Casella rises from his seat, motioning for everyone to put their guns down. "I may be many things, De Luca, but I am not stupid enough to lay a finger on your wife."

"You didn't take her as punishment for the late shipment?" I ask in confusion.

"I did not. I don't have a death wish." He stares at me. "However, if you were any other man, I might say that you do have a wish to die today. If I didn't rely on your services to deliver my goods, I wouldn't hesitate to put a bullet in your head for this interruption."

Barging in on the mob while armed and threatening isn't a smart move. But like he said, I am a necessity to his business affairs. So, I'll live to see another day.

I eye him, my gut tells me he speaks the truth about my wife. But if Casella didn't take her, then who did? I'm out of leads.

"My apologies, gentleman." I lower my gun and holster it at my waistband. Then I spin around and get the fuck out of there before any of them change their mind about letting me go, furious at myself over my false assumption.

Casella's right, as long as I've known him he's never been one to play with deadly stakes. He likes his crime easy, his women expensive, and doesn't mess around in other people's business. As Don of the Casella family, he has enough on his plate keeping his empire both profitable and peaceful.

In short, he'd never kidnap Sophia. Then who the fuck did?

I bring up Baron's contact and press call.

"De Luca, I haven't found her yet." At least he cuts to the chase. Not that I'm happy about his update.

"What's the problem?" I bite out. We're wasting precious time.

I need to find her, not only alive but unharmed. The need to get to her is visceral.

"I tracked the van to a warehouse, but that's where

the trail runs cold. I sent a team. The place is empty and the van's gone. I know it couldn't have vanished into thin air, but the team's turned up nothing helpful."

"Did you ID who took her?"

"No. They wore masks. Without the van we can't try to get prints or DNA."

"What about the plates?"

"I ran them. It's a rental under the name Peter McDonald, a dentist from New Jersey. I'm going with a case of stolen identity on this one."

"Fuck!" I slam the car door closed. "We have absolutely nothing to go on."

I spear my fingers through my hair. Knowing Sophia's out there, somewhere, in danger is killing me. Literally. I can feel my heart failing, my lungs refuse to take in sufficient air, and I'm both too hot and too cold.

I *need* to find her.

I've been a goddamn fool for not telling her how much she means to me. How much I adore the ground she walks on. How much I fucking *love* her.

Now it's too late.

No. It can't be too late. I'm going to get her back.

"We'll keep looking," Baron's voice breaks through my thoughts.

I've never felt more useless in my life. All I can do is wait. I've activated all of my resources to find her, every single one of them. Called in every favor. Nothing has pointed to a new lead.

Casella was my only potential suspect.

I was wrong.

No one else has found any trace of my wife either.

I frantically wrack my brain for what else I can do. And keep coming back to one answer: Nothing.

I such in a shuddering breath. "Keep me updated on—"

My phone vibrates with an incoming call. The caller ID shows an Unknown Number. I have to answer it, just in case it's vital news. If it's a spam caller, I swear to God I'll personally hunt them down and beat them to death with their own phone. I have nothing better to do right now.

"Hold on," I tell Baron, switching calls. "De Luca here."

A deep, Russian-accented voice speaks. "De Luca, this is Dimitri Kozlov."

Surprise and wariness hit me. "What can I do for you?"

"I was hoping you'd ask that. Though the real question is what can we do for each other? You see, I need a promise from you and your friend Blake Baron that you'll stay out of my way, and not interfere with a certain situation."

"What situation?"

"It hasn't happened yet. But it will. I'm not at liberty to discuss it right now, or ever. I need a guarantee that neither of you will intervene when it does occur."

How fucking cryptic can he get?

"I can't promise you a damn thing," I snap.

"You will once you know what I can offer you in return."

"And what's that?" I indulge his fantasy.

"Your wife. Sophia."

My heart stops. Why the fuck would he take her? He should be thanking me for outing his cousin for the rat that he was, and how he took advantage of the Kozlov Bratva for his own gain.

"You mother—"

Dimitri Kozlov cuts me off, "Nikolai faked his death. He's alive and took your wife. If you want to know where they are, then I need your promise—"

"You have it," I say without hesitation. I'll deal with Baron's part of this oath later. "Where's my wife?"

He gives me an address near the river, then hangs up. Deal done.

I text it to my driver up front, and then to Baron. The car jolts forward, and we're off.

Do I have reason to suspect this could be a trap? Possibly. Though, as far as I know, there are no hard feelings between Dimitri and myself. He has no reason to kidnap Sophia either.

But Nikolai Kozlov... he has every reason to want to hurt her.

I can't believe that piece of shit is still alive. I should have sent someone to the morgue to verify that it was his body dragged from the river, instead of taking the newspaper's word for it. How fucking stupid could I be?

Kozlov's alive. He has Sophia.

This time, I'm going to kill him.

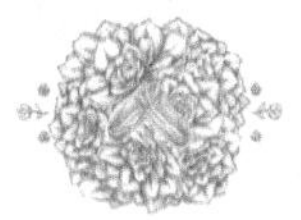

Traffic is awful and by the time we pull up to an abandoned building, I'm ready to murder half of New York City just for being in my way. I channel all that rage into dealing with Kozlov. Before the car's come to a full stop, I jump out, Ruger in hand.

Should I wait for Baron and backup? Yes.

Am I going to wait another second to rescue my wife? Absolutely not.

A quick check of the surrounding area shows it's clear. Kozlov doesn't have any men here, he's so sure his stunt worked, and no one suspects he's alive. I forgot to ask how his cousin found out.

The summer sun sets on the horizon, its warm glow in stark contrast to the cold determination in running in my veins.

Gun at the ready, I burst through the door.

Kozlov has my wife bent over the back of a chair. Skirt up around her waist. Wrists bound.

He holds a knife to the back of her neck with one hand, while he fumbles with his belt.

I see red. The fury that sweeps through me is strong enough to set my skin ablaze and melt my bones. My frozen heart shatters into a million pieces. If I'd arrived even ten seconds later...

Not so long ago, I was determined to draw out Kozlov's death, to make him suffer before giving him the mercy of death. Now I need him dead. I need his hands off my wife. His dick flaccid.

Most of all, I need her safely in my arms where she belongs.

I don't hesitate. I shoot him in the head—twice—then again in the chest. When he doesn't immediately collapse, I advance on him, popping off three more shots until he finally crumples to the floor.

Sophia lifts her head, her bruised face curtained by her tangled, blood-crusted hair.

"Behind you!"

Her warning comes in time for me to spin around. A bullet grazes my arm.

I put two rounds into the behemoth coming at me, and he drops to his knees. One more to the head and he falls sideways, bleeding out on the filthy concrete floor.

I do a full sweep of the massive space, peering into the shadows to make sure no one else is hiding in them. Once I'm certain we're alone, I go to Sophia and take her gently in my arms.

It requires all my self-restraint to not crush her body to mine. All I want to do is kiss her, hug her tight, and reassure myself that she's really here, alive. But I hold back.

First, I holster my gun, then I untie her wrists. Helping her stand upright, I brush her hair away from her face to take in the damage. Her lip is cut and bleeding. More blood crusts one side of her head. Bruises are already darkening her cheek and jaw.

She won't meet my gaze, which makes my chest

tighten. She's not crying and hasn't spoken. Is she in shock?

I need to get her to the hospital.

"Come." I reach for her, intent on carrying her out of here, when she comes in close, only to leap back almost instantly. Like touching me has burned her.

Shuffling backwards, Sophia's small hands wrap around my gun, pointing it at my chest. Her eyes finally lift to mine. Hurt, uncertainty, and fear shine in her chocolate brown orbs.

What the fuck is going on? I'm missing something vital here.

"Tell me it's all lies." Her voice is raw, broken. "Tell me you didn't push a pregnant woman down the stairs."

I hold up my hands in surrender. "No, of course not."

Fucking Kozlov. What did he tell her?

Of course he'd take the opportunity to turn her against me.

"I guarantee everything he told you is a lie." I take one step closer to her, she steps back. "We need to get you to the hospital, then I'll tell you everything. The truth. I promise."

Her hands are surprisingly steady on my gun. "Then you're not still married to Olivia?"

Guilt rattles me to the core. This is not the time or place for this conversation, but I can't lie to her right now either.

"Legally, I am," I confess. As soon as the words leave my lips, I realize they were a mistake.

Her features twist with heart wrenching agony. The pain of betrayal is clear in her voice. "She's alive. You're married."

They are statements, not questions, but I answer anyway. It's too late to backpedal now.

"Yes."

And just like that her pain vanishes, replaced by soul-deep loathing, all aimed at me. Which is exactly what I deserve. I hate myself too. So much so, that I won't ask for her forgiveness. I don't deserve it. While I never meant to harm her, I completely betrayed her trust, lied as I stood at the altar with her before man and God.

"I'm such a fool," she says in a hushed, devastated tone.

"I can explain, if you'll give me the chance. I don't expect you to forgive me but—"

"There is no *but*, Roman. You're a liar. An adulterer. Everything we have is fake." She slips her wedding and engagement rings from her finger and hurls them at me. They hit my chest and drop to the floor. "We're not even married! None of this is real. How could you do this to me?"

"I didn't mean to hurt you." I step forward.

"Stop. Don't come any closer." Her tone is hollow and cold enough to give me pause. "We're done, Roman. This sick game we've been playing is over."

No. Selfishly, I can't stand the thought of losing her. But I know it's too late and I have to let her go.

One part of me wants to drop to my knees and beg for her forgiveness. She's captured my heart and soul, and I know beyond a shadow of a doubt that I can't live without her.

While another part of me knows that this is how we end. My lies and secrets destroy us. I deserve to be alone forever. I've hurt the one person I care about in this world, and she deserves better. Better than me. She deserves a man who's not fucked up.

The second voice in my head is the one that wins. Which is why I stand frozen in place and watch Sophia leave.

Taking everything good in my world with her as she goes.

Belatedly, I realize I never even told her I love her. Now it's too late.

I stumble away from the warehouse, head throbbing, mind reeling. Devastated. Fury and despair battle for control over my emotions, wearing me down in an instant. Bone deep exhaustion settles over me.

Spotting Roman's car, I let myself into the back seat. Gun pointed at his driver, a man I've seen once or twice, and tell him to take me home. Not to Roman's house, to my parents' home.

"Straight away, Mrs. De Luca," he says, shifting into gear.

I cringe. Bile rises in the back of my throat. It's all a lie. All of it.

My father used me as his pawn my whole life. Stupidly, I thought that changed when Roman and I married. I thought I *meant* something to Roman. I thought I was special because for once in my life, someone really saw me for who I am.

But no. I simply became his tool for revenge. He doesn't care about me at all. If he did, he wouldn't have been able to treat me like this. To lie to me every step of the way.

I can't believe this is happening. But I need to come to terms with it, because the truth is: Our marriage is a sham.

Roman doesn't love me.

I'm the biggest fool for ever thinking that he did. Or that he could.

"We're here, ma'am." The driver startles me out of my spiraling thoughts. He holds my door open, and I glance around. Sure enough, we're in my parents' driveway. Only then does it occur to me that I should have gone to Ravenna's house, where I wouldn't have to confront my father. Perhaps subconsciously, I want to get this part over and done with. I need to face the man responsible for handing me over to Roman De Luca.

I step out of the car, gun in hand, and smooth the front of my dress. As I enter the house, I catch a glimpse of myself in the foyer mirror.

Hell, I look like death warmed over. Dried blood plasters my frizzy hair to one side of my face, and the other is discolored from bruising, thanks to Nik's eagerness to hit. My lip is cracked and bleeding. Somewhere along the way I lost my shoes.

Considering everything that's happened in the past few hours, I'm surprised that I don't look worse.

For a few heartbeats, I stare at my reflection and a chill races down my spine. I don't recognize this woman. She has cold, empty eyes and a gun in her hand. She scares me.

"Sophia?"

I turn my head, to find my father gaping at me in horror.

"Sophia, what happened?" When he tries to come near me, I point Roman's gun at him. He halts in his tracks.

"Roman happened," I tell him. "Well, technically, Nik happened first, then Roman. So I'm going to make this very clear. I'm not returning to Roman. I never want to see him again. If you so much as allow him to step foot in this house, so help me God, I'll shoot you."

Papa slowly nods. "You're safe here. I promise."

"Good." I storm past him, up the stairs to my old bedroom, and lock the door.

Once inside the familiar space, my world tilts. Everything comes crashing down around me as the consequences fully sink in. And it *hurts*. It hurts so much. The pain is agonizing, crushing.

Roman betrayed me.

My future is gone. Wiped away in the span of several seconds.

With no one to pay for tuition, my college dream is dead.

Most of all, my heart aches for Roman. I *loved* him. Truly and completely, with all my heart, and he destroyed that love with his lies.

Unable to hold together my broken pieces, I sink to the floor, bury my tender face in my hands, and let it all out. All the pain, all the heartache, all the anger.

Until there's nothing left to cry over. I'm empty.

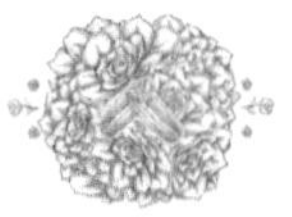

"Sophia, open the door." It's Ravenna's voice this time. She knocks again. "Open up. This is your last chance. I'm serious. Okay, that's it."

A key rattles in the lock and my bedroom door creaks open. Ravenna, Arianna, Ginevra, and Mama all rush into my room where they find me curled up on the floor.

Mama takes one look at my face and her features harden. "I'm calling the doctor. Girls, get ice for her, right now."

She and Gin leave, my sister returning moments later with two bags of frozen vegetables.

Arianna and Ravenna grab pillows and blankets from my bed, toss them on the floor, then settle down around me. Ravenna pulls a thin blanket over my shoulders as Arianna stuffs a pillow beneath my head. Gin presses a frozen bag to the side of my face.

"Did Roman do this to you?" Arianna gently asks.

I nod.

Ginevra gasps. "He beat you?"

"No." I lift the bag from my bruised cheek. "Nik did this. It's fine, he's dead now." More tears escape my eyes and I wipe them away, showing my damp fingers to my sisters and cousin. "Roman did *this*," I sob.

They come in close, rubbing my back and arms. In silence, they let me cry myself out—again.

Once it's over, Ravenna asks, "Do you want to talk about it?"

I shake my head. What is there to say? It's over.

For once, Gin doesn't press for more. Which I appreciate. She takes my hand and gives it a reassuring squeeze.

"Don't worry, Soph, we've got your back. If he ever shows his face around here again, we'll give him hell."

I nod. Grasping for a subject change, I ask, "Where's Elena?"

"She went back to Italy right after the wedding," Ravenna says. "She's not done finding herself, or whatever she's doing over there now. She says she's just visiting family, but she's been there for the better part of a year and so far has no intention of coming home. Not that I blame her."

Ravenna sometimes makes vague remarks like that about her home life, but she's never elaborated. Her father, Papa's brother, was a cold and calculating type of man. I'd never seen him show much warmth toward his daughters. He and his wife died, leaving their daughters alone in the world—except for us. They will always have us as their family.

"Maybe Elena has a secret Italian boyfriend," Gin jokes.

My temples throb. "Can we not talk about boyfriends, or weddings, or anything like that, please."

We descend into silence. Which is fine by me. I just want quiet.

CHAPTER 30

Roman

Two minutes. That's as long as I lasted before I broke and went after Sophia. Thanks to my driver, I tracked her to her parents' house, but it was too late, they wouldn't let me in.

That was five days ago. Five agonizing days.

Since then, I've called her and left a plethora of voicemails. All of them go unanswered. Same for the thousands of texts I've sent. Given that her parents won't let me inside, I've sent deliveries of flowers, chocolates, even Luis's garlic breadsticks with apology notes begging her to answer me. Nothing.

I haven't been home since then either. Every night I camp out in my car in front of her house, hoping to catch a glimpse of her through the windows. In the morning, I shower and change in my office building's locker room before heading upstairs to work.

Work which mainly consists of staring at the wall, drinking single malt Scotch until I'm wasted, and snapping at Eve every time she pokes her head in here to check on me.

She's a nuisance. I already told her to clear my schedule. No meetings. No phone calls. I don't want to be interrupted.

As if she hasn't learned her lesson already, my assistant cracks my door open again. "Boss, you have a visitor."

"I told you, I'm not seeing anybody today." I lounge on the leather sofa, half-empty Scotch bottle in hand. I gave up on glasses after day one. What's the point when I have to keep refilling it? The bottle's a better option. One of these and I manage to drift off for a couple of hours.

Passing out drunk is the only sleep I get that's not plagued by nightmares of losing Sophia, only to wake up to realize that I *have* lost Sophia. Then I repeat the cycle, again and again.

"Well, this visitor, Boss, you're going to see whether you like it or not." Eve swings the door wider and steps aside.

In my dazed state, my heart hammers, and I hope Sophia has come to see me.

That hope is blasted to smithereens, dispatched like a ship's cannon, when Baron enters my office.

I scowl at him. "What the fuck are you doing here?"

"I called him," Eve answers, earning herself my glare. "I've had enough of *this*." Her gesture encompasses me and my office. Then she faces Baron. "Good luck. You'll need it."

The door clicks shut behind Baron, who stands there and stares at me with that ever present bored expression. From experience, I know that's his sympathetic face.

"What?" I snarl. I see the fucking judgement in his eyes when they drop to the bottle in my hand.

"What indeed," he drawls. "What the fuck happened to you? You look like you haven't slept in a week, and you're clearly wasted at—" he checks his watch "—eleven in the morning. Plus, your assistant called me here to deal with you, and she's never called me before for anything. In fact, I don't think she likes me very much."

"I don't need dealing with. You can go." I shoo him away, and swallow another mouthful of fifteen-year-old single malt Scotch. Nice stuff. I wish I could still taste its subtle flavors, but now it just burns going down.

Baron, the asshole, plucks the bottle from my hands with a sneer. "That's enough of this. Where is your wife?"

My wife?

Sophia's words echo in my mind. *You're a liar. An adulterer. Everything we have is fake.*

I grimace. "My wife is right where I left her, in Rockland Psychiatric Center."

"*Sophia's* in a mental hospital?" He sets the Scotch on my desk, out of reach. "What the fuck happened to her, Roman?"

"What? No, not Sophia. Olivia. Olivia's my wife."

"Olivia's dead," Baron slowly states, trying to

gauge my level of delusion. He must think I've gone insane.

I shake my head.

Baron stands over me, studying my face. With a disgusted sneer, an expression I've earned from my best friend on multiple occasions, he goes to the windows and starts opening all the blinds. I cringe away from the glaring summer light.

When he's finished, he claims my desk chair. "Are you saying that Olivia is alive? That she's been locked up for six years?"

I shield my eyes with my arm. "Yes."

"I thought she was dead."

"That's what everyone's supposed to think. But she's very much alive. Alive and ruining my life from inside a padded cell simply by existing."

Baron mulls over that information. "You never divorced her, did you?"

"No," I groan, regretting it with every breath I take.

"Why? After everything she did to you, why not end it with her?"

"Because I wanted her locked away, for her own protection as much as a punishment, and since she has no other family, as her husband, I'm her legal guardian. I pay for her care, but I can also keep her locked away for life." I'm her fucking jailor.

Baron eyes me. "You're one twisted, self-loathing fuck, aren't you? How long are you going to drag this out, Roman? Let me guess, Sophia found out about your real wife and dumped your ass."

"That sums it up."

"And why, exactly, are you self-destructing in your office?"

I peer at him from beneath my arm. "Isn't it obvious? I want her back, but I fucked up. Royally fucked up."

He crosses his arms. "If you want her back, then go get her."

"I've tried," I snarl. "She won't see me. She's not answering my calls or texts. She hates my guts and I don't blame her for it."

He's quiet for so long that I almost forget he's there. So when he speaks again, I groan at the reminder.

"Why did you do it? Why did you have a fake wedding with Sophia if you care about her so damn much?"

"Because when I'm with Sophia I forget about Olivia and Kozlov and everything that happened. I wanted to keep my past at bay forever. And have a fresh start with Sophia. I never meant to hurt her, she wasn't supposed to find out. Fuck, I don't even know how Kozlov found out Olivia's still alive. I'm a mess."

Baron snorts. "I'm your best friend and even I didn't know your dirty little secret. So, what are you going to do now?"

"Nothing. Unless you have any bright ideas."

He hums. "Actually, I do."

I lift my arm and squint at him. "What's that?"

"Fix this, Roman." He stands, casting me one last pitiless glance. He thrives on tough love. "Pull yourself together and do what needs to be done."

"I don't know what—"

"Figure it the fuck out." He heads for the door.

"Wait! I'm serious, I don't know what else to do." I try to sit up, but the room spins too much.

"I'll give you a hint: Do what you're *terrified* of doing." With that cryptic answer, he lets himself out.

What the fuck am I terrified of doing? I'm not afraid of anything—except never seeing Sophia again. I swear, Baron comes up with the most meaningless bullshit at times.

Then it hits me.

He means confronting my past, facing my pain and guilt. He means I need to finish this and go see *her*. I need to choose Sophia over my revenge.

The days go by in an unending blur of muted memories and dulled pain. Eventually, I cry less and eat more. My family gives me space when I want it and support when I need it. Bit by bit, I manage to pull together a semblance of myself.

I wish I could simply hate Roman and never think of him again. Instead, I end up hating myself for missing him. My thoughts keep drifting to him, even my dreams focus on him more often than not. Some mornings I wake up and reach across the bed, only to discover it cold and empty. Then the memories come crashing in and I live his betrayal all over again.

Am I a glutton for punishment, or what?

I'm not sure how many days I've been home when I finally decide to join my family for dinner instead of taking it in my room. Their stunned, hesitant glances tell me they weren't expecting me to come out of my room yet. But I can't waste away in there forever.

The past is just that, over and done. Its storm has done its worst to me. I need to find solid ground beneath my feet again.

I'm strong, I'll survive this. Gradually, I'll find myself in the remains of this wreckage, patch the pieces back together, and move on with my life. It won't be so bad.

We eat in strained silence for the first ten minutes. Mama smiles encouragingly at me with each bite I take, while shooting daggers at Papa, who focuses on his plate. Ginevra and Arianna glance at each other like they're carrying on a telepathic conversation. Since when do those two get along? Maybe they're silently arguing.

"I'm sorry," Papa's voice brings everything to a halt. He glances at me. "I'm sorry for what you went through with De Luca, and I swear you'll never endure such a thing again."

I scrutinize him, attempting to get a fix on his angle. Papa never apologizes.

He wipes his mouth, then sets down his napkin. "Arranged marriages have been how we've done things for generations. The Pontrellis all the way back in Italy arranged their matches for the benefit of the family. When we came here, we kept our old ways, our traditions. Traditions that may be more harmful now than helpful."

I glance at my sisters and Mama, who are as equally astounded as I am. Papa never apologizes for anything, he thinks it shows weakness. Now he's giving us a family history lesson and saying they might have been wrong?

He continues, "Alliances with other families are important, but not at the expense of destroying my sweet daughters." His gaze trails over my face. "Nikolai Kozlov gave you those bruises. I suspected what kind of man he was, but ignored my suspicions for the sake of the alliance.

"Then I gave you to Roman De Luca without a fight, without negotiating on your behalf at all. I should have put you first, sweetheart, I should have been a better father. I'm so sorry, Sophia."

My fork hovers mid-air, I haven't dared move a muscle since he began his speech.

"I've decided that we'll have no more arranged marriages. My daughters aren't for sale, they're not pawns to be used in the games of ruthless men. From this day on, you'll choose your own husbands."

I clear my throat. "So you won't make any more deals with the Russians, or try to tie us to the Baron family?"

"No more marriage deals. You have my word." He casts his stern gaze on my sisters. "I want you both to marry for love."

"Davide, are you feeling okay?" Mama's concern is clear in her tone. She's probably on the verge of calling the doctor here again. "Where is all of this coming from?"

"I've had an entire week to think about everything while looking at my abused and heart-broken daughter. I did this to her as much as those two men."

And just like that, all the anger and hurt I've held onto towards my Papa vanishes. I forgive him.

"Thank you, Papa," I tell him. I'm not going to say that it's okay, or that there's nothing to forgive, because that would be a lie. But I can thank him for stepping up and being a better father than he's been in the past.

"One other thing," he says, his gaze on me. "I heard you were accepted into Columbia University. I'm so proud of you."

Tears sting the back of my eyes. "I was, yes. But, uh, after everything, I'm not sure how I'm going to pay for it. I should send them a letter and give up my spot to someone else."

"No, don't do that." Papa's tone softens. "I will happily pay for your college."

I thought I was surprised before, but now my mind is completely blown.

"Are you serious?" I must have misheard. Papa never once encouraged any of us to attend college. He calls it a waste of money for women who'll most likely get pregnant before they graduate and become mothers and wives, that women will never use their degree.

"If a college education is what you want, then I'll pay for it."

For the first time in too long, a smile touches my lips. "It's what I want more than anything."

"Then you will have it."

"Thank you, Papa."

He waves off my gratitude. "Everyone stop staring

at me like I've sprouted horns and eat your dinner before it gets cold."

We all obey. Except for Mama, who reaches across and entwines her fingers with Papa's. They share an intimate glance, and my guess is that Papa is out of the doghouse.

I spend the rest of dinner reeling. All at once my future has opened up again. Papa has freely given me my dreams, without any strings attached like Roman's negotiations. I have everything that I want, handed to me on a gold platter.

So why does my heart continue to ache? Why is there still this emptiness in my chest?

CHAPTER 32

Roman

"I had a feeling I'd see you again one day, Roman De Luca." Olivia stands beside a canvas she's working on. The landscape scene is exceptional in its detail and composition, she's obviously been continuing to develop her artistic talents.

"That makes one of us," I murmur, stepping closer to her secluded painting spot on the grounds. "This is not by choice."

The summer day is scorching and humid, sweat trickles down my spine. I would have dressed more casually, except that I'm here on business, this isn't a social call.

Even in the heat, Olivia looks serene. At twenty-eight she's stunning as ever, though not a single positive feeling stirs at the sight of her beauty. But neither does the usual onslaught of negative emotions. In fact, I feel nothing at all towards her.

She arches a raven brow. "Then why did you come? Who forced you?"

"We need to lay this to rest, Olivia. I'm setting you free." I retrieve an envelope from my briefcase. "All I need is your signature on these papers. I've written a proposed sum, it's not half my fortune, but it's more than you're entitled to due to the prenup agreement."

Her penetrating green eyes study me, boring a hole into the depths of my tortured soul. I set the envelope on the folding table beside her array of paints.

"My oh my, Roman De Luca fell in love, didn't he?" She sets down her palette and brush, giving me her full attention. "It's the only reason you'd deliver these papers yourself. Tell me about her."

"I'd rather not."

She sighs. "Roman, listen to me, these past seven years all I've wished for is your happiness. I'm glad you've met someone."

She must be lying. I locked her away in here and expected her to rot. Instead, she seems to have flourished.

"You don't hate me?" I warily ask.

"No. I don't hate you. But you hate me." She twirls a long strand of black hair around her finger. "But if you're willing to give me a divorce and set me free, then that means you must love her more than you hate me."

"Yes. I do."

"Good. Does she love you too?"

I inwardly cringe. "I don't know. She used to, but I fucked up."

"If it's you that messed up and not her losing interest, then I'm sure you can salvage the relationship."

"Perhaps." I nod toward the envelope. "Are you going to sign the papers?"

"Yes, but I have a couple of conditions, or rather, questions to ask first."

I narrow my eyes at her. "What do you want?"

She dives right in. "Have you seen Nikolai? How is he?"

"Dead. I shot him for attempting to rape my w— the woman I love." I deliver the news in a flat tone.

She closes her eyes and exhales a long, steady breath. "Then it's finally over. The man I've loved my whole life is dead, and now I'm free of him. I can be at peace."

"You don't hate me for killing him?" I ask, curious. This is not the reaction I expected when I told her what happened.

"Not at all." She opens her eyes, they appear brighter, clearer. "Loving a man like Nikolai Kozlov is a curse, not a blessing. I tried to love you, Roman, I really did. You were always the better man. But the heart wants what it wants, and oftentimes what it can't have. I know Nikolai never loved me in return, but it didn't matter, I was always his. Now that he's dead, I can move on."

"If I'd known, I would have killed him years ago." I mean it. Too much of my guilt comes from having watched her suffer because of her unrequited love for him, and knowing I couldn't do anything about it.

"How could you have known? We never talk about

such things. We never speak at all." She gives me a sad smile.

"What else do you want before you'll sign?"

"I want to stay here. I don't know the world outside of this place, and I don't want to know it." Olivia motions around us to the maples, the sprawling lawn, and the lake in the distance. "You thought locking me away here was a punishment, but it wasn't. I love it here. I'm happy here. Truly happy."

I nod. "The figure I've written down is enough to pay for your care here until you're one-hundred and fifty years old. It'll suffice."

"Thank you, Roman. There's one last thing."

"Name it." I demand.

"Will you forgive me? For everything I put you through?"

I hesitate. For everything? That's asking a lot of me. But I'm determined to move on and truly lay my past to rest.

Can I forgive her for cheating on me, for breaking my heart? For shattering it further when I wasn't enough, for preferring being dead than with me? All I wanted was for us to be happy together, but it was never meant to be.

"Yes. I forgive you." I can forgive her now because she no longer holds my heart, it belongs wholly to Sophia.

That sorrowful smile returns, and she reaches for the envelope. In a matter of minutes, she's initialed and signed every single sheet of paper, folded them up, and hands them back to me. Taking the envelope, I stuff it in my case.

"I see you still love to paint," I casually note to fill the awkward silence between us. It's time for me to go, for us to part ways once and for all.

"I do, yes. Do you still have any of my old paintings at the house?"

I nod. "They're in the attic."

"Oh, Roman, sell them, get rid of them, burn them if you want. Those were the worst years of your life, you shouldn't hang on to any of our memories. I want you to live every moment from this one forward for that woman who's won your heart. Cherish her until the end of your days. And be happy. Now go." Olivia returns to her painting, effectively dismissing me.

I do as she asks and retrace my steps across the lush green lawn, feeling a kind of peace I've never experienced until this moment. Olivia is finally, completely out of my life. I never realized the closure I received today is what I've needed for years.

Now I'm a free man. And I'm going to get back the woman I love, because I'm tired of hiding in the shadows, behind my half-truths, and only giving parts of myself to Sophia.

She once said she wanted all of me, even my damaged heart. She can have it. I'll give her everything she asks for and more. I just hope it's not too late. I hope I haven't broken her heart to the extent that she can no longer love me.

CHAPTER 33

Sophia

The mafia princess goes to college, I muse as I wander campus. School doesn't start for another six weeks, but I wanted to familiarize myself with the layout and where to find the dorms.

Mama and Papa said I could live at home with them, but I want the full college experience. That means roommates, dorm parties, late night study groups. All of it.

Hell, maybe I'll join a sorority.

I've already created a rule for myself: No boyfriend. Dating is fine, but no committed relationships. I'm going to fly free with absolutely no strings attached, and no falling in love. Besides, college boys are the worst.

Though, honestly, do they ever get any better? Roman, who I haven't heard from in weeks, is ten years older than me and he's still a liar. He'll do anything to get what he wants and pretends there won't be any consequences.

I know I'm better off without him, but the more I think about what happened between us the more I want to know why.

Why? That question burns in my gut.

We had sex when I was still technically his fake fiancée, he could have stopped there and rubbed that in Nik's face. Roman won their pissing contest way before we walked down the aisle. So why take it all the way to vows when he knew he was making promises he couldn't keep?

Why lead me on, through a romantic honeymoon, all the way to a real life that we couldn't have together? What was the point?

Is it me he hates, or himself? Because all I can figure is that's some sadistic, self-sabotaging bullshit. Maybe I was just the means to the end of his own destruction. Maybe, deep down, he wants me to hate him.

Not that any of it matters now. Roman has obviously moved on. I really need to do the same. I *am* doing the same. One day at a time.

Which is why it really messes with my head when I spot a man in a dark, tailored suit. He sits on a bench that I'm approaching, his back to me. Yet a tingle of awareness makes my arm hairs stand on end.

I slow my pace. As soon as I pass him, and get a peek at his face, the illusion will be over. If I draw out the moment, I can pretend that it's him for a while longer.

I never said I was *fine*. I'm moving on, that's not the same as being okay. Are these Roman fantasies that crop up every time I see a well-dressed, dark-haired man potentially harmful to my mental health? Probably. But it's my coping mechanism.

For a little while, I can pretend that he still wants me. That he seeks me out.

But, it's never actually him. And pretending lets me think about all the things I'd say to him if it were. I'd tear him a new one, that's for sure. Then I'd demand answers. I have too many *whys* nagging at me.

Would I eventually forgive him? No. I don't know. Maybe.

Those fantasies, the ones where I forgive him, are the most dangerous. In those ones, he manages to offer up a logical explanation, a heart-wrenching reason for why he did what he did, and I can't help but let him back into my heart.

As if I ever truly pushed him out of my heart. Which I can't ever do. Not fully.

I've gotten better at nipping those fantasies in the bud before they take root and I downward spiral.

None of it matters anyway because I'll never see him again. If he really wanted me, he wouldn't have given up after one week of flowers and chocolates. He would have fought for me, but obviously I'm not that important to him.

That he only gave me seven days before moving on, hurts. Did he think I'd just get over the fact that my entire life crumbled because of him? Or was he only pretending to care about me in the first place?

Either way, it sucks.

As I draw closer to the man on the bench, his head angles so that I can see his profile. My heart flip-flops because damn if this guy doesn't have a striking resemblance to Roman. The straight nose, those thick eyelashes, kissable lips.

Then, as if sensing my presence, he turns all the way around. Our gazes collide.

I stop.

My stomach's in my throat.

It's *him*.

As Roman stands up, my confrontation fantasies flee, and I have the urge to do the same. I could run away. Just spin around and never look back. But my feet won't move, it's like there's some invisible force keeping them rooted to this spot as Roman draws closer, and closer with each step.

I must look like a deer caught in the headlights because his sure gait falters and he cautiously approaches. This close I can clearly see the uncertainty in his eyes.

"Sophia." My name is soft on his lips, as if speaking too loudly would frighten me away. Which at this point, it might.

"Roman." To my astonishment, my voice is both strong and steady, though flat.

When he reaches for me, and I shy away, he redirects his hand to his jacket pocket and pulls out a neatly folded piece of paper. That movement finally snaps me out of my daze.

I spin on my heel and rush away, as a jumble of

emotions bombard my tenuous mental state. I don't want to talk to him. I can't bear being this close to him after everything he did.

"Sophia, stop." His commanding tone halts my retreat.

I don't want to face him, but I have to, one last time. If I don't do this, I'll forever regret it. I need answers.

"What are you doing?" I pivot, facing him and cross my arms. "I'm not sure I even want to speak with you."

He flinches at my harsh tone. "This was finalized this morning, I came looking for you as soon as I had it in hand. Take it."

Roman thrusts the paper towards me, and I hesitate, glancing at it, then up at him. If I take it, then I'm humoring him. Or I can really walk away, right now, and never look back. I'm torn.

Curiosity wins out. Or maybe it's a driving need for hope. *Pathetic.*

As I reach for the paper, our fingers touch, and that old familiar spark of electricity travels over my skin. I try and fail to suppress my reactive shiver.

I pluck the paper from him and unfold it. It's a divorce certificate. At first, I think that it's for us, him and I. My stomach plummets. Why would he rub our fake marriage in my face with a false divorce certificate? My teeth clench.

But then my gaze scans the page down to the two names listed: Roman De Luca and Olivia Bruno. My breath whooshes from my lungs. He's not being cruel. Or is he? I'm so confused.

"Why are you showing me this?" I glance at him. My stupid heart swelling with hope. A hope I barely dare to acknowledge.

"Because I did this for *you*. I want you back, Sophia." He drops to his knees on the walkway, earning us curious glances from the few people on campus. "I know I don't deserve you or your forgiveness. I know what I did was wrong and deeply hurtful. I'm so, *so* sorry. If you give me another chance, I'll spend the rest of my life making it up to you. Please, I'm literally begging you, to give me one more chance. I love you, Sophia. With all my heart, I love you."

I love you. Those are the words I was desperate to hear from him. I craved them for so long, before I gave up hope. Now it might be too late. How can I possibly forgive him?

"Say something, please, anything," he begs, still on his knees, hands clasped at his chest. The agony in his voice, twisting his handsome though haggard features, is enough to make the coldest heart melt. For once, Roman is an open book. His myriad emotions swim in his hazel eyes, no longer lurking behind his defenses. Remorse, desperation, and...love.

I swallow hard.

This man is the version I've always wanted. The Roman that's open and honest, afraid to let me in but willing to do it because he loves me. How do I reconcile this man with the one who married me to get revenge on another, and broke my heart? Or the monster who pushed a pregnant woman down the stairs. Then locked his wife away to punish her.

"Sophia, please."

"Get up, Roman." I walk past him to the bench and sit down. Hesitantly, he joins me. I hand him back his divorce certificate, then look him in the eyes. "Why should I ever trust you again? You married me when you were already married to another woman. How could you do that to me?"

"I made a mistake."

I scoff. "I'll say."

"My mistake wasn't marrying you, Sophia, it was not getting divorced from the woman I haven't considered my wife in *years*. A piece of paper tied me to her and that's it. My heart, my vows, everything I am and have belongs to you." He scoots closer. "I love you. No one else, only *you*."

Butterflies flutter in my stomach and my heart squeezes. Is this for real? Does he really love me?

I decide there's only one way to find out.

"Tell me everything that you've been hiding from me. I need to know the truth."

He nods. "I will do anything you ask of me, except walk away. I'll fight for you. If that means baring my soul to you, then let's start there. I married you because I am head over heels in love with you. Every vow I uttered was the truth. But you have every right to know the rest of my story, too."

Roman takes a minute to gather his thoughts before he launches into his story.

"I was fresh out of college when I met Olivia at a

party. She was nineteen, vivacious, and I instantly fell in love. Or so I thought at the time. We had a whirlwind year together before tying the knot. Shortly thereafter, everything went to shit.

"Back then, Nikolai Kozlov and I ran in some of the same circles. I was the one who introduced him and Olivia over a game of poker. She took him for all he was worth that night, but instead of being upset, Kozlov became infatuated with Olivia.

"She grew distant, and at some point I caught on to what was going on between them. As soon as I confronted Kozlov, he gave her up, because he never loved her, she was just another notch on his bedpost. But Olivia had fallen in love with him."

My heart twists hearing him tell his story. That level of betrayal makes me sick to my stomach, and I have a feeling this tale's only going to go from bad to worse.

The birds merrily chirping in the trees are a stark contrast to Roman's painful story. The warm summer breeze oddly chills my skin.

"Olivia wanted a divorce, which I wouldn't give her because no one in my family divorces. Plus, foolishly, I desperately hoped she'd fall back in love with me and forget Kozlov. But she didn't. She was heartbroken that he washed his hands of her and was completely inconsolable.

"Then she found out she was pregnant with his child. Even then I wouldn't let her go. She was a few months along when one night we were arguing on the staircase landing. I was over it, so I started up the stairs, and she turned away to go down. She must have tripped, I don't know. But I wasn't within reach to catch her, and she fell all the way down. She lost the baby."

Oh my God. Hearing Roman's version, the sorrow in his voice, tells me everything I need to know. Of course Roman wouldn't push her down the stairs.

Guilt punches me in the stomach. How could I ever have thought he'd done something so terrible?

Nik is a manipulative liar. I can't believe I listened to him and fell for his twisted lies. I'm ashamed that I let him poison me against Roman.

He continues in a more distant tone of voice. "After that is when she started trying to kill herself. Eventually, she put her life in so much danger that I had her locked away in a mental hospital where she's remained ever since. The day I delivered her the divorce papers is the first time I've seen her since I dropped her off there seven years ago.

"Over the years, I've been waiting for a chance to get back at Kozlov. He ruined not only my life, but hers, and I wanted vengeance. When your father told me about his plans to marry you to Kozlov, I saw my opportunity to strike. I'd been compiling blackmail material on him for years, but I wanted to hit him in the ego, to wound his pride by making my revenge much more personal. You were the perfect piece. So, I took you from him."

For the first time since he started talking, he glances over at me. Remorse shines in his eyes.

"My plan for you was terrible, but I won't go into

the details unless you want them. I saw you as my enemy because of your association with Kozlov. That's how I justified what I was going to do to you. But then you turned my world upside down."

He angles towards me, his fingertips lightly brush the back of my hand. "You shone a light on my loneliness, and the anger and hurt I'd been carrying around for years, festering like an untended wound. But you also breathed new life into my heart. When we were together, I started to forget about Olivia, and Kozlov, and my revenge plans. I didn't care about any of them anymore. You captured all of me, Sophia."

I turn my hand over and our fingers entwine. At the contact, his shoulders visibly relax, and my thundering pulse settles.

"At any point along the way, I should have stopped and settled my business with Olivia, but I was blinded by my ego. I thought I could have my revenge on Kozlov, keep Olivia locked away in a kind of purgatory, and have it all with you. It was wrong of me to marry you when I had no right to do so. I never meant to hurt you, I only ever wanted to have everything with you. My life is not worth living without you as the center of my universe, Sophia."

My insides swoop and dive as he does, in fact, bare his soul to me. He's an open book. In him, I see all his unspoken words too, how much those in his past hurt him, and how those scars run deep.

"I'm sorry." He sucks in a shaky breath. "Over the last month, I've dealt with my past and lain it to rest. I'm a free man now. More importantly, I've gained clarity. You see, I thought I'd fallen in love with Olivia, but I didn't know what love was until I met you. Every past emotion I've experienced pales in comparison to what I feel for you every single day. I will never let you down again if you will take a chance on me, one more time."

"Where would we even start?" I ask.

His actions and choices have deeply hurt me. But now I can at least understand why he did what he did. His apology and remorse seem sincere enough that I might give him the chance he's asking for.

Hope shines in his eyes and he scoots close enough that our knees touch. "We'd start over. This can be the first day that we meet."

"How can I ever trust you not to break my heart again, Roman?" I glance away, heat and pressure build behind my eyes. "You really hurt me. What you did is unforgivable."

He slides from the bench to his knees, kneeling in front of me. "I know. I take full responsibility for my own damage and for the heinous things I've done." Roman takes my hands in his. "I want to spend every day of the rest of my life making this up to you, earning whatever forgiveness you want to offer me. Please—" his voice breaks.

The emotional desperation in his tone makes me meet his agonized gaze. I see a broken man begging for a chance to heal.

Roman clears his throat. "Please, Sophia. My life is meaningless without you. But this isn't all about me... We're so good together. We belong with each other.

We've both seen what our life could be like together if we give this one more chance. I promise that no man will ever love you as much as I do, principessa. You have my heart, my soul, my everything. You are my everything."

Having Roman on his knees, his soul bared to me, telling me everything I've yearned to hear from him, is like a dream come true.

Can this be for real? I contemplate why he'd lie right now, and come up blank. He has nothing left to lose. I'm no longer any use to him as a pawn in his revenge game. There's no reason for him to be here other than he wants *me*. He loves me.

And the truth is, despite everything that he's done, I love him too. Is love enough to keep us together forever? To heal our wounds? There's only one way to find out.

It's a risk, but one I'm willing to take for our potential future together. If love's not worth risking everything for, then what is?

Slowly, I nod. "We can try starting over."

"You're serious? You'll give me another chance?" His brows pinch together, his gaze searches mine for the truth.

"Yes. But don't ever hurt me again."

His features soften. "I'd rather fall on my own blade than cause you harm or grief ever again, principessa. You have my word."

I smile at his archaic phrasing. I've missed him so much that it hurts. As he holds my hands, a knot deep inside loosens, unraveling until the pain begins to fade.

"Date me," he blurts, pressing a kiss to my knuckles.

A wry smirk twists my lips. "I don't know, I'm thinking of dating for a while and I'm not looking for anything exclusive." It's true. It's the promise that I made myself. One that I feel I'm ready to go back on for Roman.

"Then we'll date."

I lift a brow. "Non-exclusively?"

"Anything that you want." He squeezes my hands between his large palms.

"I think you're lying, Mr. De Luca." Slowly, I stand, pulling him up with me. Turning us, I shove his chest until he sits on the bench where I can climb into his lap and straddle his thighs, unable to keep my distance for another moment. I've missed him too much. "I think you'll tell me anything for that second chance."

"Not *tell* you anything, I'll *do* anything. And I'm not lying." He palms my ass and hauls my body into his. "We can be non-exclusive for a while. Just know that I'll never look at another woman, and any man who glances your way will find himself in a shallow grave, so don't expect many offers for a date."

A grin splits my face. "There's the Roman De Luca that I know." I trail my thumb down this jawline, my heart breaking for him all over again. "You've been through hell. So have I. And I understand you so much better now. Thank you for opening up to me, it's all I ever wanted."

"I'm so sorry for what I put you through these past

few weeks. I would have come sooner but I needed to have this out of the way first. And I'm sorry that I couldn't open up until I realized I'd lost you. I'm a fool."

"You hurt me, Roman, a lot, but I don't think you ever truly lost me because even though I should have, I never stopped loving you. You stole my heart, and I haven't been able to find it again without you."

His open gaze searches my face, seeking my sincerity. "You mean it. You love me. Does that mean you'll give us a chance? For real?"

"Yes. But I do want to start over. A clean slate. No assumptions."

"Then you shall have it. When can I take you out on our first date? Tonight?"

"How about right now?"

"Perfect." He spears his fingers into my hair and pulls me in for a mind melting, toe curling kiss. A perfect start to our first date.

CHAPTER 34

The town car pulls up to the Pontrelli house so that I can collect Sophia for our thirty-ninth date. In the last six weeks, we've had a date night, or afternoon, several times a week. Everything from fancy dinners to catching a matinee to simply sitting in the park and talking for hours.

It's been the best month and a half of my life.

My knock on the front door is answered by Mr. Pontrelli, who narrows his eyes in greeting. At least he's finally dispensed with the death threats—those lasted three whole weeks. We eventually had to sit down and talk, man to man. During that conversation, I gave him express permission to kill me if I ever break his daughter's heart again. I made sure Baron understood as well, given that he's my insurance policy against such things.

Then we fought over who gets to pay for Sophia's college. In the end we settled on a fifty-fifty arrangement. Neither of us was thrilled by that decision, but we both knew the other would never back down.

Now, I'm pretty sure Pontrelli's biding his time, waiting for me to fuck up again so he can pull the trigger. Unfortunately for him, I'm not going to. Ever. His daughter's the center of my universe and at some point, he'll come to realize that.

"Good evening," I drawl.

His glare deepens.

"Roman!" Sophia races down the stairs, a vision in a black skirt and a crimson silk top. I told her tonight would be casual. "Bye, Papa." She kisses her father's cheek on the way out the door.

I open the car door, letting her inside before I climb in. "Continue to our destination," I tell the driver, missing Enzo and his quiet efficiency. He never had to be told when to stop and start the car. It's strange not having him around anymore after so many years of service.

"And where is our destination?" Sophia asks, wrapping her arms around mine.

"You will just have to wait and see once we arrive."

"So mysterious," she teases.

"Yes." It's meant to be a surprise, so hopefully she'll like it.

Sophia's made it clear that she wants to fully experience college, including living in the dorms, so that's what she's getting. I just hope she likes what I've done with the place.

Either she'll love it, or she'll tell me I overstepped. We'll see.

We pull onto campus and up to her building. She cranes her neck out the window, and I can already tell there are a thousand questions zinging through her mind.

"We're going to my dorm? Why?"

"Patience, principessa." Taking her hand, we exit the car and I lead her up to her private room on the top floor. After going through orientation with the seventeen and eighteen-year-olds who will be her fellow freshmen, she opted for her own space and privacy. As a woman of twenty-one, I don't blame her. I'm sure she'll make plenty of friends without having roommates.

Glancing nervously at me, she lets us into her dorm room that's more like a studio apartment, and flicks on the light.

Her gasp warms my heart. She takes it all in, from the brand-new bed, to the high-end appliances, to the wall art. The amazement in her eyes tells me I did well. Cool relief floods my bloodstream.

"Roman...what did you do?"

"I call it an upgrade."

"An upgrade?" She makes a beeline for one of the hanging pieces of art. "Is this a Monet? Oh my God, Roman, this is an *original*. How...?"

I shrug. "I have an acquaintance in the art world who hooked me up with some collectors who were willing to sell. As for the rest of it, Ravenna and Eve did most of the work. You can thank them later."

"That sneaky cousin of mine." She spins full circle in her new space. "This is perfect. I love it."

"And I love you."

With an excited squeak, she leaps into my arms, peppering my face with kisses. I let her have her way with me for a moment before I wrap my fingers around her neck and capture her mouth with mine. My tongue demands entry, and she opens up so I can taste her.

Her soft moan is my cue to pull away. "There's more. This was only our first stop."

"More? More of what?"

I take her hand in mine. "Come with me and find out."

Nerves jumbled from what I'm about to show her next, we walk through campus, and across the street. Again, the potential for overstepping is high. What can I say, it's in my nature.

"How far are we going?" she asks.

"Not far. We're in this building right here." I lead us into the glass lobby where we take an elevator up to the penthouse.

"Who are we going to see? Who lives here, Roman?" She's practically bubbling with anticipation.

I click my tongue. "So many questions. All of which will be answered through this door." I enter the key code and we step inside. "Welcome to my new home away from home."

"You bought a place across the street from campus?"

"Of course. You didn't think I could stand living an hour away from you, did you? This way we can be close, but you'll still have your own space."

She beams up at me. "It's lovely, Roman."

I'm so glad she wants me close. I'd be devastated if she ever told me to go back to my country estate and leave her alone.

"I'm glad it meets with your approval. Now let's eat."

CHAPTER 35

Sophia

"Luis! How are you?" I haven't seen him in ages. Roman and I have been sticking around Manhattan, and honestly, I'm beginning to miss his peaceful estate in the country, and Luis and Diana.

"Good, good, Miss Sophia." He motions us toward a candlelit table. "Dinner is prepared. You two have a good evening, I'm going to see myself out. Goodnight, sir," he says on his way past Roman.

Roman pulls out my chair, and I take a seat, then he pours us each a glass of wine before sitting across from me. The table is laden with all of my favorite food, from Luis's amazing pasta to garlic breadsticks to apple tarts. He went above and beyond tonight.

"To starting college." Roman raises his glass.

"Thank you." I sip my wine. That's right, tomorrow I officially begin attending classes. I'm settled in, I have my schedule, and I'm ready. Now I have a gorgeous dorm room too.

Outside of preparing for school, Roman has taken up most of my time this summer. He's held true to his word. He spends every single day making me feel special, cherished, and loved.

He sends me texts from work. Little desserts with love notes, he sends to the house on the evenings we don't spend together. But most importantly, he tells me he loves me, and I believe every word.

Physically we've taken things slow, not going beyond making out. It feels right to reconnect emotionally and mentally first, but I'd be lying if I said I don't miss the sex. Like, really miss it. I want all of Roman. I think I'm ready.

Dinner is amazing, the food tastes richer than before, everything about spending time with Roman since we agreed to start over is brighter, fuller, deeper. It's simply...*more*.

I gaze across the table at this incredible man. His angular features are sharper in the candlelight, cast in ever moving shadows. He really is gorgeous, reminding me of a Greek God with his straight nose and full lips. Not to mention the rest of his body is a sculpted masterpiece.

I bite down on my lip, trying and failing to keep my lustful thoughts at bay. Honestly, I'm not sure how I've gone this long without touching him.

He watches me watch him. "Penny for your thoughts."

"I'm sure you know exactly what I'm thinking." My voice is breathy.

A smirk twists his cruel lips, he's a master at reading my body language. With two fingers he summons me to him. As soon as I'm within arm's reach, he catches me around the waist, sits me on his lap, and presses my back to his chest. I'm caged in by his arms and I am loving every moment.

"Elevated heart rate, wide pupils, flushed skin," he murmurs in my ear. "I think you're thinking about me doing naughty things to you, principessa. Do you want me to bend you over this table and fuck you within an inch of your life?"

My panties dampen and I roll my hips, riding Roman's thigh. "Yes."

"Yes *what?*"

"Yes, please. Yes, sir."

"That's my good girl."

Roman lifts me from his lap, and presses my body forward over the table. In a matter of seconds my skirt is up around my waist, my panties are gone, and Roman's on his knees, his hot tongue licking my pussy. I grab fistfuls of the tablecloth and hang on for what's sure to be a wild ride.

He fucks me with his tongue, his fingers teasing my clit. It's been so long that I'm instantly quivering, thighs shaking, and muscles clenching. The orgasm tears through me like a tsunami.

"Oh my God, Roman!" I cry into the tablecloth.

"That's right, principessa, right now I am your

God." He buries his cock in my sensitive pussy, and I cry out again.

Roman does what he promised, fucking me with punishing thrusts. The table creaks, dishes rattle, and our wine glasses topple, but neither of us pay the destruction much mind.

He smooths his palms over my ass, kneading, caressing, and I know what's coming next. One solid smack, and my pussy clenches around him, another orgasm sends me into oblivion.

"*Fuck.*" Roman rocks his hips, riding through it. Then he withdraws, flips me over, and enters me with languid, but powerful thrusts. He smooths my hair away from my face and rests his forehead on mine.

Suddenly, the entire energy of what we're doing shifts. We stare into each other's eyes. Into the other's heart and soul. The amount of love I find in his gaze, beaming at me, is more than one person could possibly hold for another. Yet it's there, clear as a summer's day.

Our bodies move together, a primal dance, the physical manifestation of what our hearts are saying to each other.

I love you.

I cherish you.

I want forever with you.

We're no longer fucking, we're making love.

This time, we come together in a mind-shattering, soul-bending release that strips us both down to nothing, then rebuilds us in a new form, one whole from two halves.

"I love you," he whispers. "Forever and always."

"I love you, too."

"Good, because…" Roman picks me up, and settles us on the floor, on our knees. He reaches into his trousers pocket and pulls out a small square box.

My heart flutters with anticipation.

"Sophia, will you marry me?"

The ring nestled in the jewelry box is my old engagement ring. The beautiful diamond from *Maçon*. I can't tear my gaze away from it.

"If it holds too many bad memories, I'll have a new one made for you," Roman says, his voice hesitant, gaze searching my expression.

"I'm so sorry I threw this at you." Tears well in my eyes at the memory. "I'm sorry that I let Nik's twisted version of the truth ruin what we had."

"There's nothing to forgive." He wraps me in his arms, holding me close. "If I'd told you the truth, his words wouldn't have held any power over us. If I'd told you how much I love you, you never would have doubted my intentions. That's all on me, principessa, not you."

"Dammit," he curses under his breath. "I knew I should have had a new ring made for you."

"No." I pull away. "No, this one's perfect."

He peers into my face. "Is that a…*yes?*"

"Yes." I smile.

He beams, and quickly slips the ring on my finger, as if he's afraid I'll change my mind. There's no chance in hell of that happening. I want this. I want *us*.

He holds my hand in his. "With this ring I vow to love you every day, to have no secrets between us, and to give you my body, heart, and soul. All of me is yours. Forever."

"Are we not negotiating this time?" I tease, the butterflies in my stomach going wild.

"This isn't a business deal, principessa. I want to marry you because I love you."

"And I want to marry you because I love you, too, Roman. With all my heart. I'm yours."

"Damn right, you're *mine*," he growls.

We seal our future with a soulful kiss. The kind of kiss that's all-consuming, full of hope and promises. A silent vow shared between us.

CHAPTER 36

Five months later

Sophia

"**R**oman, what is this place?" We're in the middle of a vehicle procession, rolling along and stopping every few feet, waiting our turn at the building's entrance. The lone structure was erected in the Greek Revival era, resembling the White House and other such buildings of that time.

As we get closer to the palatial entrance, I read the words illuminated across its front: *Only the sons of lions shall enter.*

"Roman?" I question again, glancing at his handsome face. This is our first New Year's Eve together and I still can't believe he's mine. All mine. And our wedding is planned for this coming summer—in Italy.

"We're at the *Leonidas Gentleman's Club*," he murmurs, gazing at the building as if trying to see it through fresh eyes.

"You brought me to a strip club?"

He gaze snaps to mine, then softens. "Precisely," his tone drips with sarcasm. "That's why you're wearing a one of a kind dress by Skye Adair."

I bite down on my bottom lip to stop myself from rolling my eyes at his teasing tone, and glance at my dress. It's a crimson and gold gown that's breathtaking in the way the fabric catches the light.

Fashion designer Skye Adair has seemingly come out of nowhere and taken the world by storm. Her designs are coveted, selling out as soon as they're available through her boutique. To be honest, I'm not sure how Roman managed to get his hands on this dress.

Not just a Skye Adair gown, but a one of a kind? Roman truly is amazing.

Finally, it's our turn, and Roman helps me out of the car. He still hasn't given me much information to go on about this place.

My arm wrapped around his, we pass across the threshold into a stunning foyer with gleaming marble floors, a soaring ceiling, decorated in glittering silver and massive, elaborate ice sculptures.

One masterpiece is a full-sized carriage pulled by four unicorns. Another is a towering Poseidon, God of the Sea, standing amid crashing waves, trident held high in the air.

Once again I ask him, "What is this place?"

"It's an exclusive club. They have the best New Year's Eve parties, and it's about time that I introduced you to this part of my world. Come."

I'm in awe as Roman leads me further into the

club. We poke our heads into various rooms: A darkened ballroom, a smokey gambling den, and a quiet library. Then we enter a decent sized space where the booths and tables all face a stage.

Blake Baron waves us over to his booth against the far wall. Like all the men here, he's wearing a tuxedo, but I notice that he's without a date. Though, come to think of it, I've never seen him *with* a date, even when he was the best man at my fake wedding.

"Baron," Roman says in greeting, lettings me slide into the booth first.

Blake's gaze flicks to me and I see the usual indifference in his eyes. Then the faintest curve of his lips. Is that a smile?

Stop the presses, Blake Baron smiled on New Year's Eve. If that's not news worthy, I don't know what is.

"Are you bidding, or putting yourself up for auction tonight?" Baron asks Roman.

My interest is piqued.

Roman helps himself to the bottle of *Dom Pérignon* on the table, pouring us each a champagne flute. "Neither. We're simply here for the entertainment, unless something irresistible presents itself."

"What would you bid on?" I ask, curious about what he'd consider irresistible.

Roman gazes at me. "I'd certainly bid on *you*, principessa."

"Is that so? And where do the proceeds go?"

Baron answers. "It's a charity auction. This year it's an orphanage, or is it something environmental? I don't remember. A good cause, for sure. The usual." He waves dismissively.

Beneath the table, I run my hand up Roman's thigh, and delight in the way his muscles tense. We've been together, this time, for a little over four and a half months now, and he's been true to his word, making me feel cherished every single day.

I lean into him. "How about if I auction off a kiss. It's for a good cause, right?"

"If that's what you want to do. Just know that your kiss will belong to me." He moves in to claim my mouth and I duck away.

"Not so fast, you haven't won it yet." I nudge him until he reluctantly lets me out of the booth.

I sign myself up for the charity auction and then return to our table to wait for the event to begin. By the time the host steps on stage, the room is packed and noisy.

"Welcome to our annual charity auction!" The elegantly dressed host speaks into a microphone and the crowd grows quiet. "We have a delicious line-up for you tonight. Let's begin..."

The first piece is a gorgeous emerald necklace donated from one of New York's wealthiest families. The next auction is for one night with a handsome bachelor from Boston.

I glance at Baron. "You're a bachelor, are you going to put yourself up there?"

"I'd rather eat nails," he drawls.

Roman snorts a laugh.

Okay then, I'll take that as a *no*.

The auction goes on until they're close to calling my number. I excuse myself, shoot Roman a seductive smile, then make my way toward the stage. This should be fun.

Normally, I wouldn't dream of doing something like this. But I know that Roman will win this bid. So I'm safe.

Roman

When Sophia climbs the stage and the auctioneer introduces her, I'm instantly aware of everyone's gazes on my beautiful fiancée. I'm both proud to be her man and irritated by all of these men's, and women's, open and admiring stares.

"Miss Sophia Pontrelli is offering a single kiss."

Her name should be Sophia *De Luca*. I'll be remedying that in six months. Six months too long. If I had it my way, I'd already have put a wedding band on her finger.

"Bidding will start at ten thousand dollars. Do I have—"

I raise my hand.

"Very good, Mr. De Luca, ten thousand. Can I get fifteen? Thank you, Mr. Baron."

I glare at my friend. "What do you think you're doing?"

"You wouldn't want Sophia's kiss to go for too cheap, would you? I'm simply adding value." He smirks.

"Twenty thousand?"

I raise my hand again.

From across the room, someone calls out, "Thirty thousand!"

Baron releases a low whistle, and relaxes back into his seat to enjoy the show. "It seems like you'll have some actual competition after all."

I crane my neck to see who has the fucking balls to bid against me for my own fiancée. My glower deepens when I spot Malachy Bane along with his brothers Eoin and Alistair. To my surprise, Skye Adair is also seated at their table. Sophia likes her clothing designs, too bad the woman has terrible taste in men.

"Fifty thousand," I shout.

"Sixty," Malachy counters, his gaze fixed on me now.

"Seventy-five."

"Eighty-five."

Son of a bitch. I'm going to kill him.

"One hundred and fifty thousand." There's no way in hell I'm letting that Bane bastard lay a single finger on my girl, not to mention his goddamn lips.

The crowd watches us with interest, murmurs erupting as we volley back and forth all the way up to two hundred thousand dollars.

The auctioneer speaks. "Going once, twice... Sold to Mr. De Luca. Congratulations!"

The room breaks out in applause. Malachy sits back in his chair with a smug expression. His only aim was to get under my skin, and he did. I'll make him pay for it later.

I climb the stage and reach for my prize.

"Roman." Sophia steps into my waiting arms. "I'm so sorry, I didn't mean for that to get so out of hand. Who is that man?"

"He's no one." I sweep her into a backward bend and capture her lips with mine. This kiss is pure possessiveness, a public claiming of what's mine.

Sophia opens up for me, and I deepen our kiss, our tongues licking and tangling. The crowd goes wild, cheering us on.

Only when we're both breathless, do I set her upright on her feet. Sophia's tan skin is flushed, her chest rapidly rises and falls, and she's absolutely stunning. Gorgeous.

I cup her face.

"Now that," I say against her swollen lips, "was worth every penny."

Epilogue

Sophia

"**B**y the power vested in me, I now pronounce you husband and wife. You may kiss the bride." As our wedding concludes, the crowd applauds.

Roman dips me, his nose hovering mere centimeters from mine.

"*Mrs. De Luca,*" he growls the words, before claiming my lips. I wrap my arms around his neck and kiss him back until our tongues tangle and the cheers around us morph into whistles and cat-calls. Only then does he set me upright on my feet again.

The smile straining my cheeks is almost painful, but I bear it. On the Mediterranean coast, shaded from a beaming June sun, we've tied the knot. For real this time. I'm officially Sophia De Luca. And Roman is mine.

We walk into the sea of people who witnessed our vows. It's all friends and family this time. My parents are here with my sisters and cousins, as well as Roman's mother. Blake Baron had the honor of being the best man for a second time. Given the deep scowl on his face, I don't think he sees it as a privilege.

No matter. At least my sisters and cousins were happy to be bridesmaids again, with new dresses, of course. And a destination wedding? Few can say no to that.

The rest of our gathering includes extended family from Italy, and the cluster of women who we refer to as the *aunties*—widowed or older unwed women who belong to the Pontrelli clan. Or as I like to call them... gossips and troublemakers.

We walk by them, when one of the cackles. "We knew you two would end up together."

Uh-huh. I bet they did.

Taking Roman's hand, I lead us through the congratulatory crowd to the tables set in front of the villa. Once we're seated everyone else settles down, so we can dig into the delicious food, speeches, and toasts.

Arianna sits at my side, Blake is on Roman's other side, and Ginevra and my cousins take the places across from us. Cian O'Rourke squeezes in his large frame beside Ravenna. Her sister, Elena, claims a spot as far from him as possible.

I don't blame her, he's a mean looking giant. Though he seems to treat Ravenna with complete adoration.

Our family just keeps growing. Now that Arianna

and Gin are allowed to date, I'm curious who they'll be bringing home.

"Open up." Roman hovers a piece of bread dipped in olive oil in front of my lips.

I do as he commands, open my mouth and let him feed me. Our gazes lock as I suck on his fingers. Beneath the table, his free hand hikes up my wedding gown until he can dip his fingers between my thighs. Where he leaves them, teasing my heated flesh, throughout the rest of dinner.

"Where are you honeymooning this time?" Gin asks between bites.

I glance at Roman. "As usual, it's a surprise."

He ducks in close, whispering in my ear. "This time I'm keeping you in bed for two full weeks. We're going to turn off our phones, order room service for every meal, and I'm going to worship every inch of your body—again."

I shiver as lust rushes through my body.

"Ah, I heard part of that." Arianna purses her lips, side eyeing us. "Don't you want to do something more productive, like tour Italy or England?"

"Obviously," Roman levels his gaze on her, "you've never been attracted to another person. Much less in love."

"Love is an emotion. You can be in love with someone without jumping into bed with them every chance you get. That's lust, not love."

"It's a package deal." Roman sips his wine, his fingers finding my clit.

I sharply inhale.

Arianna glances at me. "Are you okay?"

"Fine. Just fine." I shoot a half-hearted glare at Roman and shake my head. He gives me a devilish smile and continues pleasuring me. He's so naughty.

"Sophia, can you pass the pepper, please?" Ravenna asks, and I hand it to her.

Arianna gasps. Everyone in the vicinity glances her way.

"What's wrong?" I ask, noting that she has a death grip on her phone beneath the table. She can't see what Roman's doing to me under here, can she?

"Nothing." She blanches. "It's nothing. Please excuse me." She rushes inside and I catch the tremble in her hands.

It's not Roman's hands on me that are upsetting her, it's something else.

"I need to go see what's going on."

Reluctantly, Roman nods, and fixes my dress before I stand up to follow Arianna. Gin, never wanting to miss out on an ounce of drama, is hot on my heels. Out of the corner of my eye, I catch Blake Baron's gaze flick to Ginevra then back to his plate.

We find Arianna in the hallway, pacing and staring at her phone. Something is obviously wrong.

"What is it?" I ask, and she startles like she didn't hear our heels clicking on the marble floor as we approached.

She licks her lips and pockets her phone. "Really it's nothing. My stomach just doesn't feel so well all of a sudden."

I place my hands on my hips and cock my head. "Liar."

"Something's up," Ginevra pipes in. "You've been checking your phone all day. That's not like you. Oh! Is it a boy?" Her eyes brighten with excitement.

"No," Arianna snaps. Her features scrunch and she chokes on a sob. Gin blinks at her, taken aback.

I drop the tough older sister act and come in close. "Oh my God, Arianna, what's going on? Are you in trouble?"

"I-I don't know. Maybe."

"Come on, just tell us." Gin rubs her shoulder. "Together we'll figure it out. Whatever it is."

Arianna chews on her bottom lip, clearly debating about how much to tell us.

"Okay," she says. "Th-these started about two weeks ago." She retrieves her phone and flips through several photos of her, candid shots, taken around the city.

"Someone's taking pictures of you?" Ginevra asks. "Why?"

Arianna shakes her head as if to clear it. "They're sent with these text messages."

I take her cell from her and scroll through the text thread.

UNKNOWN

I see you, Kisa.

ARIANNA PONTRELLI

Who is this?

UNKNOWN

I want you. You're mine.

ARIANNA PONTRELLI

Stop texting me or you'll be in huge trouble.

UNKNOWN

Shh, Kisa, you tell a soul and I'll have to kill them.

ARIANNA PONTRELLI

Go away.

UNKNOWN

Such a pretty girl, this photo is my favorite.

A shiver crawls down my spine as I continue reading the creepy messages. What the hell is this all about?

I glance at Arianna. "*Kisa?* What's that?"

"I looked it up, and it means like kitty or kitten in Russian." She nervously licks her lips. "I think he's Russian."

I nod. "It looks like you have a stalker. Why didn't you tell Papa?"

"You saw what he wrote. He'll kill anyone if I tell them. I shouldn't even be talking to you two about this, but hopefully he hasn't followed me here." She rakes her fingers through her styled hair. "What am I going to do? I'm terrified to go back home."

Gin and I exchange a worried look. Yeah, this is a serious problem. One we need to solve. I feel so sorry for Arianna and how she's been living in terror for weeks because of this creep.

"Are you sure you don't know who it is?" I ask. "You haven't met anyone recently who seems a little... off?"

"No, no one."

Ginevra clutches our hands. "I've got it! What if you don't come back with us? You could stay here with Elena for a while. Maybe the creep will get bored and go away, then you can come home."

It's not a bad idea. No one would question Arianna wanting to stay here with her cousin for a few more weeks.

"I don't know..." Arianna glances over her shoulder, the worry in her eyes tugs at my heartstrings. "I guess I could stay."

"I think it's a good idea. We don't have to tell Papa and Mama what's going on, though I think we should just in case this escalates."

Arianna sighs. "I guess you're right. I just wish I knew who this guy is, you know?"

"Well, we think he's Russian, so..."

Russian. Nik. The Kozlov Bratva. Of course, how could I be so blind?

Gin nudges me. "You just had an epiphany. What are you thinking?"

"Has Papa mentioned anything about the Kozlovs since we broke our agreement with them and I married Roman?"

"I don't think so." Ginevra looks to Arianna for confirmation.

I didn't think it possible for Arianna to be any paler, but all the remaining blood drains from her face.

"Oh my God," she whispers in horror. "Could it be Dimitri Kozlov? He's second in command and he was the backup groom if anything were to happen to Nikolai. Now that he's dead... And I'm the backup bride if anything happened to you, Sophia. Now you're married and I'm—" She cuts herself off.

I hadn't realized marrying Roman would put my sister in this situation. Of course Dimitri wouldn't let this go. He probably thinks my family betrayed him by going back on our word. But Arianna can't marry *him*. I've met him once, and I guarantee he's worse than Nik.

I've never seen such cold and dead green eyes before Dimitri's gaze briefly settled on me when we met. I wouldn't dare spend a minute alone in a room with him.

What have I done?

Arianna's phone pings with an incoming text. All three of us lean in to read it.

UNKNOWN

See you soon, Kisa.

The attached picture shows a plane ticket from New York City to Catania, Italy.

Dimitri's coming for Arianna. Right now. We need to leave before it's too late.

Thank you for reading *Stolen Vows!* If you enjoyed Roman and Sophia's story, please leave a review. Reviews are like tips for authors and I'd be forever grateful if you'd leave one for this book!

Her family reneged on their promise, now he'll take what's owed to him. Read FORCED UNION for Dimitri and Arianna's story.

Do you want more of Roman and Sophia? Grab their bonus epilogue here: https://subscribepage.io/stolen-vows-bonus

XX,
Cassia

Newsletter Signup

For works in progress updates and new release announcements, as well as giveaways, author life snippets, and more, sign up for Cassia Quinn's newsletter: www.CassiaQuinn.com

Acknowledgments

First, and foremost, I'd like to thank my husband for always being there to bounce ideas off of, ponder plot points, and his never-ending support. As well as his love of commas. Love you.

Andra Kapule, your support means the world to me! Thank you for being there to encourage me to continue when the writing road gets rough, give your honest and blunt feedback, and for your friendship.

Fellow author and friend, Luna Pierce, our brainstorming and shit-shooting sessions are the best! You're awesome and I appreciate you so much.

I'd also like to thank about a million people in the romance writing community, especially those in my writer groups on Facebook and Discord. Over the years I've learned invaluable lessons from you all. Thank you.

And last, but certainly not least, I'd like to thank my editor, Geissa Cecilia with GP Author Services. Thanks for all of your hard work!

Cassia Quinn writes dark and angsty billionaire romance. She currently resides in the Pacific Northwest with her husband and kitty fur babies. Her favorite activity is reading on rainy days with a glass of wine.

Keep In Touch With Cassia Quinn

Website:
www.CassiaQuinn.com

Instagram:
https://www.instagram.com/cassiaquinnauthor/

TikTok:
https://www.tiktok.com/@cassiaquinnauthor

BookBub:
https://www.bookbub.com/profile/cassia-quinn

GoodReads:
https://www.goodreads.com/cassiaquinn